Wendy Sam Miller, owner of Too Good to be Threw, is on the case

Bill drove Elsie in to work. He was looking pretty spiffy and I told him so. "Lands' End," he said. "Elsie's revamping my wardrobe."

"From that twinkle in your eye that's not all she's revamping," I said. I love to tease older men.

" Feeling like a million, now, I am. After that tonic."

"Five hundred thousand," Elsie called from the lingerie rack.

"What. He's only half as good as he thinks he is?"

"No, he's ever bit as good. Just takes my five hundred thousand to make a million." She was holding a lace peignoir set in front of her tiny body.

Bill had to turn his head. I think we were embarrassing him. Ain't it fun?

"Tonic?," I said. "Where'd you get it?"

"Now that's quite a story," he began.

"From Chloe," Elsie shouted from the dressing room. She came out in the lace nightwear. Didn't have the same effect over her floral shirt and with her little Keds sticking out.

"Now Elsie, let me tell."

"Just, I start work in ten minutes, and your stories take, oh, at least half an hour," Elsie said.

Also by Kate Holmes

Too Good to be Threw: The Complete Operations
Manual for Consignment and Resale Shops

Windows that Sell
Words that Sell
109 Promotion Ideas Especially for Resale Shops
Staffing your Store
Secrets of Successful Resalers

The Picker Who Perished

A Too Good to be Threw Consignment Shop Mystery

Kate Holmes

Katydid Press
Sarasota Florida
www.tgtbt.com

ATTENTION CONSIGNMENT, RESALE, THRIFT SHOPS,
LIBRARIES, AND PROFESSIONAL ASSOCIATIONS:
Quantity discounts are available on bulk purchases of this book
for resale, gift purposes, or as premiums.
For information,
please see our Web site at http://www.tgtbt.com or contact
Katydid Press, 4736 Meadowview Blvd., Sarasota FL 34233,
Voice 941-924-4142, Fax 941-922-5902

The morning after

The flamboyant colors of her scarf stained the puddle at the bottom of the stairs. Her nose was in the blue-tinged water, but it didn't matter. The gay petals of the cranesbill were all around her, its pot broken beside her.

A leg was broken, too, but that didn't matter either. She wouldn't scramble up, twitch her soggy skirts away from her legs, fling her hair out of her eyes, turn and gather the scattered box of vintage linens to heave them into her Jeep for the ride to her destination.

At the top of the stairs which hung on the side of the building, her screen door slammed back and forth in the thunderstorm. The inner door was propped open by a second box of linens, which were now as sodden as her skirts. Wind-blown rain soaked the boomerang pattern linoleum that was most of the reason, she had joked, she'd rented the apartment at the head of the canal.

The contents of her handbag were scattered around her body. Keys, lip gloss, wallet, phone, all those things a woman carries every day. It didn't matter. She wouldn't need them any more.

1

My margarita had sweated its way through the pasteboard coaster and was creating its own little Florida salt marsh on the glass tabletop as Ilene continued her tirade on Sarasota's headlong flight into East-Coastdom.

"Most people settle on this coast instead of West Palm and Boca because they want to live in a real town instead of a strip mall," she said. "So when they get here, what do they do? Turn it into the East Coast. We're going to turn into another Palm Springs if we're not careful."

"Palm Beach," Patty said. Ilene waved her hand to say *Yeh you know I meant that.* Patty and I were used to Ilene's habit of mixing up names. We knew she meant Palm Beach, as in Florida, not Palm Springs, as in California. Or is it Arizona? I'm not much better than Ilene.

"Unbelievable, isn't it?" I said as I repinned my hair, trying to tame the curls that kept flying in my eyes. "People move here for the climate and then use their air conditioning from February to November. They love nature but rip it all up to plant lawns that suck up what water we have."

"Only God can make a live oak," waxed Patty, on her third Mai Tai. "But only developers can put an English etched glass door on a Spanish Mediterranean house with a made-in-Mexico Italianate fountain out front."

Ilene fished the fringe of her scarf out of her beer, blotted it with her napkin, and reached for another shrimp. As she peeled it, she sighed. "I know I make my living off of people moving. I just wish that the bulldozers weren't idling in their driveways, waiting to rip up the palmetto to build a house four times as big and ten times as pretentious as the original one."

Since it was so muggy, the patio at Marina Jack's wasn't crowded. Most of the patrons were inside in air-conditioned comfort. But some of us were enjoying the sea breeze that always comes at sunset, the breeze that made Bird Key and Lido ideal places to live.

We three were doing our Monday-night girl-bonding bit, and as usual our fourth, Chloe, was late. Sure, she lives way inland, so her herbs have sprawling room, but still, you'd think she'd figured out by now how long the drive in takes. It was hard, sticking to the promise we'd all made when we started meeting: no talking about whoever's absent. We had no compunctions about talking about each other to our faces, and we'd had some doozies of discussions when all of us were there. But Chloe's late arrival always cut into our dishing time.

We'd wandered off into fashion: boring for me since it was shop talk, of little interest to Patty who insisted she was just grateful to find anything to cover her ample body, and beneath contempt to Ilene, whose vintage wardrobe refused to answer to fashion's dictates. So why were we bothering? Might be because we were trying so hard to not talk about Chloe, who had told us, last time, that she was finally going to own her land. We were dying to find out how she was going to manage that. She had a small income from the house sales she ran on a sporadic basis. Other than that, Chloe had no income we knew of except for her little herbal business, which couldn't be terribly lucrative. Maybe someone died and left her money. *Bite your tongue, Wendy Sam,* I said to myself. *What a terrible thing to think.*

"There's Chloe, finally," Patty said, who always chose the chair facing the entry. Ilene and I twisted in our seats and started to wave but stopped when we saw a trim, well-dressed man waylay Chloe and manoeuver her into the far corner of the copper-sheathed bar. He had his hand on her forearm and was leaning in to talk into her ear. His silk shirt and draped twill trousers whispered money.

"Aha," said Patty, peeling another shrimp. "I deduce a budding romance, what say you?" Patty talked that way a lot,

8

thinking it made her sound more like a detective and less like a collection agent. Sherlock Holmes, not the Repo Man.

"God, I hope not," said Ilene. "That guy's scum. And married scum at that. That's Barry Cobb."

Huh. Barry Cobb. I'd seen his picture on the society page, generally half-hidden behind his wife at some expensive fund-raiser. She was Sarina Jefferson Cobb, grande dame of Sarasota billionaires, leader of the Botox Brigade of do-gooders, board member of a dozen charities. On top of all this she was also head of the Cobb Foundation, which donated money to the arts, and Too Good to be Threw consignor #1156. Barry was a land developer who built megahouses on spec, thus Ilene's description of him as scum. His latest project was an enclave of six Godzilla houses shoe-horned in on one oversized lot where a 1950's ranch had sat gently on the shoreline for fifty years. Each of the six was listed for more than $3 million, turning a $450,000 lot into over $18 million. That $450,000 he paid the elderly couple was probably twenty times what they'd bought their little snowbird house for way back when, so they were undoubtedly happy. I hoped the money was enough to see them through their lives in assisted living. And that they didn't have any kids to see what had happened to their childhood paradise with the rickety dock, now dredged out and awaiting air-conditioned yachts no one would use because they were too busy paying for it all to enjoy life.

"You'd think the man had enough money," Ilene went on. "But no, he always wants more. God, I hate him. He was even nosing around a sale this last weekend, trying to scope out the land. He always shows up whenever there's a house sale on waterfront property. Gives me the creeps."

We all goggled with no shame whatsoever as Chloe shook her head at Cobb and said something short and emphatic. He replied with force and shoved what looked like a business card into her hand. Chloe's shoulders slumped as she tucked it into her pocket. With downcast eyes she made her way towards our table. Almost to us, she glanced back at the man, but he was heading inside to the air conditioning.

"Looks like he was waiting for you," Ilene said as Chloe dragged a chair over from another table and we rearranged glasses and shrimp shell piles to make room.

"Who? Oh, Barry? Nah, he just said something about the farm. He's my landlord, you know."

No, I didn't, and from the looks on Ilene's and Patty's faces, they didn't either. We knew Chloe leased her herb farm but she had never mentioned from whom. Besides, that little scene didn't look like a landlord-type discussion to me. More like a lovers' quarrel if my romance radar was working.

We ordered another round and enjoyed the bay breeze. Even with the construction cranes looming on the ever-taller skyline, this was still enough of a small town that we could spend the evening at a waterside café for the cost of a few drinks and a platter of shrimp.

Patty and I were discussing whether the Key lime pie here was worth the calories when Chloe's voice got loud enough to interfere with our debate. "You haven't seen what I have," she was saying to Ilene. "Old ladies who don't know what day it is, old men who've given up on their own health. They can die just because they're alone. You know that."

Ilene nodded. "Yes, we both know that's happened. There's that service now, though. I saw a note on the fridge at the sale Saturday. But you still have to realize that these people have to have the choice. It's not for us to force any decision on them."

Chloe was shaking her head. "Listen, sometimes they can't make that choice on their own. They won't come to grips with the fact that they're failing. They simply don't know what's best for them."

Ilene stared at her. "If they don't know, how can anyone else? It's not for us to say."

"We have the responsibility," Chloe insisted. "We're the ones who see them, who deal with them. You can't say you haven't seen old people who'd be better off some place where people could watch them."

Ilene shook her head. "We're never going to agree,

Chloe. Let's skip it."

"Alright, then, but don't you come crying to me again like you did Saturday. That woman was a menace to herself." Chloe gathered up her handbag, threw some bills down on the table, and said, "Good night all, it's a long trip inland."

"Well," said Patty as Chloe swept out of the restaurant. "What started all that?"

Ilene didn't answer. She was bent down towards the floor, and straightened up with something in her hand. "Nothing, just that we ran into each other and, oh, never mind. We had words, I guess you'd say." She looked down at what she'd picked up.

It was the business card Chloe had taken from Cobb. It must have fallen out of Chloe's pocket when she made her flamboyant exit. Ilene read it and her face got hard. Avoiding our eyes, she palmed the card and called for another round.

"Not me," I said. "Three's my limit."

I should have wondered what could be on a business card that would make Ilene so mad. I didn't. Maybe if I had, I'd still have my friend. Alive and healthy.

2

You could smell the salt in the onshore breeze. Candles flickered, protected within glass chimneys. My special invention, scarf flags (I love scarves but can't stand to wear them, so I fly them from bamboo poles instead), snapped. Which reminded me, I was snapping gum, a nervous habit I indulge in only before the parties I love to give but which give me heebie-jeebies for days before. Clang, clang went the brass ship's bell that served as my front door buzzer; flip flop went my stomach.

Spitting out the gum into a paper cocktail napkin on my way through the house, I answered the door, only to see the top of Susan's head and her arm, grasping her husband's shoulder. Susan was the manager of my shop.

"See you got a fresh load of shells in your driveway. Coulda told me before I wore my sexy sandals." She was hopping on one foot, wiggling the other to get rid of the shards that had made their way into her shoe. They *were* sexy.

"Hi, Wendy Sam, how ya doin'?" asked Drew, Susan's spectacularly average-looking husband as he grinned around his wife and waved a bottle of spiced rum. Ah, he may look average, but he's above that in thoughtfulness.

As I got them drink-and-nibbled in the backyard, more friends poured in. First to arrive was the rest of my shop crew. Annie brought some tattooed guy whose name I didn't bother learning because I'd never see him again. Then Elsie with a new beau, Bill, whose name I made a point to remember because Elsie only brought around keepers. Bonita entered wearing a spectacular embroidered shawl her mother had sent her from Merida. Bonita's mother had raised seven kids and had seen all but one move to the U.S. Bonita was our work neighbor,

12

employed at Mocha Mama's, the café by my shop. Dom, my next-door neighbor, brought over the stuffed mushrooms I'd borrowed his oven for, holding the baking dish in a snowy-white dish towel carefully away from his brown polyester Sansbelt slacks.

Ilene arrived in a swirl of fabric, layered just so. I loved the outfits she put together even if I could never get away with them myself. Today's ensemble was a thrift shop bias-cut 1930's slip, topped with a 1940's lace jabot and a cerise poodle cloth 1950's bolero, accented with a poison yellow leather beret trimmed in what she swore were not white egret feathers. White egrets had almost gone extinct in the early 1900's because their breeding feathers were so prized for ladies' hats. Fortunately the fashion passed and egrets now abound in lakes, retention ponds, and roadside ditches.

"For me?" I asked when she dug into her sequined tote and pulled out her hand, opened it palm up, and there sat the most exquisite sterling palm tree. She was always bringing me little things she'd found on her picking forays. Last time, it had been a cunning little blue glass Scottie that now guarded my row of blue bottles in the east window.

"Of course it's for you. You owe me a whole jar of silver polish. It was just black when I found it," she said.

"I love it, thanks. So. No guy tonight?"

"Oh, you're right." Ilene looked around as though she'd momentarily misplaced some hunky date. "I forgot. I've been kind of busy." Oh, well, no sense worrying about Ilene's love life, which was much more active than mine. You wouldn't believe the number of guys who aren't put off by poodle cloth. Maybe I'll deep-six my date uniform of slub silk and pearls for something vintage. That is, if I ever have a date again. It's been a while.

Speaking of which, the next arrivals were my favorite instead-of dates: James and Michael. They brought me an over-the-top orchid corsage with satin ribbons. They grow their own. Orchids, not ribbons. May be a strange hobby for two retired Cleveland cops, but hey, someone's gotta do it. James and Michael did it so well they won growers' awards that they proudly

13

hung on their wall, right next to their certificates of firearms accuracy and commendations for bravery. That's what I love about early retirement. We all get to be different people than we used to be.

For example, Ilene had been a dancer in her past life. Since moving here from Iowa or Illinois or one of those "I" states, she's become a picker. A picker is someone who finds used stuff, antiques or collectibles or tongue-in-chic pieces at estate sales, flea markets and thrift stores. Then, after a bit of elbow grease is applied, a picker will resell or consign them to antique shops or shops like mine. That's how we had met. Ilene brought in a batch of items to my shop, we got along, and we became friends. Normally, Ilene's stories of sleazy characters and amazing possessions and the way she finds both are a highlight of any gathering, but tonight she was quiet. Others kept the party lively though, as talk meandered from the upcoming art festival to the President's latest delusion that the world was a conundrum for him to solve. Restaurant reviews were featured topics (we love to eat out in Sarasota) as was the perennial water shortage. My personal solution to that was covering my tiny lot in shell, then tucking potted plants in next to the palms and sea grape. Low maintenance, my motto. Save the Earth, my mission.

I was digging in the fridge for the roast beast horseradish roll-ups I'd forgotten to put out when the Poltergeist Guy pinched my butt. I banged my head on the freezer door, almost dropped my favorite platter, and kissed him soundly on the lips.

Herb Geist got his nickname from the stories he loves to tell. Poltergeists are ghosts which make a lot of noise and throw things about. Herb does both. He has an amazing collection of totally worthless facts and can throw one out to suit any occasion. I suspect he makes some up. Facts, not occasions.

"Hey, Wendy Sam, wazzup? What are those?" He gobbled a few as I struggled to get the plastic wrap off, and said "Yum. You know, horseradish is an antiseptic. Next time you bang your head like that, let's glue one of these things to it." I was busy swabbing my skinned forehead with gin, which was closer than the antiseptic in the bathroom. Polter wandered off, no doubt looking for someone else to thrill and amaze with his grasp of the really important things in life. Did you know most male birds don't have penises? I did, thanks to the Poltergeist.

The party was going strong and some folks wandered down the street to Lido Beach for a dip, then back for grilled sausages and veggie kebabs. Susan and Drew were using my outdoor shower to rinse the salt off when the side gate swung open banging into them. Ah, Chloe had arrived. Drew swung his towel at her but missed. It wouldn't surprise me if Chloe had lurked in the front yard until someone was in the shower just to have the opportunity to stage her arrival.

This sounds like I don't like Chloe. I do. It's just that she tends to be a bit more dramatic than strictly necessary. Like that swirling exit from Girls' Night Out. What was *that* all about?

And Chloe was always pushing her herbal concoctions on anyone who'd stand still. Here came one now, a milk-white jar with a label that read *Skin So Supple*.

"Wendy Sam, Wendy Sam," she cooed. "A lovely aloe lotion, your hands are always so dry. Milked my own aloes and added an infusion of cucumber and just a touch of tansy plus a bit of scorpionstail for luck." Not for Chloe the bath shop at the mall. Where she figured out the concoctions she came up with was a mystery. I mean, she was a graduate of Florida State. I don't think they taught that stuff there. By the way, scorpionstail is a weed— pardon me, a native plant— not what it sounds like. I am pretty good at Florida flora and fauna, but I don't infuse things. I just yank them out.

"Smells great, Chloe, thanks. Have a drink."

"Thanks, brought my own herbal tea. Here, try some."

"Nope, Drew brought rum. Try the couscous, I put mint in it just for you." I motioned her towards the buffet table.

Out in the yard, the discussion around Ilene's table had gotten into over-development, traffic, and how the new houses loomed over the bay instead of snuggling into the landscape the way the old homes had.

"Some developer's even tearing down the old Girl Scout camp in Osprey," Ilene said. "Remember, Wendy Sam? The one you missed buying three years ago?" I didn't want to remember the prize I'd missed by, literally, an hour. Even though I loved this place, I still dreamed of the low wooden building, the long porches, the live oaks dripping Spanish moss over the sandy road that led to a community dock. I never stopped to look at it now; some developer was building three houses on the property, trying to save the oaks with berms. They'd be dead within five years.

"There's way too many people moving here," someone said.

"We're losing all our small-town charm," said another.

"Traffic's terrible," said a third. "Can't even get a table at a decent restaurant now."

"Buncha city folks bringin' their city ways," said the first.

"Losin' our orange groves and cattle ranches," said the second.

I had to say something. "Hey guys, we're all from somewhere else. Where would we all be, if those groves and ranches hadn't become houses and condos?" And if there were fewer folks, would we have all those wonderful restaurants to patronize?

Ilene said, "I'm just saying that new houses should respect the land. Acknowledge the landscape. Fit in instead of trying to conquer."

Of course I agreed. Most of us did, so we all murmured agreeably.

"Developers build what people will buy. Might as well learn to live with it. That's progress," said Chloe.

Ilene glared at her. "Progress? It's greed is what it is. They build these 7000 square-foot marble and gilt monstrosities for some Type A who lives in it three weeks a year. And the folks who used to live there end up in a one-bedroom in some assisted living place inland."

Chloe sniffed over her herbal tea. It looked like twigs and debris were floating in it, and I noticed no one else had taken up her offer to share. "Get over it, hon. No one forced anyone off any land. People get old, they move into a nursing home. Or hell, they die, that's just one generation making room for the next. Natural selection. Then someone buys the old place and tears it down. Progress, that's all it is. It's not like Simon Legree."

Ilene turned pale, then red, then stood abruptly. "You're pretty cozy with Simon Legree, aren't you?" She strode off towards the house.

Huh? What's this about Simon Legree? And that attitude? Granted, Ilene and Chloe weren't best friends or anything, but still. After all, they ran into each other a lot, since Chloe's sales were one source of Ilene's consignable treasures. Usually, they got along fine.

Maybe Chloe had overpriced something Ilene had her eye on. Ilene would get over it. With old folks constantly moving into small condos or senior care facilities, there were plenty of garage-sale bargains to go around.

Meanwhile, Evil Thalia was holding court over under the bougainvillea. We didn't call her that of course, just Thalia, but Ilene and I had come up with that name one wine-filled evening. Thalia was evil because she drove an old Jaguar 3.8 saloon, my dream car, and because she had a terrific figure and dozens of men doting on her and because her vintage clothing shop did better business than my shop. Ilene and I figured she had to have a deal with the devil. Plus, she seemed forever amused at Ilene's mix-to-not-match outfits and my oh-so-comfortable getups. Thalia herself seldom wore her own vintage stock. She dressed severely and elegantly in things that looked like origami. You'd call her Evil, too, if you had to inhabit the same universe with her.

Right now, Evil T was coolly peering over her wine glass (correction, *my* wine glass. *Why* did I invite her to start with? Oh yes, networking. Damn this unretirement anyway.) and listening to some man I didn't recognize try to impress her. She shook her head at him and moved off. He looked longingly after her. Handsome fellow, but if he liked Thalia's peroxide blonde waterfall of hair and her lip-liner mouth he probably wasn't into outspoken rounded brunettes who more often than not forgot all about lipstick.

I pursed my naked lips. Thalia seems to be happy single. So does Ilene and so does Chloe. Was I the only one who yearned for a companion, for someone who'd be there at the end of a long day, who'd care whether, indeed, I showed up or not? What was Ilene's secret of happiness alone? I'd ask her after the party. She always stayed late, helped me clean up. Good time for a serious discussion, after a party, full of food and booze. Now that the party was going, I really enjoyed myself. I always do. You don't think I'd give parties otherwise, do you?

Half an hour later, I went into the house to use up a little more of the rum Drew had brought and to change the CDs. I could overhear the Poltergeist saying "Night-blooming cereus, yes. Rather potent drug. Slows down the heartbeat and lessens blood pressure." A female voice replied *Better not give any to my Ronnie, then, he's already half-dead.* Laughter and one masculine voice saying *I'll show you how dead I am* and some scuffling and giggling on the new shell, then the sound of guests reshuffling themselves into different conversations.

I smiled, thinking how well my friends got along. Usually. As I turned to go back into the back yard, Ilene came up, extending her hand, taking her leave. Ilene, who invariably was the last to leave?

"Going already, Ilene?"

"It's been a busy week. There seems to be a lot going on."

"But it's summertime, slow season," I said.

"Oh, not business. Something I ran into." Ilene's mood was distant, distracted.

"It's still early. Stay."

"I was out at Chloe's earlier this week."

I was confused by the non sequitur. "And?"

"Do you think she knows what she's doing?"

"Doing with what?"

"Oh, never mind." Ilene darted a quick glance over her

shoulder into the back yard, where all our friends were gathered. "If she really feels that way, then she..."

"You're upset about Chloe's opinions? Ignore her. How can you worry about someone who grows weeds?" I grinned.

"Weeds. No, it's probably nothing, never mind, it could be innocent, gotta go, see you, see you at the shop. Thanks for the party." And she was off in a flurry of lace and scarves and feathers.

Ilene always came in the shop Wednesday mornings with her week's worth of treasures she found at house sales, flea markets, and thrift stores. She would perch on the high stool by my desk and sip the double lattes with extra cinnamon she got us from Mocha Mama's as I entered her consignments in the computer, paid her for the previous week's sales, and commented on her latest outfit of bits and pieces any sane 21st century shopper would pass up. But then again, I was not overly fond of sane 21st century shoppers and adored Ilene.

We never had those double lattes. Wednesday Ilene was dead.

3

Girls' Night Out again, and this time, we opted for The Grill, a stylish restaurant near the north Siesta bridge. What the point is of sitting on a sidewalk getting Hummer exhaust in your drink and Lexus dust in your hair is beyond me. But Chloe had suggested The Grill, and Patty had wanted to dress up, so here we were, Chic Central. There were an awful lot of overly-well-groomed young ladies at the bar. They were surrounded by gentlemen of a certain age. I guess the gentlemen's wives were still at the gym, trying to hang onto the taut bodies the young women at the bar possessed but weren't old enough to appreciate yet.

Patty was looking good. Really. I mean, personally I think wrinkled white linen makes anyone over a size ten max look like an unmade bed, but on Patty, it didn't look half bad. I was wearing my emerald silk sheath, fuchsia sandals, and sapphire beaded bag. I believe in standing out in the crowd, and knowing that Ilene would be decked out in her usual vintage array, I opted for simple. Simple but bright. Kinda like the way I think of myself.

Chloe must have forgotten that we were dressing. She straddled her café chair in jeans with a faint but definite manure aura about them, laced boots still spilling muck and sand from the laces, and a T-shirt that read *I didn't say it was your fault. I said I was going to blame you.* She'd been at the table before Patty and I got there, and I had the feeling she was a few drinks ahead of us.

She was leaning over to the next table, confiding in two strangers that she'd grown up in foster homes, "never had a thing of my own. Never got to see the seeds I'd planted grow. Always sent on, to another family. That's why I have a firm, I mean a farm, now. Did I tell you I have a farm? Herbs, you know."

The strangers looked at each other and waved for their

check. They left in a hurry, leaving too big a tip.

We ordered appetizers, waiting for Ilene to join us. Chloe just drank. And talked. About herbs and house sales and whatever came into her mind. As long as she didn't start in again on her foster-child upbringing. It was sad, and it left Chloe rather needy, but I didn't want to hear it tonight. So we listened to Chloe's bragging about what a good head for business she had, and how wonderful and useful her herbs were. Patty and I sat there in amazement at the words pouring nonstop from her mouth. I'd never seen Chloe drunk before, but that's what she was: drunk.

"The woman has absolutely no business sense." Chloe was intense, waving her drink around, and people were starting to shift their chairs away from our table. "She can't even see that it's *for their own good.*"

"What woman?"

"Ilene." Chloe said. "Sanctimonious Ilene. Oh-so-pure Ilene. Former oh-so-elegant dancer Ilene. Ha."

Patty leaned in towards Chloe and said quietly, "No talking about absent friends." Our rule.

"Friends? When she's just about accused us of thievery? She has no idea... " Chloe's drunken shriek drew the host from behind his stand. I got Chloe to her feet. Patty tossed some bills on the table and we hustled out of there.

We leaned Chloe up against Patty's van, debating who got to care for her tonight. We sure weren't driving her fourteen miles inland. I lost the toss and bundled her into my car. I drove up Orange to avoid the traffic on the Trail. The scent of flowers filled my car, making Chloe's drunken muttering more bearable if not any more understandable. What was it she was going on about, Ilene, thieves? Must have been some dispute on prices, I decided. Those house sales could get pretty cut-throat.

The woods on the west side of the road, full of palmettos and long-leaf pine, was now barely visible behind a big sign that read *Sandpiper Close: Another Sunshine Improvement from BB Construction Inc.* My jaw tensed. How can you improve on sunshine? Am I becoming an old curmudgeon?

21

"I can't get over how everyone's always out for the bucks. My liability insurance is major money, because everyone's always trying to sue. Jeez, you trip, it's your fault. People act like everything is someone else's fault. No one takes responsibility." Patty munched on her dill pickle. "Ain't that the truth. Always got excuses. You should hear some of the ones I do. Frizzle your hair."

I patted my hair gently. One does not say the word frizzle around my hair. It'll get ideas.

After strudel, Patty left to sneak around the golf course and I went back to the shop. Susan and I, between us, got the day's intake of consignments entered in the computer, tagged, and hung in stock.

Susan Grimes had started working for me as soon as I could afford to pay her. Not that I paid her much, but she loved the shop and because of that, I loved her. We couldn't be less alike: she was willowy and graceful and graced with a husband and three kids and a full slate of soccer dates and ballet classes and skateboard competitions. I couldn't figure out how she managed to work for me on top of all that, but whenever she mentioned in passing the price of cleats and tu-tus and broken arms, I saw the necessity.

Late in the day, a cute little old man came in with several boxes of knick-knacks to consign. A taxi idled outside waiting for him. Most of his things weren't very clean, with a sheen of old dirt and dust, but I could wash them and save myself the embarrassment of pointing that out to him. I was glad I'd already decided to do so when he peered at me and said, "My eyesight's going all of a sudden. Had to stop driving a month or two ago, and those taxis," here he waved vaguely in the direction of my parking lot, "cost a bundle. Can't keep the house very clean either. So I'm thinking of moving to the old folks' home."

"I hear the retirement communities are lovely," I said. I was surprised to hear him call them old folks' homes. Guess euphemisms don't appeal to those they are meant to soothe.

"Lovely. Can't say as I ever wanted to live somewhere

26

lovely," the old man, whose name was Otto Bruniger, said. "But I can get enough for my place to buy a nice apartment there, the real estate guy says. But I don't know. Any buyer'd prob'ly rip down my Dorothy's place and build one of those fake castles. Dot sure did like our little home, but she's been gone a while now and I can't keep it up."

Fake castles, I thought when Mr. Bruniger left. That's a good description of the new houses going up in town. I could certainly understand Ilene's rants about them. They sat high on the land, as though shunning the sand. What was left of their yards after the house took up all the land was carpeted with plastic-feeling grass that required incredible amounts of water and fertilizer to survive. Paver-block driveways instead of crushed shell, windows that didn't open. Even turrets and battlements, as though we had to battle anything except mosquitoes and hurricanes down here.

I couldn't imagine living that way, but an awful lot of people must want to. Obviously. Every time I saw a new house going up, I kept my fingers crossed that it would be a reasonably-sized, climate-friendly house, like the Florida House, the ecological showcase on Proctor Road. I loved that house, and if I had the money to build a new one, that's what I'd build. Guess I dance to a different drummer though.

James and Michael and I met for dinner that evening, at a place near their condo. They knew the waiter, and were commiserating over some customer stealing tips left on tables before the waiters could collect them.

"What low life," I said as I slid into the booth. Not that the tip was probably very much, I reflected as my pants caught on the duct tape. But the food was supposed to be the best Mexican in town.

"Speaking of low life, guess who we saw at lunch today, whispering with a married man," James said. I swear, these guys eat every meal out.

27

"The Thymely Lady," Michael finished. They did that a lot, finish each other's sentences. I guess when you've been together for thirty years, you do that. Not that I ever would be together with anyone for thirty years. By then I'll be in a nursing home. The joys of singlehood.

"Chloe? Serious? Where, who, what?"

"At Coral's, the one on University, back corner, behind a fishtail palm, Barry Cobb," summarized Michael. I searched my memory bank for the name and came up empty. I looked to James, the chattier of the two.

"You know, Barry Cobb, the guy who's always building those spec mansions. Cobb the Cobbler, those pretentious pink palaces he cobbles together with an excess of Corian and crown moldings and crap."

"My, my, James, you're a poet." I grinned at his alliteration. "Of course. Barry Cobb and Sarina Jefferson Cobb." Sarina's cast-offs were a best-seller in my shop. Her maid brought Sarina's worn-once size 2 outfits to our shop; Sarina came in person to tuck her earnings into one of her Kate Spade handbags. Why she needed the money, who knows. But her glamorous getups made my shoppers happy so I wouldn't complain.

"Yup, but it was little Chloe's ear he was nuzzling there behind the greenery. She was looking like she needed a little persuading. A little nudge. Maybe he's trying to get her to buy one of his $3 million houses? The batch down by Ibis Creek are almost ready."

I groaned. That's where I used to launch my kayak for a paddle around the mangrove islets in Little Sarasota Bay. There had been an abandoned cottage on the property, and word was it took Cobb years to find the owners, persuade them to sell, and find an architect clever enough to squeeze four monstrosities onto the acre or so. No more launching for me or anyone unless they were the millionaires with the security code to the overwrought-iron gate that now kept the rabble away from the bay.

"I doubt Barry Cobb would consider Chloe a possible buyer," I said. "She can barely afford the free compost from the

28

dump, to hear her talk. Besides, he's way too old for her. What is he, fifty-five or something?"

"There's a law that fifty-five-year-old men can't lust after thirty-somethings? Hey, Michael, hear that? A whole new class of criminals."

"Another victimless crime." Michael raised his glass in mock salute to his partner. "Surprised the politicians haven't criminalized that. Must have overlooked it."

"Maybe they were talking about her farm. Now where did I hear that Cobb's her landlord?" I said.

"What, you think they were discussing rent?" James' eyebrows were wonderfully expressive.

"You know what I find really pretentious about Cobb?" Michael asked. I looked at him in surprise. He usually abstains from saying anything bitchy.

"That damn XLR convertible of his. He never puts the top up. It was ninety-five today, more in the parking lot at the restaurant. And there his car sat, parked right in front by the valet, top down."

James laughed. "One night we saw him zipping down Mcintosh in the rain. Top down, one of those British racing caps pulled down low to shield his eyes. Guess he figured if he drove fast enough, the raindrops wouldn't catch him."

"Everything catches up with you in the end," I said, and rose my Margarita high. I didn't really mean anything by it, just seemed an appropriate gesture at the time.

The nachos grandes came, we were aural recipients of the day's specials in glowing restaurant-speak, and we ordered.

6

It was raining. I had to sit at my kitchen counter to drink my coffee, something I normally did out in the yard.

I skimmed the paper, keeping an eye out for any news items that might affect business. Sale at that ritzy dress shop downtown: good, because my ritzy consignors would need room in their closets for new stuff so I'd get some gently-used goodies. State legislature decides against back-to-school sales tax holiday: bad, because now I'd have to pay it for my customers as a sales incentive. The society page had shots of last night's glittering Midnight Madness ball at a mansion on Casey Key and I studied the elegant gowns, sure that they'd be coming in to me soon. Usually, I sold these on-line to women in other parts of the country who were equally as glamourous, but more frugal (or sensible. I consider the words synonyms.) than their Southern sisters. Sarina Jefferson Cobb was sure to bring me that satin number she had on. It was terrific: a wide portrait neckline that framed her elaborate braided up-do and her signature diamonds. Her possibly-philandering husband looked equally elegant in his tuxedo. Those weren't really diamond studs in his shirt, were they? I shook my head in amazement over how people spent their money. The ball was to raise money to support the faction of local boaters and land speculators who wanted Midnight Pass reopened. If those folks had just not bought all new clothes and chowed down on caviar crepes and champagne, a lot of money would have been freed up for their cause. But then consignment shops and caterers would not prosper. Damned if you do, damned if you don't. I sighed as I closed the paper.

Well, it might have been a sleep-in morning for society ladies, but I hauled my butt out of the kitchen, into the shower, and into my car. I reminded myself that it had been my decision to open a shop and rejoin the working world.

The rain began to let up around nine as I was driving over the John Ringling Bridge on my way to work. Looked like it had rained hard overnight. At least I wouldn't have to water the flower boxes in front of our shop windows today. I waved at Bonita over at Mocha Mama's and let myself in. Dragged the vacuum out of the back room and used it, then cleaned the dressing room mirrors. Looked like the last customer yesterday had licked her reflection in the mirror. Then I wiped down the bathroom. The boss gets all the good jobs.

Finally, I plopped on my stool. "Enough already. I'm gonna go get a latte in a moment. Want one?"

"Coffee with skim milk for me. Don't hold with those fancy names. If you can't say it in American, I don't want to eat or drink it. Did you know the French eat frog legs?" said Elsie Martini, my "volunteer" three days a week. "Now your cooking I like. Good party last Friday. Those little green ballsy things were good. Bring me the recipe."

Elsie always cheers me up. I had had to smile this morning when she had arrived splashing through the puddles, gingham umbrella swinging, plaid lunch box in hand. Now you might think from that description that Elsie was eight or so, and you'd be right. If the "or so" translated to "and seven decades."

Yup, Elsie Martini, seventy-eight (and three quarters, if we're sticking to the juvenile angle here), carries her lunch in a plaid lunch box that she swears is identical to the ones she packed with PB&J and Oreos for her kids back in the 'Fifties. She cackled the day it came in, elbowed me rather painfully in the ribs, and said, "See, Wen, that's why I volunteer here. To get the good stuff."

Now let me get it straight. I don't allow a seventy-eight-year-old woman to work for free in my shop. After all, we are not a charity. I pay her. We just don't tell the Social Security folks that. Elsie says the same thing my mother always used to: "No sense people knowing all your business. Men like a bit of mystery."

But Elsie treasures the treasures that come into the shop a lot more than the meager pay envelope she gets. In fact, most of the envelope's contents end right back in the cash register, as Elsie finds arm-loads to buy every week. I have no idea where she puts all the stuff she buys, since she lives in a 20-foot trailer in Sun N Fun, a trailer park (oops, sorry, RV resort) on Fruitville Road. Maybe she has a storage unit. I wouldn't be surprised.

I needed to remember to bring her the recipe for spinach bites. Little green ballsy things, indeed. Smile.

As I sipped my $5 caffeine, I redid the display window. To brighten up the grey day, I chose clothes and knick-knacks in lime and lemon, with a soupçon of teal. I was expecting Ilene on her usual Wednesday morning visit. So where was she?

Ilene had been one of my first consignors. She stopped by on Wednesdays because it was a slow day in the picker business. I liked her quirky sense of humor, the odd things she found for my shop, and her air of been there, done that in zebra-striped sateen. I could never figure out how she could load and unload her Jeep with fringe dangling fore and aft and layers of skirts swirling around her legs. Whenever I had to haul stuff around, I dressed in capri tights and a big T-shirt, which isn't the best look for a fanny-rich forty-some, but what the heck, hauling isn't the proper time for a fashion statement in my mind. In Ilene's mind, life was one big fashion statement.

By eleven, I was getting concerned. Especially considering her abrupt departure from my party. I'd tried her cell a couple of times, but she didn't pick up.

"Ilene didn't call when I ran over for coffee, did she?" I asked Elsie.

"No. Expecting her?"

"Maybe she went to Corinthia's." Corinthia was the woman who did up all of Ilene's vintage linens. A proud, feisty African-American woman with a thriving alterations business in her front parlor, pillar of her church, neighborhood leader,

Corinthia was an honest-to-goodness native Sarasotan. She lived in a brightly-painted wooden house in Newtown with carefully-raked gravel for a yard and several mongrels under the porch. I loved that house. It had been built when people knew the value of cross-breezes and didn't just crank up the AC. I could understand Ilene wanting to linger there hearing old Sarasota tales on a rainy day, but not to answer her phone? That was totally unlike her. I called Corinthia's number.

"No, Wendy Sam, she's not here and I'm mighty peeved with her. I stayed home from Circle just because she said she'd be by, and she hasn't. When you find that girl you tell her Corinthia is not at all happy with her." Corinthia hung up abruptly. That's just her way. Once she's said whatever she meant to say, she sees no reason to keep yammering.

"Elsie, I'm going to run over to Ilene's." I could understand if she was running late, but apparently it was more than that. She'd never risk getting on Corinthia's bad side.

"No problem. It's slow because of the rain." Sarasotans think they'll melt if they go out in the rain. Or that it will stop any minute, and then they'll run their errands. So no sense wearing out the wiper blades.

7

It was only a few miles down Tamiami Trail to Ilene's apartment, but the rain had gotten heavy aagain by the time I pulled into the sand drive next to the two-story building and peered through the windshield at her windows. No lights on, which meant she probably wasn't home. Dang. The first floor of the small building was dark too, but that wasn't surprising. It's a storage space or workshop or something.

Since I couldn't see Ilene's parking space from the drive, and her door was on the far side of the building, facing the canal, I got out. By now, the rain was down to just a light sprinkle. Rain in Florida does that.

Ilene's Jeep was there. Puzzled —why hadn't she answered her phone when I called? —I rounded the next corner.

My mind couldn't take it in. Why was there a lump of clothing at the base of her steps? Why were linens scattered all the way down? Why was there a overturned flower pot on the ground?

My body reacted before my brain, and I was on my knees beside Ilene, turning her over by her shoulders. I had never touched a dead person before, but the heaviness told me she was. Then I noticed that her slick skin and the soft rain were the same temperature. Her striped scarf floated in a puddle.

I don't have a cell phone and I couldn't bear to use Ilene's, which was lying in a puddle next to her purse, which had spilt its contents. I had to go up into the apartment to call. All the way up, I kept thinking *I don't want to call 911, there's no emergency, but how else do I call the police?* I actually spent several minutes looking for Wendy's phone book before I took hold of myself, reasoned it was an emergency for *me*, and punched in 911. They said they'd be right out. I told them no rush, then embarrassed myself by giggling. I hung up.

I stood numbly in the kitchen. On the window ledge above the sink, she'd started rooting some bits of plants and vines in old bottles. They would live on, although their gardener was dead. I stared out the window and saw the sky was beginning to clear. But Ilene was still dead.

That's when I saw the bottle. I love blue bottles. It was a clear cobalt, with high shoulders, square in shape, and empty. It was the only empty one. I tucked it into my purse. I wasn't sure I should be doing that but I did anyway. It would be a lovely reminder of my friend. Probably Ilene had meant to give it to me for my collection.

I jumped as the phone rang. Were the police calling back? What, were they trying to make sure it hadn't been a prank call, like pizza-delivery places do?

"Hello?" I said in what sounded, even to me, to be a teeny voice.

"Ms. Brown, Sam Bennett here. I thought we had an appointment? It must be today, my flight's first thing tomorrow. You insisted it was urgent. I will, after all, need several hours to run the tests."

"Excuse me," I said. "Ilene Brown isn't available right now." I had no idea who this person was but he was bossing me around and I hate that. "May I take your number and call you back?"

He was very displeased, but I couldn't help that and I couldn't deal with it. I wrote the number down and stuck it in my pocket.

8

I was sitting on the bottom step, shoulders hunched, staring at Ilene's body, when the cops came. Or cop, singular. By then I was as wet as Ilene, for the rain had come back full force. Ilene's record book, which I had seen so often as she recorded her purchases and sales, was in my hand. I had fished it out of a puddle before it got soaked. I tucked it out of sight into my waistband as I rose to meet the officer.

It was a woman, so small that I had the inane and sexist thought *Isn't there a height minimum?* She couldn't have been more than a size 4. If she hadn't had that bulky equipment belt on, she'd have looked like a 16-year-old camp counselor in her polyester uniform.

"Did you find her like this?" The cop motioned towards Ilene, whom I had covered with an oval tablecloth cross-stitched in cabbage roses. I'd tampered with the scene of the crime, which any mystery reader knows not to do. But then, it wasn't the scene of a crime, it was an accident. Right?

Soon the drive was filled with emergency vehicles. The woman cop, Lucy Goodman, had me in the back of her patrol car, and the marina guy was leaning in handing me a cup of coffee. I'd seen him around but didn't remember his name. Ilene had said he gave her the willies and I could see why. He wasn't very clean and he seemed awfully calm to be on the scene of a death. He backed away with a slight smile. Creepy.

The coffee was the worst I've ever had, in a mug that indicated he didn't wash mugs any more often than he did his body. I couldn't stop shaking. Never thought of myself as the fragile type, but then I never discovered a friend dead before. And the rain made it worse.

36

Lucy opened the car door, stuck her head in, and said, "The inspector's here. Can he speak to you?" What was I going to say, *No, thank you, I want to go home and take a bubble bath?*

He folded himself into the back seat next to me. My age, good shape, plain unadorned face. Just a guy in a suit.

"Ms. Miller, my name is Tom Litwin. I understand you called the body in?"

I shifted in my seat. "I reported the death of my friend, yes."

"Sorry. Not always as tactful as I should be. Officer Goodman got the necessary information, but can we talk about your relationship with the deceased?" Do police really talk like that?

"I'm sorry," I said stiffly, "but I really am not up to this right now and I'm wet and uncomfortable. I need to get back to work." I told him my shop name and address.

He looked sharply at me, then nodded. "What time do you close? I can come by then. Maybe you'll be able to talk about it then."

He handed me out of the car. As I stood up, I felt Ilene's record book slip from my waistband into my panties. Maybe I would have given it to him then, but I couldn't see myself digging into my underwear to haul it out. Maybe if I had, though, it would all have ended much better.

I got back to the shop and sent Elsie home. I didn't say why. She took one look at me and left. Then I flipped the sign to closed, put on dry clothes and turned on the answering machine. Turned off most of the lights too, so people wouldn't try the door to see if we were open in spite of the sign. I felt guilty, because a store's supposed to be open when it says it will be, but I just couldn't.

Because I needed to devote all my attention to colorizing the earrings. This is what I do when I am worried and need to think. All the greens on this stand, from celery to forest, all the blues there, from aqua to navy. A silly thing, but one that calms me and lets my mind wander.

What could have happened? Were the steps just wet, and Ilene, carrying a box of linens, careless? How did the cranesbill planter fall as well? I shuddered as I remembered the small, gay petals of the flowers plastered onto Ilene's cold cheeks. Would she have grabbed for a hanging plant when she missed a step?

But she was, I assumed, carrying the box. Her hands wouldn't have been free. Did she hit the pot with her shoulder on the way down? I tried to dig back into high school physics. If her shoulder dislodged the pot from its bracket, it would have traveled down the stairs along with Ilene, wouldn't it? Then how did it end up on her head?

I'd never seen Ilene so much as stumble. But it was raining, and old wood gets slippery, especially in this climate. It was probably an accident, but is it likely she would be dead from falling down stairs? Unless the flowerpot did it. Still didn't seem likely to me. Sprains, bruises, even broken ankles and concussions, but dead?

Why did Ilene's rushing out of my party last Friday come into my mind? And what did her phone call to me Monday mean? *She thinks she knows what's going on, but she doesn't. I don't think I do either.*

That makes three of us. Me, Chloe, and Ilene. Except Ilene is dead.

It was just a little before six when a dark four-door sedan pulled up in front of the shop. Tom Litwin got out and peered through the window glass, shading his eyes from the sun so he could see into the dimness. Now the sun comes out, I thought. Where would Ilene's body be? Would the police have called her family? Come to think of it, I wasn't real sure Ilene had family, although I thought I remembered something about her mother, a nursing home, and California. Everyone in Sarasota (well, not Corinthia, but everyone else) is from somewhere else, so we don't tend to know much about each other's previous life. Even the obituaries in the Herald-Tribune read "born in so-and-so, came to Sarasota from such-and-such 12 years ago." Life starts when you reach the county line.

I let Litwin in and led him to my back room.

Mistake. I'd forgotten how little my office is, since I am in it so seldom and never, to my recollection, with a man. A man in a suit. By the time we were both seated, our knees kept touching. I straightened up and put my hands in my lap. So did he. In his lap, I mean.

"Can you tell me about Ilene Brown? Her neighbors barely knew her and the landlord's in North Carolina for the summer. Can't seem to find any employment on her."

I'd only known Ilene for about two years, but we'd seen each other two or three times a week, and even gone on two long weekend trips together, once to the Keys, once to Miami. Guess I knew her as well as anyone else. "She didn't work for anyone, she was a picker."

"You'll have to explain that to me."

So I did. I took him out onto the sales floor and showed him some of the things Ilene had brought in and I could see the look in his eyes: *Who would want to deal in secondhand stuff?* Immediately I disliked him. Secondhand stuff is my life. It has supported me for years, I like turning one man's trash into you-know-what, and I actually *prefer* used to new. Those whose imagination is so lacking that only new and shiny will do are distinctly lesser beings as far as I'm concerned. Shame. The way his hair curled on his neck had begun to appeal to me. Probably married, anyway.

I explained how the shop worked, and that Ilene usually came Wednesday mornings to bring things in, and that I'd been expecting her, and how Corinthia called and that's why I went over to Ilene's. I noticed he didn't write all that down.

He was getting ready to leave when I asked if Ilene's mother had been notified. Litwin said he'd talked to the manager of the nursing home in Ojai (that's it, now I remember) and that she wanted to break the news to Mrs. Brown herself, gently.

39

"I just can't understand that Ilene would have slipped on the stairs, even if they were wet. She was always so sure-footed," I said as I escorted him to the door. "And for a fall to kill her..."

"The steps weren't wet," said Litwin. "At least not when she fell. The ground underneath her was dry."

I stopped dead. Not the best choice of words, but I was shocked. "If the steps weren't wet why did she fall?"

"Well, it looked like she was carrying that box of tablecloths. Probably she missed a step. Then she must have grabbed for that flower, it broke lose and hit her in the head."

"How do you grab for something when you're carrying a box in both hands?" I couldn't visualize any scenario where the flower pot would have come down.

"Ms. Miller, accidents happen. I'm sorry this one happened to your friend, but..."

"You're sure it was an accident? Why?"

The detective sighed, put his hand on the door, and as he pushed it open, said "There's no reason to think it anything but an accident. Her place didn't seem to be burglarized, the keys were in her ignition, her wallet was right there in plain sight..."

"Maybe she was murdered."

He sighed rather dramatically this time. "Ms. Miller, if you know something you haven't told me, I'll be glad to listen. But believe me, it's an accident. Who'd want to kill a junk dealer?"

There he went again. I bit back my standard lecture on the difference between junk and the underappreciated remnants of human history, ignored his well-shaped hand on my glass door, and bid him good night. I had a lot to think about.

9

So, if someone did kill Ilene, why? I drove home, parking and grabbing the mail from my box automatically. Bills, bank statement, circulars, and an actual real letter. I get so few personal letters, I ripped it open immediately, realizing as I did so that I recognized the handwriting. It was from Ilene. Enclosed was a key.

Going out of town for a bit. Need to think what to do. Something's not right, it's gone beyond greed. I'm getting a bad feeling. Will you feed the fish? I'll leave their food on the counter. Should be back in a few days. I'll call. Mucho, I.

What's gone beyond greed? Where was Ilene going? I'd seen no indication that Ilene was leaving town. No packed suitcase in the car or her living room. What kind of bad feeling? What was going on?

And if she was going out of town, why didn't she just drop off her key at the shop? She's done that before when she'd gone across state to auctions or major sales. What had been going on in Ilene's life? Had it gotten her killed?

For such a short note, it sure raised a lot of questions. And since it was probably the last thing Ilene wrote, I felt tears welling up again. She must have written it yesterday. Her last day on Earth. I put the letter on my entry table, attached Ilene's key to my key ring, and shut the door firmly behind me. I needed a dose of sunset and I needed it right now. I saw Dom a few houses ahead of me with the same destination in mind. I caught up with him when he had to wait for a couple of Harleys to go by on Ben Franklin Drive, and we crossed together.

I waited until we'd kicked off our sandals and sunk our feet into the sand. Then I broke the news about Ilene to him. He put an arm around my shoulders and murmured "Ah cara mia." I patted his arm thank-you, then stepped into the water to walk in the ankle-deep waves. Dom always stayed three steps above the waterline, and we continued north this way until it was quite dark. I was too absorbed in my thoughts to even notice the sunset, but it still lent peace to my soul.

As we turned to head back home, Dom insisted I join him for snapper piccata. He used to be a restaurant chef. I had missed lunch. I said yes.

Dom's place is the other half of my place, but the two couldn't be more dissimilar. Dom was widowed fifteen years ago and moved to Sarasota the week after he buried his wife. None of his kids back in Jersey wanted anything from the family home, and Dom didn't think he should make any rash decisions, so he brought it all down with him and crammed it all into his two-bedroom, 800-square-foot beach cottage. And there it sat, Bleeding Heart of Jesus, velvet draperies, crocheted toilet-paper cozies and all. He even arranged the shelves with his wife's collection of porcelain shepherdesses and bisque song birds. Doesn't make for a swinging senior bachelor type of place, and Ilene was always teasing him that he needed to clean out some of the clutter, but he always said he'd will the lot to her.

My eyes welled up at that thought and I could barely swallow the luscious fish. With a sip of wine, I managed, and then asked Dom, "Would you think I'm crazy if I said I think someone killed Ilene?"

He patted his lips, then put his napkin beside his plate. "Why do you think such a thing? Who would want to kill her?"

"I don't know, but the police think it's an accident, so they won't go looking. I just can't believe that Ilene would slip on dry steps. The policeman told me she fell before it rained."

Dom swirled his wine in his glass, wet his thumb to pick up a few bread crumbs off the tablecloth, and realigned his plate with the edge of the table. He did all this without looking at me. "Anyone can trip, hit their head," he said quietly.

"Dom, you knew Ilene. She wasn't clumsy."

"Wendy Sam, you have no reason to think someone killed her. Or do you?" He looked up, finally, sharply. "Do you know something I don't?"

I told him about what Ilene had said about Chloe in her phone call, and their argument at my party, and about Ilene's note with her key. *I'm getting a bad feeling about all this.*

"None of that sounds like something worth killing over," Dom said when I was through.

I poured myself just a splash more wine and sat back in my chair. Why was I so sure it wasn't a simple accident? Why could I picture someone shoving Ilene, someone taking the planter and smashing it down on her as she lay there? I shuddered. I could picture it, but I couldn't *see* it, if you know what I mean. Try as I might, I couldn't imagine who might want Ilene dead. Want it badly enough to kill her.

"I have to find out," I said. "She was my friend."

Dom patted my hand, muttered something that sounded disapproving, but said out loud that if there was anything he could do to help...

A change of intensity was called for before I started crying. But I couldn't change the topic.

"What do you suppose happens to all of Ilene's stuff now? In her own way, she had as much as you do here," waving my wineglass around Signora Dom's earthly goods.

Dom looked closely at me. I think he was judging whether I should have had that last glass of wine. "Her mother's the only family member, right?" I nodded as Dom continued, "I doubt she could handle it if she's in a nursing home. Maybe you should call her and volunteer."

"I suppose so. And there's Ilene's goldfish she wanted me to see after. How often do you have to feed fish, anyway?"

Dom had no idea. He got up from the table, cleared the plates, then brought out home-made tira misu. "Absolutely not," I said. He looked hurt. "Dom, I'm stuffed. I can't possibly."

10

I didn't get out of there without a healthy portion of the rich cake "for breakfast." Just what my hips needed.

Getting ready for bed, I started thinking again of how Ilene died. It seemed to me that someone must have pushed her, then slammed the flower pot down on her as she lay stunned at the foot of the steps. But who, and why? I washed my face and donned my favorite nightie.

That detective didn't think it was a robber. Neither did I. I had to admit that it was unlikely a robber wouldn't at least take Ilene's wallet, and her apartment wasn't a mess when I went in to call the police. Well, not any more of a mess than usual.

To kill someone, especially with a flowerpot, you had to have a reason, and so it must have been someone she knew. Most murders, they say, are personal. I thought over Ilene's personal life as I flossed. A while back there was a Richard but he didn't last long, and before that a Jack, or was Joe before him? Men were all in and out of Ilene's life too quickly, I thought, to feel driven to murder.

No, her personal life, as far as I knew, didn't seem passionate enough to lead to murder. Could it have to do with her business? After all she did run across a lot of eccentric people. She had to buy low to make a profit. Had she crossed someone somehow?

But most of the people Ilene bought things from were elderly, and most of them were frail. They were tickled to get rid of a lifetime's accumulation of material goods. I couldn't imagine some disgruntled eighty-year-old climbing Ilene's rickety staircase, pushing her, then heaving a pot at her.

44

Material goods. Was a robber involved: someone Ilene had bought things from and she discovered the goods were hot, and threatened to report the thief? Or could it be that somehow, Ilene was involved with thieves and there was a falling-out? I didn't want to think of my friend like that but anything's possible... like Patty and I were talking, everyone's got an excuse.

The phone rang. It was Chloe.

"Oh God, Wendy Sam, I've got to apologize. That was totally not *comme il faut*, Monday. I can't tell you how embarrassed I am, being such an ass. It's taken me this long to work up the courage to call you and apologize."

"Hey, Chloe, doesn't matter. We've all been there. My couch is your couch. Where are you?"

"Home, why?"

"Sit down," I said. I hated to do this and didn't know how. "Chloe, Ilene is dead."

There was a silence on the other end. A long, empty silence.

"Chloe?"

"I'm here. Ilene. How? Why?"

So I told her. Just about the fall, not about my suspicions that it wasn't an accident. She listened so quietly that a couple of times I had to say "Chloe? You there?" When I was done I took a shaky breath. Still, Chloe didn't say anything.

"Wendy Sam," she finally said. I could hear the miles between us, me here by the Gulf of Mexico and the beach and the bougainvillea, Chloe out in the dry pastureland and orange groves with her herbs and barb wire.

Her voice seemed to be borne to me on an off-shore breeze. "What are the chances you'd die, falling down steps?"

We talked for another ten minutes or so. As we were saying goodbye Chloe said something strange. "Did you talk to Ilene this week?"

"Monday night, yes. Not since. Why?"

"Never mind." Chloe's voice was getting farther and farther away, as though she was drifting away from me. I noticed my fist was wrapped around the handset so tightly the plastic was creaking. "No, wait," I said. "Why?"

"Just wondered what she'd been doing. She hung around with some shady characters. Thought I heard that she'd been getting close to some guys with records."

"Records?" I was thinking LPs.

"Criminal records. Burglaries. Doesn't matter now."

Burglaries? Ilene had been seen with such people? I couldn't believe it.

I tried to get Chloe to tell me more, but she wouldn't. *Never mind, shouldn't speak ill of the dead,* she said. She reminded me that she'd given me a jar of herbal tea for my birthday, and that I should brew some up "to soothe your mind, Wendy Sam. That's why herbs work, it's really mental more than anything else. Take the tea." I promised I would, we said goodbye and hung up. As I waited for the kettle to boil, it finally sunk in. Ilene. Stolen goods. It might be true.

My God, what if the items Ilene brought to my shop were stolen goods? Was I an accomplice? Would my shop's reputation be ruined? I reached into my cupboard for a mug when the tea kettle started to whistle. It was blue, which made me remember the blue bottle from Ilene's that I'd tucked in the bottom of my purse. While the tea brewed, I got the bottle out and uncorked it to rinse it under the tap.

What a strange smell. I sniffed the bottle more closely. Turpentine? Skunk? Something unpleasant mixed with something sweet: Lavender? Orange blossoms? I washed it out well, sniffed again. Mostly gone. I replaced the cork, dried the bottle, and found a spot for it on the shelf. By now, my tea was cool enough to drink so I did, vowed to look into Ilene's items at my shop in the morning, crawled into bed and cried for my lost friend.

11

Looking through Ilene's consignment account, I did see a pattern, but it was only a pattern that matched the sales I remember her talking about. Here was a batch of 1940's-style items, including a great horsehead-shaped lamp I remembered a delighted New Yorker snatching up.

Other batches also had themes, it seemed, when I looked at them as a whole. Here's one with a lot of masculine stuff like brocade smoking jackets and curly-maple pipe-racks and a brass ship's compass. Surprisingly, the two pipe racks had sold within a day. Dang, must have priced them too low. Who knew? I thought there were fewer smokers around nowadays. Supply and demand in action: as things get harder to find in the "real" stores, they become more valuable in consignment shops.

I sighed, exited Ilene's account, and went to unlock the front doors and turn the sign to *Open! Browsers welcome, Buyers adored.* As usual, my third helper was scurrying across the street, just barely on-time enough that I wouldn't mention it. Ah, youth. When the nights are such fun, it's hard to get up and get to work on time. Couldn't remember the last time that had happened to me.

Annie Driscoll was a sweet soul, twenty-one, college dropout, tattoos and belly-button ring. For all her attention to fads, though, she had zero taste. It was all I could do to deter her from doing displays around the shop, and she was specifically forbidden to do our window displays, lest the passing public got the idea that this was a head shop or something. I mean, hot pink vinyl and leopard velveteen has its place, but not in Too Good to be Threw's windows. We did let Annie have her way with the back left-hand corner, which is traditionally the lowest-value area of any shop. She'd found an old worn Oriental for the floor, made a bamboo structure that held a chartreuse plastic tiki awning, and zealously combed our racks for the tackiest, showiest, sleaziest stuff we had. Not that I'd tell her that. And I had to admit, it did look just like the stuff her age group wore, and it did attract a whole new customer base to the shop. Was it P. T. Barnum who said you'd never go broke underestimating the taste of the American public?

For all Annie's youthful flamboyance, she was raised right. She hugged me, said she was sorry about Ilene, patted my shoulder and hitched up a bra strap and down her mini.

"God, I hope she wasn't hung over or anything," Annie said, hesitating noticeably after the "or." "The paper said she fell. Maybe she was just tired. That's it, it must have been late."

"What are you talking about?" I said a bit too sharply and Annie took a half-step back from me. I tend to forget that I'm old enough to be her mother so sometimes our relationship gets a little weird.

"Nothing."

Ten minutes later, though, as we readied the shop for business, Annie said, "Ilene was at the club the night before, Tuesday night. I've never seen her there before. She was over at the bar, drinking with some guy..." Her voice trailed off as she reached high to dust the top shelves. From the rear view of Annie's lack of skirt length, I was glad we weren't open yet.

"Your club, Demon Den or whatever it is?" I was surprised. I never knew Ilene was the loud-music-watered-drinks club type.

"The Sand Box." Annie rolled her eyes just like I was her mother. Great.

"Sorry," I said. "What was she doing there?"

"Nothing. I mean, not dancing or anything. But the guy she was talking to..." The dust cloth suddenly became exceedingly interesting to her.

"Talking to or drinking with? There's a difference."

Annie nodded. "Yeh, ain't there? Talking to, mostly.

48

Looked like question and answer time. Her questions, his answers. Thing is, though, the guy's..." again with the trailing voice, but this time she was just standing there, avoiding my eyes.

"The guy is..." I led in my most motherly voice.

"He's a dealer. Not a big one, but he can get what you need. I mean what they need, what people want, uh, ya know."

I took pity on her then. Nothing like trying to keep your boss from knowing your illegal habits. "What's his name?"

"Mark. They call him Mark Four 'cause that's what he drives, a big old Lincoln. I never heard a real name. Just Mark Four."

"Did you see her leave? Did she leave with him?"

"I don't think so. Later on, maybe an hour or so later, I saw her leaving, and the guy, Mark, was still at the bar. And there was some older guy at a table, who stood up when Ilene left."

"Did this guy follow Ilene out?"

Annie shook her head. "Sorry, Wendy Sam. I must have got side-tracked. I don't remember one way or the other. In fact I forgot about it. Until I heard the news."

What was Ilene doing in a club she was fifteen or twenty years too old for, talking to a drug dealer? What was she asking him about? Who was the guy watching her leave? Was Ilene dealing in drugs? Drugs *and* stolen goods? Did I really know my friend at all? Was she living the kind of life where you get murdered? My funny, quirky friend Ilene? And did I really want to know all this? A quick little thought crept into my mind: *The police think it's an accident. Better that than a drug deal gone sour, for the sake of her reputation.* I shook myself. No. I wouldn't let her death go unavenged. Even if she was dealing, she didn't deserve to die at the foot of her own steps with her own flowerpot smashed at her side. I didn't know how, but I was going to find her killer.

Our first customer of the morning came in and asked if we took old clothes. With an invisible, I hope, sigh, I led her to the counter and handed her a brochure which explains how we operate. As she read, I played my little mind game of what she might bring in.

You could tell she was a teacher by the way she held herself, as though perpetually in front of a pod of pernicious pre-pubescents. *See, I can be alliterative too, James,* I thought, thinking of my orchid-growing ex-cop friends.

As she read the brochure, I worried that my wording could probably use some work. *Please God, make her a math teacher, not an English teacher.*

She looked up and smiled a tight little teacher smile. I instantly felt thirteen again. "You got consignor and consignee right. The last shop I was in didn't. I'll get my clothes out of the car."

Well whoop-de-doo. I'd passed. I would be permitted to handle her old clothes after all.

And sure enough, teacher clothes. Polyester blouses and pleated plaid flannel skirts. Prissy suits and I swear, even a dickie or two, one with a ladybug embroidered on the collar. Where had this woman been the past two decades?

Well, I got Ms. Teacher sorted out, and was tagging the dozen items I figured were saleable while Annie helped a couple of society matrons going through the designer racks. Amazing how the belly ring didn't bother them. Probably Annie reminded them of their daughters.

The door opened and I looked up, my standard welcoming smile in place.

It was that detective again. Litwin, Tom Litwin. I wasn't very good with names, but his I remembered. Of course it had only been yesterday when I met him, well, saw him twice. Today he was wearing an awfully-yellow Oxford shirt, chinos, and a mahogany-brown windbreaker that matched his eyes exactly.

"Ms. Miller, do you have ten minutes? Could we talk?"

I remembered how our knees touched in my back room and decided Mocha Mama's would be better. Annie would be fine for ten minutes, as long as she didn't blow up the computer or something.

"Sure, next door okay?"

The door banged behind us at the café and Bonita looked up. She gave us a moment to settle in a booth, then came over and offered her condolences. "Ilene was so interested in everything. Those stories about old folks, they made me laugh. And she loved the Internet, always she wanted sites. We will miss her, yes, Wendy Sam?" Bonita had dreams of being a web-site designer, and knew more about it than anyone I knew.

She left to fetch our coffees after flirting a bit with my detective, finally persuading him that today's special pastry, flan Danish, was just what he needed. Only in Florida would you get flan Danish. Caribbean and North European in one fattening dish, guaranteed to clog arteries even further than either culture could separately. I passed.

Litwin played with the sweetener packets, arranging them in their little square dish white, blue, pink, white, blue, pink. I couldn't think why we were here, so I just sat.

"Does everyone call you Wendy Sam?" he asked when the silence continued long enough. "I assumed Sam was a middle name."

"Nope, I have a two-name first name. My parents couldn't decide which grandfather got the middle name instead of the first, so, Wendy Sam all in one. No middle name."

"Grandfathers?" Litwin paused in his packet filing and looked at me finally. "I never met a woman named after her grandfathers."

"Yup, Wendell and Samuel. Guess I should be thankful they weren't John and Joseph. Don't see myself as Johnnie Jo," I said.

"Neither do I. Johnnie Jo would be perky."

So he didn't think of me as perky. Big deal. After all, we'd met over my friend's dead body. And what the hell did I care if he thought I was perky? And who the hell wanted to be perky anyway.

"So," I said as the coffee came. "What can I do for you,

51

Detective?" Time to get down to business.

"Tom, please," he said. "That way I can call you Wendy Sam."

"Mmmph," I said in my coffee. Did I want to be on a first-name basis with a police detective? One who wore exceedingly-yellow shirts?

"I need to complete my report on Ms. Brown's accidental death." He pulled a small spiral notebook from a pocket. "May I ask you a couple of questions?"

"Why do you insist it was accidental? Did the doctor tell you that? Was there an autopsy?"

Tom sighed. "No. It wasn't necessary. Her body was examined at the hospital, as the law requires. Death was from an accidental fall."

"So why are you here?" I asked. The image of Ilene's body in the morgue was not one I wished to dwell on.

"I need to track her movements that morning. Get a time frame for my report. The medical examiner needs a time frame. You can't go on internal body temperature in Florida."

My mouth must have been hanging open, because he muttered something about being sorry and stirred his coffee.

After a moment he continued. "There's no real neighbors near by, since she lived in the marina. The manager of the marina..." Here Tom flipped through his notebook.

"The guy who sent the coffee over," I said. "I don't know his name. Thick-set, beard, always wears cutoffs."

"Yeh, umm, Gary Beeton. He came to work around seven, saw a silver Mercedes leaving the lot faster than would seem normal. He knows it was a Mercedes, but not what model."

"Probably two-thirds of the cars in this town are silver because silver reflects the heat. And three-quarters of the people in this town drive faster than they should. And there's a lot of Mercedes in Sarasota."

"Don't I know it." Tom grimaced and took another sip of his coffee, which had to be cold by now.

"It's a marina. There are some nice boats there. The

Mercedes could be anyone's."

Bonita came back and refilled our coffee cups.

Tom smiled his thanks at her, which I took as a good sign. So many men act like women, from waitresses to wives, are put on this earth to serve them. It's nice to see a guy who doesn't feel entitled, just because he has an outie instead of an innie.

"Most of the boats are closed up for the summer, though," I mused. "They belong to snowbirds. The only person leaving a marina at seven would have been a fisherman back with his dawn catch, and somehow I can't see someone carrying dead fish in a Mercedes."

"Well, at any rate, the Mercedes driver would not necessarily have seen the deceased. Her apartment faces away from the parking lot."

"She's not the deceased. She's my friend Ilene who wore outrageous clothes and loved Sarasota and knew all the old folks in town and. . ." I dug in my purse for a hankie. A hankie, I realized as I dug it out, that Ilene had given me for my last birthday, a hankie with fancy perfume bottles and lipsticks printed on it, from the 1950's. I sobbed out loud.

Tom buried his face in the coffee cup. I wiped my eyes and apologized.

He waved his hand for *apology not needed.* That was nice, a man who didn't get all bent out of shape by a little justified emotion. Nicer than the average guy, I decided.

He said, "She was on her way to your shop?"

"She was going to make a stop first. That's why I got worried. Because she hadn't gone there either."

I'd told him all this yesterday.

"Are you asking me all this again to make sure I'm telling the truth?"

"Did you tell me this before? Sorry. You said a lot of things yesterday. I must have missed this."

Some detective. Shouldn't detectives listen? At least he had the grace to look abashed. Actually, he looked kinda cute abashed, like a third-grader who had been caught with a frog in his pocket.

So I explained about Ilene's usually coming around opening, at ten, and how she didn't and how I called Corinthia.

"It wouldn't have taken Ilene two or three hours to run that errand, would it?" Tom asked. "Or would it?"

"I wouldn't think so. Corinthia can talk a lot, but not that much."

"So why would Ms. Brown be loading up her car so early in the morning? Seems like seven's early to leave home, especially for someone without a job."

"She had a job, I told you that yesterday. Just because she didn't have to report to an office doesn't mean she was lazy," I snapped.

"Sorry, didn't mean to suggest anything. I was just wondering where she might have been going so early."

"Not to see me," I said. "I'm still in my nightie at seven most mornings." Then I blushed, thinking how intimate the word "nightie" was to use to a stranger.

He dabbed at a bit of flan that had landed on his incredibly-yellow shirt. I just had to say something.

"That's a very yellow shirt," I said.

"Yeh." He grimaced down at it. "Gift from my Mom. You can always tell when I'm getting to the bottom of my dresser drawers. It's past time for me to take my shirts to the laundry."

"Your wife doesn't do that?"

"No wife," he said. "You?"

"No, I don't have a wife either."

Well, we didn't get established where Ilene might have been going so early, but he did tell me again, as we parted at the cashier counter, "I'm sorry about the accident." There seemed to be a stress on the "accident" part. Was he telling me the case was closed, that my friend, who might have been murdered, was going to go down as a clumsy clod? I couldn't abide that. If Ilene was murdered, I couldn't let the murderer go unpunished. But how the heck was I, a distinctly non-perky "retired" shopkeeper, going to find out who murdered Ilene?

12

I stayed behind in the café, waiting for a break in Bonita's routine to follow up on something that struck me as a little odd: what internet sites had Ilene been interested in? I knew she used the internet at the library, but I'd never heard her mention anything but the obvious places for pickers, like eBay and antique collectors' sites.

Boss was presiding over the bakery case and cash register, and his ample tummy was covered with a crisp white apron. His name wasn't Boss, of course, but we couldn't very well call him Mocha Mama, not with his 11 a.m. shadow and the hound-dog face that it covered. He shaved, I guess, at five in the morning or thereabouts, before he came in to bake. Whenever he was asked his name, he said "Boss." I hated to call him that at first, because all my life I've worked hard not to have a boss. He must have had a real name, but I guess nobody cared enough to find out what it was. So Boss it was. By now, it was just a name to me, not a title.

"Gonna miss that crazy lady," Boss declared now. "She sure did love my guava roll."

We paused, thinking how alive and happy Ilene'd always been. She loved what she was doing, she adored the old people she bought from, and she was always so interested in what the town was like in the past. She especially liked photos of old Sarasota and I always kept an eye out for them for her.

Bonita finally got all her customers to a point where she could leave them for a few minutes and came up to us. "So sad, so sad," she patted my on the arm. Her soft Mexican accent made it sound even sadder, and tears came to my eyes. But I had to find out what Ilene might have been looking at on the web.

"Recipes," Bonita said when I asked.

"Did she say why?" I asked.

"I made dinner for her one night. A real Mexican meal, like in my village. Vegetable pancakes with a fruit and black beans sauce herba de Santa Maria. She liked it, wanted to find out more about Mexican cooking."

That was odd. I'd never seen Ilene cook. Isn't it sad. She wanted to learn something new, and then she was dead.

That guy Annie saw Ilene talking to at the bar, I pondered as I worked in the shop that afternoon. Was Ilene involved in drug dealing? Did she poke her nose around too much and someone killed her for that?

Chloe's a grower. Well, of herbs, but hey, marijuana's an herb, right? And opium, that comes from poppies. The only person I knew who was into plants was Chloe. Maybe Ilene thought Chloe had some drug connection. Chloe and Ilene seemed severely on the outs. Did drugs have anything to do with their disagreement? Or maybe Ilene and Chloe into something together? On the phone, Monday night, Ilene had said *Chloe's scaring me. She thinks she knows what's going on, but she doesn't.*

I had to talk to Chloe soon. But life goes on, and I had to work. Annie was a great help, but she wasn't up to running the shop by herself. In fact, Annie left a bit early, and I was left to close up myself. I was doing just that when Elsie came rushing in, her arms open wide. "Aw, honey," she said, and I broke down.

Being hugged by Elsie is a very active state. Squeeze squeeze, pat pat. It felt good. No one had hugged me so good since my grandma died. Finally, she sat me down on the husband settee and told me about the last time she'd seen Ilene.

"Bill and I ran into her at Sugar and Spice," she started. "Don't you love their peach pie? Anyway, she joined us for dinner and we had a nice visit. Thing was, though, she embarrassed poor Bill when I went to the little girls'."

"How so?"

56

"Well, you see Ilene had met Bill just a few weeks ago, at his sale, when she bought a batch of things. Remember, I took that day off to help Bill? I don't know why men wait until after they've moved to have a moving sale, seems silly to me." Elsie shook her head at the strange ways of men.

"Anyway, when Ilene was at the sale, she saw some medicine Bill had on his kitchen counter, you know, with his vitamins and such, and she asked him about it. But she waited until I left the table."

"And that embarrassed Bill?"

"Well, I should think so! It was for, umm..."

"For what?"

Elsie put her hand to the side of her mouth as though to prevent others from hearing. "You know, like Viagra?"

"Elsie, there's no one in the shop."

She looked around. "Oh."

"Bill told you about this conversation?"

"Kind of."

"What do you mean, kind of? Elsie, tell me."

"Young woman, you are being nosey. That's personal."

"Elsie, I'm just trying to figure out what Ilene was doing before she was murdered."

Elsie sat back and stared at me. "Murdered?"

It was my turn to hug Elsie. I probably didn't do it as well as she did, but being the hugger is almost as good as being the huggee. "I think so," I said. Her shellacked beauty-parlor do was tickling my nose, so I let go.

I explained why I thought it was murder, and no, the police didn't think so, and yes, I was going to try to figure it out. And yes, I would be careful and no, I wouldn't do anything foolish, and what does the name of the policeman who took the report have to do with anything.

I realized that I didn't know when Ilene and Bill had had this conversation. "When was this?" I asked Elsie.

"Just last Saturday," Elsie said. "The day after your party."

13

That evening I nestled into my ticking-covered couch, pulled a barkcloth foliage-printed pillow over my tummy for comfort, and opened Ilene's record book. It was a small brown leather binder, filled with accountant-neat entries of expenditures and income, addresses and contacts. Ilene might have seemed casual, but she kept careful records.

I'd opened the book to see if any of the items in her apartment needed to be delivered to buyers. There had seemed to be more there than usual, but maybe it was simply the shock of her death that had made the place seem claustrophobic.

Each expenditure was listed with the seller's name and address. Income, too, had names, but mostly abbreviations. I spotted TGtbT, my shop of course, as well as Snips & Snails, the childrenswear shop near mine, abbreviated S&S, and even Thalia's The Witch in the Wardrobe, listed as Witch. Appropriate, I grinned, then remembered these were my dead friend's notes. Some income listings I could guess at: BradAnt was probably the monthly antique show in Bradenton, and VV was probably the Venice vintage festival. Others were probably antique dealers, of which there were dozens in town and hundreds within easy driving distance.

I flipped to the last pages, where Ilene had noted upcoming sales or people who wanted to clean out so their kids wouldn't have to "when the time comes." There were also some delivery notes, what and when, all the past dates neatly Xd out. Sure enough, a few were due soon. I'd have to see about those. I could deliver the things myself. Oops, *oak brkfrnt* to Tampa. I'd have to find a trucker of some sort to do that one. Who did Ilene use?

Maybe she had a business card from her delivery service. There was a flap inside the back cover of the book stuffed with cards, and I fanned them out to look. Antique shops, real estate agents, auctioneers, refinishers, appraisers. But no delivery service. Several cards had notes on the back, which made me look at each one carefully, front and back. One agent's card had a photo, a friendly-looking bald man in tennis whites. Going for the Baby Boomer market, I guessed. But what was even more interesting than his hail-fellow-well-met visage was a list on the back of his card. In Ilene's favorite turquoise pen was *Jolly Johnson, Sandpiper, Ugly Ct, Wm from Wisc , Liverwurst, Blowfish Bayou?, Epazote/ St J? AM!, Loquat.* What was that all about? Strange list. Had Ilene just used the card as a handy piece of paper, or could that salesman have some connection to the list? Could the list tell me why Ilene died? I decided to go visit the man the next day. At last, some clues to follow. I felt like Nancy Drew. I really would have enjoyed this, if only it wasn't Ilene's death I was trying to solve.

14

It was very early but the real estate office was already awash with noise. Voices, printers, and fax machine beeps clamored for attention. The coffee machine in the lobby was sputtering as though dying. The receptionist said Laurence Pease was in a meeting. Would I like to wait?

Not particularly, but I did. I flipped through a magazine of houses for sale, choosing which one I'd buy if money were no object. All the houses I liked were labeled "tear-downs." At the prices they were asking, I'd want a house, not just the lot. I sighed. The coffee tasted like it was indeed in imminent peril of death. Maybe the Styrofoam cup was killing it. I made a face.

"Nasty stuff, huh?"

I looked up, and there was Laurence Pease. I recognized him from his business card, even though he was now wearing a striped golf shirt instead of the tennis whites in the photo. Covering all the sports fans who might need a new house, I guess.

"There's better in my office," he said, leading me through corridors formed by fuzzy tweed cubicle walls. His office was no cubicle, though. Windows looked over a manicured yard with a covered picnic bench where several office staff sat and smoked. Sunlight danced on the inside wall of his office, covered edge to edge with brass plaques proclaiming Pease Salesman of the Month, Year, Decade, and for all I knew Century. The desk was piled neatly with files and color photos and more brass, these in the form of tennis racquet paperweights and golf club letter openers and sailboat statuettes.

An assistant who looked like an overworked single mother brought a sheaf of pink message sheets. "Coffee," said Pease to her. "Now." She left.

I was trying to figure out how to approach asking Pease about Ilene's list when another person entered quietly, a young man who begged Pease's pardon as he slipped behind the great man.

There was a big map of Sarasota on that wall, and the young man removed an orange dot and replaced it with a gold star. When he left, I saw the location was only a block or two away from my place, which had no dot or star or anything.

Laurence waved expansively at the map and said, "Another *SOLD by Laurence Pease*. We have a man in the field with a cell phone, so he'll get the sign up immediately. My tenth this week."

How can one man sell ten houses in one week? Probably has a whole platoon of poltroons. "That's just over from my place," I said.

"Really? Your address?"

Nonplused, I gave it to him. He twirled around to the computer on his right, tapped a few keys, and told me how much my house was worth today.

I blinked. "That's more than three times what I paid."

"That's what beach property goes for in today's market. Tell you what, why don't I stop over, see the place, bring some papers. Get it on the market next week. How's this evening sound?" he said, uncovering his daily agenda and uncapping a fountain pen which had a dollar sign for a clip.

I shifted in my chair. I didn't want him to think I had gotten into his office under false pretenses, but apparently the receptionist hadn't passed on the message that I needed his help. Or maybe real estate help was the first thing this dynamo thought of. That's probably what made him a dynamo.

After explaining that I couldn't afford to sell my house, even if I wanted to, because what would I replace it with (he had plenty of ideas on that), I pulled out his card with Ilene's list on the back of it and asked him about it.

Yes, Ilene had been to see him—he remembered her by her style of dress once I described it—earlier in the week, maybe

Monday? He could get an assistant to look it up, they kept track of every contact for him. I'll bet they did. Didn't matter, he remembered she was interested in waterfront. Didn't look like she could afford it, but "I didn't get where I am in this business by prejudging people. Let me tell you about this German professor who came in one day. . ."

As I listened to his story, I realized how Ilene had ended up with a list on the back of his card. He mentioned names, dropped tidbits of fact or fiction, speculated wildly as to people's sources of income. The man was a gossip. And the stereotype is a gossiping woman. Go figure. Ilene probably made the list in her car, after she left his office. But why? And what did it all mean?

When he came up for breath from his story, which seemed to involve how brilliantly he got the German professor to spend more money than God has, I asked for help on the names on Ilene's list. He unfolded a pair of tortoise half-lens reading glasses and took the business card from me. "*Jolly Johnson, Sandpiper, Ugly Ct, Wm from Wisc, Liverwurst, Blowfish Bayou?, Epazote/ St J? AM!, Loquat.* Strange list."

"Yeh," I said. "How about that first one, Jolly Johnson? Do you recall talking to Ilene about someone with that name?"

The harried assistant interrupted us with coffee. "Sorry, I had to make fresh." Pease glared at her. When she left, closing the door after her, he snorted. "These temps nowadays. What was your question again?"

"This first name, Jolly Johnson. Did Ilene ask about him?"

He frowned. "All the young lady and I talked about was waterfront property and how she'd go about finding something she could afford. Seemed to think I would give her some inside knowledge that would let her bypass real estate people." He paused until the assistant left the room. "I thought it was naive of her to think I'd cheat myself out of a commission, but then I thought, *Hey, play along, she'll end up a client yet.* So, she really in the market?"

"I doubt it. She's dead. Fell down a flight of stairs."

He removed the glasses to look at me. "I read that in the paper, didn't connect the name. I usually recommend clients stay away from two-story homes."

"How about this other name, William from Wisconsin?" I couldn't believe the man's self-centeredness, but since the list was on the back of one of his cards, I had to assume it had something to do with the conversation Ilene had had with him, so I soldiered on.

He shrugged. "Common name. Common state. When did she make this list? Maybe she just didn't have anything else to write on one day, so she used the back of my card." He looked sour, as if the thought of his business card as scratch paper offended his very soul. He handed me back the card and adjusted his body, as though starting to stand up.

"How about Blowfish Bayou?" I was determined to get through the list before he dismissed me.

He stood. "Not a very appealing name, is it. You got your Pelican Cove and Paradise Shores and Holiday Harbor, but Blowfish Bayou? Never heard of it, and I'd recommend they change the name to Heron Heights or something if I had. Gotta have an appealing name, get folks to open their wallets."

True, I thought. Blowfish Bayou must be an original name. Not many of those left. Shake-It Creek became Shakett, and Slaughterhouse Road became Cattlemen Road. Buying and selling land had been the main business in Sarasota since Mrs. Potter Palmer arrived in her private rail car from Chicago in 1910. Gotta have appealing names to wheel and deal in land in the Sunshine State.

He'd come out from behind his desk and was flipping through some files, telegraphing *I'm a busy man.*

The young male assistant tapped and immediately entered again, this time with two dots stuck to his left index finger. He peeled them off one by one and placed them on the map south of Bee Ridge Road, holding his tongue between his teeth as he did so. A very earnest young man.

"What about Ugly Court? That's not a very saleable

name, is it?" I persisted.

Pease looked at me silently for an extra beat more than normal.

The assistant looked eager to please. "Ugly? That's over by Mineola and Valencia and Mandarin. Southgate." He thumped the map with a knuckle. "Varieties of citrus. Ugli is that lumpy fruit they sell in the grocery now. Ugli Court dead-ends into the river. Nice views." The streets in Southgate had been named after the citrus that used to be grown on the land.

"Yes John, thank you, get on to that call list, will you?" said Pease. John nodded timorously and left again. Pease was doing the body language thing to me again, the polite version of the bum's rush. I stayed seated.

"Oh, ugli with an I." I had heard ugly like unattractive, and I guess Ilene had done the same. "What about it? What's Ugli Court like?"

"I wouldn't know," he said. "I sell the better listings. You'll have to excuse me, I have a meeting coming up."

It was time for me to leave, I guess. But I hadn't asked him about the strangest item on the list. Epazote/ St. J. I asked Pease if the words meant anything to him. I thought Epazote was a pretty good name for a development, myself. Epazote Estates? The Manors at Epazote?

"Nope, never heard of anything called that. Sorry, I really must..."

"Epazote must have meant something to Ilene. Maybe it's in Bradenton or North Port? She traveled all over for her stock."

"Stock?" Pease said. "She had a lot of stock? Land's a lot better investment than the stock market right now, I can tell you. Darn, I should have gotten her out of the market and into real property."

"No, stock, as in stuff to sell. She was a junk dealer." I said a little prayer to Ilene's spirit for calling her that, but the urge to prick the prick's balloon was just too strong. It worked. Pease looked aghast, as though he'd shamed himself by trying to sell a house to a junk dealer.

64

On the way out I asked again when Ilene had been to see him. He sighed and asked his assistant to look it up. The woman fumbled a bit on the computer keyboard, biting her lip. "Sukie here's just a temp," Pease said. "Don't worry, honey," he said to the woman, squeezing her shoulder, "take your time."

The woman winced, whether at his condescending tone or the overly-familiar gesture was hard to say. She hit enter a few times and pointed at the screen. "There. Tuesday," she said, glancing up at me with tired eyes. *Tuesday*, I thought as I got into my car, being careful not to ding the green convertible in the next slot. The day before her death. She'd told me Monday night she had to find something out the next morning. That was Tuesday. She went to a real-estate office about waterfront property, she wrote a cryptic list, she talked to a drug dealer, and the next day she died.

It never occurred to me to wonder why, of all the real-estate people in Sarasota, Ilene had gone to see Laurence Pease.

15

When I got to work, I was still thinking about the names on Ilene's list. Laurence Pease hadn't helped a lot, but at least I knew it was Ugli Court with an I. I looked the street up on my map, planning to drive over there after work. Pease's assistant had been right. Ugli Court was so small, I could barely read the name.

Otto Bruniger, the old man with the dusty knick-knacks, came in with another box, this one so heavy that the taxi driver had to carry it in for him. Otto got settled in a chair to wait for me to sort through his consignment, and the cab driver decided to poke around a bit in our air conditioning rather than wait in the car.

"So how long have you lived in Sarasota, Mr. B?" I asked as I dug into his box.

"Let's see, Dotty and me, we came down a couple of years after I sold the hardware store. Didn't see any reason to go through those Ohio winters no more, selling snow shovels, and we didn't have any family. Musta been 1968, maybe '69. We only stayed down here in the winters, though, for a long time. Snowbirds, we were."

"Sarasota must have been a lot different then, huh?" My fanny was up in the air as I bent down into the box, but that's never stopped me from carrying on a conversation.

"Oh my yes. Bought our place the next year, after we'd looked around a bit. Didn't spend more'n twenty, twenty-two thousand on it. Dot could tell you to the penny if she was here. She sure loved our place. We sold up Back Home in, oh, '76 maybe? Yes, '76. That was the Bicentennial, right? All those fire plugs painted like Colonial heroes? There was one outside the hardware store. Back Home."

Amazing. The man had lived her off-and-on for over thirty years, but Up North was still Back Home.

"Hmm." From the look of the items in this box, Dorothy had loved to shop for her home. Unfortunately it looked like her shopping sprees stopped in about the avocado-and-burnt orange age.

The old man readjusted his hands on his cane and settled in for a good long chat. What had I done? He was turning out to be one of those oldsters who'd talk your ear off. Normally, I don't mind. You hear some great stories that way. But I was preoccupied, and wanted to get out of the shop early and go see what I could see on Ugli Court. Not that I knew what I was looking for. But I hoped I would when I saw it.

"Why, the road wasn't even paved then, just the Johannsens and the Madisons and us on it, guess they figured we weren't worth paving for," the old man continued. The look in his eyes, pale and watery as they were, was that of a younger man. "Yeh, the three families shared a boat, we kept it docked at Blowfish Bayou. We were all snowbirds back then. Sure had some good times, the six of us. There was Olaf and Inge—was it Inge?—no, Ingrid. I think."

"Did you say Blowfish Bayou?" I tried not to shriek. "Where's that?"

"Oh, honey, that was just our little joke because we always blew our fishing. Blowfish Bayou was just a little swampy spot with a tackle shack and docks for, oh maybe six or eight boats. Gone now." He shook his head. *So much gone now.*

"But where was it?"

"Golly, haven't thought about Blowfish Bayou in years. I'm the only one left now, the Johannsens both passed and Jack Madison did too. His wife, let me see, Mildred? Martha? Dotty'd know if she was here. Anyway, she remarried and wouldn't you know, ended up back here in Florida in Bradenton. Or was it Brandon? Haven't seen her in years, but she still sends a Christmas card every year." He chuckled. "Always has a damn kitten on it one way or the other. Mildred sure loved her cats.

67

There, Mildred, see? Now was it Bradenton or Brandon?" His eyes grew older. "Dot would know."

Off the top of my head, I made up an excuse to visit Mr. Bruniger later at home. I wanted to see if somehow I could contact Mrs. Madison, Mildred or Martha or whatever her name might turn out to be, and talk to her. Hopefully her memory for details would be better than his. Ugli Court would have to wait.

Later that day, after the rush was over, I went to Mr. B's.

"Thanks, Mr. Bruniger, this will be easier, to look at what you want to get rid of here, rather than at the shop." He had dressed up: a clean grey plaid shirt buttoned to the neck, less-than-clean black trousers, and soft felt slippers. In the kitchen a teapot sat with tea bags already in it, waiting for the boiling water, and a plate of packaged cookies was on the dining room table. My heart ached with the loneliness this bespoke, but I steeled myself to my cause and oh-so-casually said, "We sell Christmas items really well. Would you like me to help you go through them?"

He led me to the back bedroom which served as a storage unit. In Florida, a "Florida basement" means a garage or a spare bedroom, anything *but* a basement, since our high water table doesn't allow for such luxuries. He waved towards the left rear corner where Dorothy had stored the holiday decor, and toddled off to make the tea.

By the time he returned, carefully balancing a tarnished silver tray with two filled teacups and the plate of cookies, I'd found Dorothy's Christmas card list. On it, Mehitabel Madison Frazier's Bartow address. Mr. B must be in worse shape than he seemed, to forget a name like Mehitabel. Or maybe he just wasn't a fan of Don Marquis.

As we sipped our tea (Lipton's, lukewarm, too weak) and cookies (stale), he showed me his pride and joy, the sunroom. It was lovely in a 1970's sort of way.

He excused himself at one point, and came back with a pill bottle. "Sorry," he said. "I have to take one of these horse pills. Damn kidneys. Don't get old," and he waggled his finger at me as though I would be a naughty girl if I did.

"I'll try not to," I said, and he laughed as he downed the pill with his tea.

Mr. Bruniger might not have been a lucky fisherman, but he had been an enthusiastic one, and he showed me the rods hung on the walls, lures carefully laid out in metal tackle boxes, and shelves full of how-to-hook-the-big-ones books. More interesting to me were the family photos, lovingly framed in dime-store frames. Ilene would have loved them. Pictures of people in boats holding up their gear, people at back-yard barbeques, people toasting each other at parties in fancy clothes. I especially loved one that showed all six of the Blowfish Bayou buddies: Olaf and Inge-maybe-Ingrid Johannsen, the Madisons and the Brunigers in their boat, waving upwards towards the camera. One of the women had on striped capris and a tall-crowned sunhat tied under her chin, while the other two wore swimsuits and scarves over beauty-parlor 'dos. The men didn't look much different than men nowadays. They looked happy and sunburnt and Floridian. I wondered who had taken the photo.

16

Later that evening, but not too late (I didn't want to wake Mrs. Frazier), I called her, with a little help from Directory Assistance.

After ten minutes of *How are you* and *How is he* we settled down to real talk. I heard the rasp of a kitchen match and a deep inhalation: Mrs. Frazier, bless her 70+ years, needed a cigarette to talk on the phone.

"Oh those guys. Dot 'n Ot, we called them. We had some fun in that old boat. There were six of us, and sometimes more if the kids was visiting. Ingrid always brought creamed herring and Dot her seven-layer salad. Good thing, that herring. We never caught much fish, but boy we had fun. Lotsa Dixie beers, lotsa jokes, lotsa songs. Did Ot tell you what a beautiful voice Dot had? Me, I can hardly croak along, but I make a mean meat-loaf sandwich. Or at least I did when I had folks to cook for."

"Mrs. Frazier, Otto mentioned Blowfish Bayou but he was kind of hazy on exactly where it was. Could you tell me how to get there?" I asked.

"Haven't thought of BB for years. Let's see. . ." I could imagine her shutting her eyes, trying to concentrate. "It was south of the south bridge to Siesta, past a lot of woods. We turned west, towards the water, down a road that wasn't really a turn, kinda a right fork. There was a house in that neighborhood I loved, a stucco thing with wood balconies and what looked like a bell tower. Always looked so romantic to me."

I knew a house like that, and thought it was in Vamo. I interrupted. "Vamo? Would Blowfish Bayou have been in Vamo maybe?"

70

"Yes, that's it," she exclaimed. I heard the pop of a beer can opening, to accompany her cigarette no doubt. God bless her.

Nowadays, to tell someone something was in Vamo, all you'd have to say was it was opposite the mall. But back then, Vamo was its own little village. Well, a development, to be honest, just a development that predated deed-restricted subdivisions. Named after the two home states of its developers, Virginia and Missouri (and yes, there is a Mova Street within Vamo), it was a pleasantly-homey, slightly-seedy area of modest homes, the waterfront now almost solid mega-mansions. Only in Sarasota can you drive through a neighborhood of rusted pick-ups up on blocks and arrive at $4 million homes.

"That young man that owned the bait shop. He was real tickled to hear us call the place Blowfish Bayou. Seems to me he even had a sign painted and hung it over the gutting tables." Mrs. Madison took a swig from the sound of it. "Yeh, I can see that sign now. Bright red paint, kinda curly, Blowfish Bayou. We drank a toast to it when young Bartram hung it."

"Bartram? That was the name of the bait shack owner?" I interrupted. "Unusual name."

"It was a family name maybe. But we called him Barty? Bart? Something like that. The young man was what our mothers would have called a whippersnapper. Always on the go. Always tryin' to cut deals, buyin' and sellin', bait, boats, motors, whatever. He's probably some big mucky-muck now, that or a penniless bum."

Since I couldn't recall any local mucky-mucks named Bartram, the bait-shack owner must have faded into bumhood. After a few polite noises about she really must drive down to see Otto (I hoped she'd sleep off the beers first and doubted she'd ever make the trip), we made our goodbyes.

I leaned back in my chair and looked at my notes. Blowfish Bayou = Vamo. Bartram = Bart(y)? What could memories of fishing trips have to do with Ilene's entry on her list of Blowfish Bayou? Why was she interested in what went on in the 1970's? She was just a kid then. And as I recall, lived in

71

Alabama or Arkansas or some "A" state. Or was it an "I" state? Geography was never my strong suit. Wasn't Ilene's, either. We used to laugh about it, how vague we both were.

But I did know California was three hours earlier than Florida, so I thought it might be a good time to call Ilene's mother and see if she wanted my help clearing out Ilene's apartment. First I had to call Tom Litwin to get her number.

I took Tom's card out and held it in my hand a moment. He'd given it to me at Mocha Mama's, flipping it over to hand-write his home number on it. I wondered why, if cops gave out their number so readily, his home number wasn't printed on it like his office number. His handwriting looked strong. If you could tell that from seven numbers and a dash.

I dialed, practiced my mantra *I am calm I am calm*, and winced when a young voice answered. "Litwins." Did he have a nymphet girlfriend?

"May I speak to the inspector, please?" I figured, if it was his girlfriend, no sense getting him in trouble by asking for Tom.

The receiver was dropped, I could tell by the sound, and then a voice, "Dad! For you!"

Dad? Tom hadn't mentioned any kids. And this one sounded big enough that he wasn't likely to have forgotten it, the way I imagine one could forget a little baby.

"Litwin here."

"Tom, it's Wendy Sam. Sorry to bother you at home, but I was thinking I'd call Mrs. Brown and express my condolences and I forgot to ask you for her number."

"Just a minute, let me get my notebook." No *hi, how are ya doin', nice to hear from you*. I sighed. I was just part of a case to him. Not even a case, since the police thought it was an accident. I was just part of an incident to him.

I heard a doorbell in the background, then Tom's voice saying *Here's a twenty, tip him three, count the change* and then he was back on the line.

"Here it is. Got a pen?" He gave me the number.

"Thanks," I said. "I didn't know you had a child," I

added, hoping for at least a word or two extra.

"Oh, that's Joshua, my son. I take him to baseball practice every Saturday, so he spends Friday night. That way we get all of Saturday. Great kid, except he likes pineapple on his pizzas."

"Ugh," I agreed. "But I like anchovies, so who am I to talk?"

"Anchovies?" I could hear his nose wrinkle, I swear. "Gimmee pepperoni and sausage anytime."

"Maybe I will," I said, and said goodbye. I sat there with my hand still on the phone, feeling the blush go from cheeks to forehead and back down to neck. Had I really made an innuendo to a police officer? I was mortified.

Well, kinda.

17

The call to California went smoothly, except that they thought Mrs. Brown was probably still in the dining hall instead of her apartment. I asked them to try ringing the apartment anyway, and sure enough, Mrs. Brown answered. She said she was tired of always-fried-fish on Fridays and I concurred.

We talked about Ilene and her life, and that her ashes would be sent to California, for a while. I didn't think it was a good idea to tell the old woman that I thought her daughter had been murdered, so I didn't.

"Mrs. Brown, would you like me to go through Ilene's belongings and ship you anything I think might be valuable?" I finally asked.

"Oh dear, I hadn't thought about that. How well did you say you knew her?"

"We were personal friends as well as business associates. She and I took a couple of trips together, and we were always over to each others' places. I remember the photo album, you'll want that."

Mrs. Brown didn't answer for a moment, and I worried that I'd increased her pain. "Mrs. Brown," I said gently, "perhaps you can give me an idea of what you'd like to have of Ilene's, and what you want me to do with the rest."

"Thank you, dear, of course the album, and there were a few things of my mother's that Ilene cherished. A little brass figurine of a old man holding a dog and her monogrammed train case. The initials were E. H. MacK. Elaine Harriet MacKenzie. I can't think of anything else. You'll know best which charities to use," she said.

"If I have any doubts, I'll put things aside and call you

and ask," I said. "If that's all right with you."

"Of course, and thank you. You're very kind." She paused. "May I ask you a question that's been bothering me?"

"Please," I said, dreading whatever was coming. I wasn't quite as close to tears as Mrs. Brown sounded, but I wasn't far behind either.

"Did she have a boyfriend? Someone she was afraid of? I wish I could remember the name, but she had so many and she was always changing them. Gary? Gary. Gary something to do with vegetables. Bean maybe? Gary Bean? Oh, old age is awful. I'm sorry, but I can't remember his name."

My turn to pause. "I can't imagine Ilene having a boyfriend she was afraid of. She wouldn't put up with that, would she?" I asked. The Ilene I knew wouldn't have, but maybe her mother knew a different side of her.

"Well, not afraid like for herself, but afraid that he was up to no good. The reason I ask is she said something like *he doesn't care about anyone except his own wallet.* That's why I remembered it. She said any*one*, not any*thing*. Like he was hurting people somehow."

"The name's not ringing a bell," I said, "but I'll keep an eye out in her apartment and let you know if I find anything."

After arranging for shipping whatever I thought she'd want, giving her my number in case she thought of anything else and promising to keep in touch, we hung up. I'm sure she sat there staring into space thinking of Ilene longer than I did, and I did for hours, before I roused myself out of the chair, and rustled myself off to bed.

But not to sleep. Gary? I couldn't think of any Gary in Ilene's life, yet alone a Gary Somethingvegetably. But of course she certainly knew people she never mentioned to me. I'd watch for anything in her apartment.

Could this be a clue? Was Gary Whatever a murderer? I wondered how detectives ever figured out anything. All I had so far was a belief in my dead friend's sense of balance, a note about something *gone beyond greed*, a sighting of her in of all places a nightclub talking to of all people a drug dealer named after an old American car, and a mysterious list that might not have anything to do with anything at all. I thought about my phone calls to Mrs. Frazier and Ilene's mother. There was something tugging at a corner of my mind, kind of twisting and rolling the edge of my understanding. One of them had said something that needed more thinking about. What was it?

Must be that name. Gary Somethingvegetably. A ridiculous clue, totally unprofessional. And somehow I didn't think that's what was nagging at me.

I dreamt of carrots dancing with asparagus with beets cha-chaing around, a little boy named Joshua who looked like his daddy, and Ilene falling forever.

18

I woke up with tears in my eyes. And the determination to find whoever killed Ilene. If I was wrong and Ilene wasn't killed, there would be no one to find. But until I reached a dead end, I was going to look.

Something, I couldn't remember what, that Mehitabel Madison Frazier said stuck in my mind. After I turned on the coffee, I looked at my notes again. There. That scribbled doodle at the bottom of the page. BB/ BB/ BB. Blowfish Bayou, of course, but why did BB stick in my mind?

I've learned to let things simmer in the back of my brain for a while, so that's where I stuck BB. I took out Ilene's list on Pease's business card again and looked at it. Then I got her record book and sat at the table. There was a great blue heron standing statue-still and peering into my goldfish pond intently. Then he looked up at me, or at least at my French door from the dining room to the patio.

I'd forgotten to restock the pond with fish. I buy them at the pet store. Actually, several pet stores, because I buy a lot and I don't want the clerks knowing I feed them to the birds. Yes I know there's plenty of food for them in the wild but it's like a birdfeeder, you feed them to watch them. Herons like strips of baloney, too. A couple of my visitors will eat them out of my hand, and one, an egret I call Birdie (hey, I'm not very imaginative but I am kind-hearted), will walk right into the house if I leave the door open.

I got up and shredded some baloney. Kosher all beef, of course. The heron flew off when I opened the door, but I laid the strips down near the water. He'd be back, or a cousin of his would.

I laid Ilene's list down next to her record book and compared the two. No Johnson that I could find, no William, but I struck gold with AM. Looks like she sold *Italian vase ($16), 2 paperweights ($5) & grocery scale ($13)* to AM just a few weeks earlier for $95. Nice profit margin. Wish I had that. Then again, my consignors came to me. I didn't have to drive all over three counties to get my merchandise like Ilene did. Did do. Used to.

I paged backward through Ilene's records and found some other references of sales to AM. So who was AM and why was he or she on Ilene's list? Probably an antique dealer. I pulled out the Yellow Pages.

There's three pages of antique dealers in the Sarasota book, most noting *Buying Now! Top Dollar Paid!* I wondered how many old folks turned to these pages, hoping to fill the gap between Social Security and the cost of living. Or how many bereaved children did, clearing out Mom's home.

I didn't think real detectives had such maudlin feelings on a case, so I shook myself and ran my finger down the listings. There's an Antique Mall of Oviedo. Is that AM? I made a note of it. Amelia's Memories in Osprey? Not likely, sounds more like a gift shop, but I noted it too. Ah, here's something more likely, and closer, too. AM might be Anciennes Modernes, Proprietor Henri Pousse, Dealer in XXth Century Artifacts. That's mostly what Ilene dealt in, too, but she'd call them knick-knacks. I added his name to my notes, and decided it was still too early to go antiquing, so I'd go house-hunting instead.

I gathered my things together, put a fresh bottle of water in my car, rechecked the map, and set out across the Ringling Bridge for Ugli Court and whatever I could learn about why it was on Ilene's list.

19

There were only three homes left on Ugli Court. Three homes and one almost-completed Godzilla which loomed like a gargoyle, complete with four or five different styles of windows (and that was just on the front), more gables and parapets in the roof than trees in the yard, and even—could it be?—a watch tower. I decided it must be the elevator shaft. The concrete block, of which almost all houses are built down here in Florida, was still unfinished and gave the looming structure all the charm of an over-decorated prison.

The three original houses, no beauties true but at least human-scale, had decent-sized yards around them, and the breezes off the creek rustled the exotic foliage. In the gargoyle's corner there was no land left for plantings. Or breezes. The gargoyle's future inhabitants were obviously Carrier stockholders, who wouldn't care if they were in Alhambra, Florida, or New Jersey. Just crank up the a.c.

I walked around the construction site. The rustling in the greenery became louder, and I looked over. Between the allamanda bushes beamed a friendly lined face which turned out to belong to a Mrs. Biddy Amberson. She even gave me lemonade, served on a glass-topped iron table in her Florida room.

"Yes, it's awful all right, but we can't complain I guess." Mrs. Amberson was concentrating so hard on keeping her balance that her tongue peeked out between her thinned but carefully lipsticked lips as she poured the lemonade. The generation that put on lipstick Saturday mornings is shrinking all the time. It did my heart good to see Mrs. Amberson and her plaster dolphin plaques and the vinyl lounger in front of the TV and her basket of granny squares close by. "Makes our property values go up, so when we're ready to sell we can afford a better old folks' place."

"How much did the house sell for?" I asked, trying not to wince at the over-sweetness of the lemonade. It was from a mix, too. I guess picking those lemons outside and squeezing them and all is more bother than you're willing to take when you're old.

"Oh, a good price," she said. "Charlotte had some agent come by to give her an idea what it was worth but she didn't sign a contract. Said he was pushy, made her tired just to listen to him. While she was still deciding, some stranger knocked on her door and offered more than the agent estimated, cash, straight out. So she figured that was easiest and sold it. Charlotte said it was a good deal because she was getting more than that salesman said and she didn't have to pay commission. The man who bought it told her she saved even more, no lawyers and so on. Said he didn't need an inspection, that he'd catch any problems himself when he remodeled. He even did all the paperwork for her. Wasn't that nice? Charlotte wasn't feeling real well so it was a blessing. And she and her Albert had only paid $32,000 and the mortgage was paid off. So she just took that man's offer and moved to the old folks' home. I've been there. It's real nice. She's got her own patio and all. She's feeling a lot better there so it's good for her."

"And she has lots of folks to talk to," I added, thinking that's what Mrs. Amberson could use as well.

"Well, yes. That would be nice. Days go by and all I talk to are store clerks. Sometimes I catch the mail man in his little white truck, but he always seems to be in a hurry." I had to remember I was being a detective so my heart wouldn't ache again like it did at Otto Bruniger's. Such loneliness that anyone might be a friend.

"But the man who bought Charlotte's house didn't remodel, did he?" I said, waving my hand at the wall of concrete block that was three times the height of Mrs. A's house.

"Turns out it wouldn't be wise, that folks these days

wanted grander houses. I talked to him one day. Nice fellow, dapper, but here I thought he was buying the house for himself. Turns out he just wanted to build a house to sell. Don't know why people always want bigger. Just more to vacuum."

Before I excused myself, I asked for Charlotte's last name, which was Penzar, and her address, which was Apartment 42, Morning has Broken Estate, on Fruitville Road. I didn't know why I needed this information, but I might, and it seemed a detective-y kind of thing to do.

I was standing on Mrs. A's front stoop, trying to make a graceful exit, while she was using up her day's worth of words on me. I was guiltily letting them waft over my head, unheard, until she said "Eh?" and peered at me over her bifocals.

"I'm sorry, I didn't catch that," I said.

"I said, you know that other girl? That one who was here last week? She looked kinda like you. But she didn't like my lemonade as much as you do."

Could that have been Ilene? Ugli Court was on her list. "She looked like me?" I asked. "How like me?" I was pudgy with curly dark hair, Ilene was slender and blonde.

"Well, young," Mrs. Amberson said. "And real interested in that house next door. Said she knew Charlotte. That was, well, it must have been Sunday, because the mail man doesn't come on Sundays."

Could it have been Ilene? And if it was, what did that mean?

"Did she dress funny?" I asked. That's how I perceived Mrs. A would think of Ilene, if it was Ilene. "Drive a big Jeep?"

"Yes, she had a big car, I remember she had to kind of hop up into it. Don't know if it was a Jeep or not. But no, she wasn't dressed funny. Had the dearest pink rosebud print dress and pink pearl button earrings and three-strand necklace. Reminded me of myself in my younger years. I don't know why young girls don't dress like that more often. Maybe it's coming back?" she asked with a glimmer of hope in her eyes.

She looked at my denim shorts and striped t-shirt and the

glimmer died.

I headed south on Tamiami Trail towards Osprey. I was already halfway there, I figured, and Amelia's Memories was probably open. I could work on that AM clue I got from Ilene's list. So far, though, nothing on the list seemed really to be a clue. Maybe it was just a to-do list, people to see and all that.

Think, Wendy Sam, think. Ilene went to Ugli Court last Sunday. But she didn't write the list, I didn't think, until she'd gone to see Laurence Pease. What was special about Ugli Court, and why Pease? I had a lot to learn about being a detective. It all didn't make sense. A made-up name for Vamo, a bulldozed house, and an over-achieving salesman. Combined with a fall that Ilene couldn't have taken, not with her dancer background, the list seemed sinister. Had Ilene learned something that someone had to kill her for? Cold chills ran across my scalp, and I didn't even have the air conditioning on in my car.

Here, just past the old Osprey School, which sat on the Trail and was used nowadays as the visitor center for Historic Spanish Point, was Osprey. I was hoping Amelia's would be open. I could take a look around, and if it was just a new-merchandise gift shop, leave. But if I saw some Ilene-type merchandise, I could question the owner. If the owner was there. And if I could figure out what questions to ask. Damn, I wish I was a detective and knew what I was doing.

The shop was in need of fresh paint, but cute for all that, hibiscus spilling onto the walkway, plastic flamingoes pushed into the garden here and there. The shutters had cut-out silhouettes of leaping dolphins. An old-fashioned brass bell jingled in an old-fashioned sort of way, brushed by the door as I opened it. As I stepped over the threshold a voice called out, "Welcome, come in!" I did.

A quick shopkeeper-scan (when you're a shopkeeper, you case other shops automatically) told me I was right, it was a gift shop. Victorian-era, I guess you'd call it. Fairy-rampant stationery and stained-plexiglass lamps and place mats with Latin names of flowers, that kind of a thing. The air reeked of potpourri that was probably called "Garden Delight" or "Honeysuckle Dreams." I hate potpourri.

Just as I decided that Amelia's Memories was not the AM Ilene had had both on her list and in her record book, the proprietress stuck her head out of the back room and immediately followed it with a figure that was even zaftiger than mine, and I'll match zaftig with the best of them.

Aha, becoming a great detective, am I? How'd I know she was the shop's owner and not an employee? Simple. No boss would allow a helper to dress in such an outrageous manner. First thing I saw, and what told me Ilene had left her mark on Amelia's Memories, was the hat. Faded pink straw, possibly once red, picture-hat style, no crown, navy velvet ribbon and peacock feathers and bits of sequins and lace and netting hinter and yon. Once seen that hat could never be forgotten. And I had seen it on the top of a box of goodies destined for "a new customer" at Ilene's apartment a few months ago.

I took another quick scan of the shop as we said hello. Yes! Under the new merchandise was an assortment of oak bric-a-brac tables, a black curio shelf, and a small corner cupboard in neo-Colonial style, that ghastly stuff we all grew up with. The stuff that Annie's generation, as soon as it got out of the tongue-stud period, would think cute and kitschy. Ilene must have sold the woman the furniture being using as store fixtures.

"Are you Amelia? I'm Wendy Sam Miller. I own Too Good to be Threw up in Gulf Gate. Charming shop you have here."

"Well, really it's Amy, but I use Amelia for the shop. Sounds cuter, don't you think?" She adjusted the hat, which matched the genie-style purple embroidered gauze pants, which clashed with the orange tank top. High platform shoes with pansies embroidered on the toes completed the ensemble. Did I mention she was obviously the boss?

Okay, so she was the AM in Ilene's record book. Now

how did I go about figuring out if she was the AM on the list, and what that meant? I fiddled with some bottle-stoppers topped with tiny carvings of song birds while I thought. Well, bull by the horns, I guess.

"Did you know Ilene Brown?" I asked.

"Oh, I read about the accident in the paper. Yes, Ilene helped me get started. She sold me some shelves and things and showed me how to arrange stuff and like that." She touched her hat. "Ilene gave this to me as a grand-opening present. Wasn't it awful, her dying like that?"

I didn't want to tell her I thought it was murder. After all, she might be the murderer. Jeez, I didn't think about that. Here I was, alone and unarmed in a shop with a potential murderer. I looked quickly about. Surely she must sell letter-openers, they're Victorian, aren't they? I could defend myself with one. If I could just find one.

I took a breath, realized I was gripping a goldfinch-topped wine stopper so tightly it was leaving dents in my palm, and agreed. "Yes, terrible. I was wondering. Did you talk to Ilene in the last two weeks or so?"

"Why, yes, how'd you know? She came by with lunch. I closed up, and we walked down to the bay and sat on the dock."

"Did you talk about anything in particular?" I tried to sound casual. *Like drugs*, I thought. *Or hot goods.*

"Oh, this and that, you know. What's selling, what should she keep an eye out for me, for my shop. I want a slipper chair for my back corner. About a house she was clearing out and how the seller was feeling so relieved. I knew what she meant. Keeping a house up can be terrible when you're old and sick. I have a couple of customers, same problem. One old lady practically fainted in my shop one day. Really scared me. But once she took a slug of her medicine, she seemed better, and her sister said she'd drive home so I didn't call the squad."

"A slug of medicine? What'd she do, carry it in a hip flask?" I was amused by Amy's choice of words.

"No, an old bottle. Really pretty one, blue. Wouldn't

have minded buying it for my shop."

She shook her head. "Funny thing. The last time I talked to Ilene was last Sunday. She called me at home, which she never did. She asked me about that bottle. What color it was. Strange question, don't you think?"

Why would the color of the bottle matter to Ilene? Maybe she wanted to buy it, for me, for my blue glass collection? Maybe it was the one I'd taken from Ilene's apartment?

"Did she buy the bottle from you?" I asked Amy.

"Why no, I don't have it. It was just a story, about the two ladies. Just a funny story. But Ilene wanted to know what color it was. Strange, huh?

"Ilene taught me about mixing some old things in with the new," Amy continued. "She said it would give my shop an aura."

Anything but "Honeysuckle Dreams" would be an improvement, I thought as I said goodbye.

20

It was only one o'clock, so after I grabbed a quick lunch at the Spanish Point Pub (fish and chips in one of those flimsy plastic baskets, but a great view over to Casey Key) I drove back north into downtown Sarasota, to the area called Herald Square, after the old newspaper plant building that was there.

The other AM I'd figured likely was Anciennes Modernes, Henri Pousse, Proprietor. The shop was in the triangular building that formed the heart of the antique district. By the time I got there, it was almost closing time. Summertime slow season, tourist-oriented business, I figured it would close at two or so. I wasn't far off. The hours posted in the window said he closed at three.

Okay, I admit it. I figured Henri Pousse, Dealer in XXth Century Artifacts, would be gay, or at least effeminate. If the guy at the Spinet desk was Henri, perhaps I was wrong. Major hunk. Dark hair, flopping over gold eyeglass frames, crisp white-on-white shirt, alligator belt and loafers, slub silk trousers that hung just right when he stood up, greeted me, and extended his right hand. Fifty-ish, I thought, possibly a sailor, looking at the pale crows-feet I could see when he took off his glasses. Enough taller than me that I had to look up. I took his hand.

"I'm Wendy Sam Miller," I said. "Are you Mr. Pousse?"

"No," he said and smiled. "I'm Henri. My father is Mr. Pousse."

So okay, it's an old line, but in a new, most attractive voice.

I had to force myself to do the shopkeeper scan. His eyes were more interesting than his shop, and the shop was fascinating. I wondered why I'd never been in before. Then I remembered

86

that golly gee, I was a shopkeeper, and didn't normally get out to other businesses too much since our hours generally coincided. Mentally I reviewed my shop's budget. Surely I could afford my helpers for a few more hours a week, if it meant getting out and meeting people such as Henri Pousse.

"And were you looking for a specific item, or just admiring it all?" Henri asked. My silly smile he misread for pleasure at his stock in trade.

"Actually, it all looks great," I said, "but I was really here to ask you a few questions." There, I sounded like more of a detective with every drive up and down Tamiami Trail.

"Then please, sit, may I offer you a sherry? Saturdays in August are usually slow."

I haven't been offered a sherry since my last visit to my great-aunt's in Wapakoneta. "Please," I said, continuing the genteel theme.

It came in a tiny roly-poly glass that was tinted aquamarine. Henri's was amethyst. I loved the glasses, coveted them, but figured asking the price was crass. Maybe next visit.

"I was a friend of Ilene Brown," I began.

"Ah, Ilene, such a tragedy. She was so full of life."

"So you did have dealings with her?" I asked. "She had AM in her record book but I wasn't sure it was you."

"Yes, Ilene had a good eye for what I could use here. Why? Is there something wrong?" He looked a bit alarmed. I guess every dealer in used goods is a little afraid that not everything has arrived at the business from its rightful owner.

"Not that I know of. I'm trying to trace her last couple of weeks. When did you last see her?"

Henri refilled our roly-polys. "Not long ago. Usually I could look her visit up in my account book, but that time, I didn't buy anything. We just... talked." He didn't look up at me.

"Oh, what about?" I used my most innocent tone and expression.

He stared off into a corner. "Hmm. Changes. Shops going out of business. New ones coming in. Hoity-toity, she called them. Not the kind of shops who'd be interested in the items she dealt in. She was upset about all the growth. Northerners moving in, changing the way of life."

"Did you agree?"

"Not really. It's not like she or me or most of us are from here. We moved in and changed the town too. It's that old close-the-gate-behind-me mentality. But I let her talk."

"What did she mean, change the town? More traffic? Better restaurants? Not enough beach parking?"

"She was upset that the laid-back old feeling was gone, that everything was gated and guarded," Henri's eyes were back on mine. Nice feeling.

"Yeh, I know. The little places I used to be able to put my kayak in the bay are all fenced off now. Like I'm going to damage their property values," I said.

"You kayak? So do I. Perhaps we could one day together."

"Sounds good," I said. "Here's my card, call me." At that, I made my exit, before he could see the glassy glitter of my eyes. Yum.

I'm beginning to like this detective stuff. Might even get a date out of it. Goodness knows I've tried everything else.

Back down Tamiami to my shop. A budding detective I might be, but I still have a business to run. Susan and Annie were hard at work when I arrived, and Saturday's consignments were backed up. I uncovered the first batch. It was a new consignor, and Susan had done everything right, because there was the signed agreement and the notation that the consignor said it was all right to donate any no-thank-yous to charity. From the looks of the batch, that could well be everything. I looked at the name on the agreement. Lucy Goodman. Just at that moment, Annie came over. "The woman who left these was a cop. Wearing a gun. Cool, huh? I wonder if I'd like being a cop?" I resisted saying anything about gun belts getting hung up on belly-button rings. Sometimes

I can be a good girl.

Lordy, now what? I didn't want to upset a cop in the case I was working on. What a lovely phrase, *case I was working on.* But these clothes really weren't what I wanted in my shop. Too old to be fashionable, not old enough for my vintage area, not weird enough for Annie's funky tiki hut.

I reminded myself to stick to my standards, managed to find a few things that weren't too bad, and set the majority of them aside for pick-up by the free clothing pantry.

The phone rang. "Ms. Miller? This is Sukie Grimes? Do you remember me? Mr. Pease's office?" Oh, the overworked temporary assistant that Pease had been so condescending to.

"Yes, of course, hello."

"It's just, well, I couldn't help but overhear about Jolly Johnson?"

"Of course not." I figure when someone talks in questions, she's nervous. I tried to soothe her.

"There couldn't be two of him, could there?"

I ignored the metaphysical implications of that. "Probably not," I said. "And who is he?"

"He's something to do with Every Little Sparrow?"

The all-question format was getting old. "And Every Little Sparrow is..."

"A senior watch program? My mother has a flier with his name on it, that if there's an emergency he should be called? She thinks it will save me the trouble if she, well, if she dies?"

"Your mother's going to die?" I asked.

Sukie Grimes gave a hysterical giggle. "Not before she drives me as batty as she is."

Turns out, her mother lived alone, and was getting a touch forgetful, and Sukie had a hard time of it, dealing with several (I never did get straight how many) teenage children, a husband who couldn't seem to find a job, her own job and that senile mother. The adult day-care center Sukie's mother would sometimes go to handed out these fliers.

"I could call and find out who he is, then?"

89

"Oh that's not necessary? The flier said he lived at Windmill Village? I remember because it's right around the corner from my doctor?"

"Your doctor?"

"My stress doctor? I have a lot of that?"

I could tell.

"Funny thing about that, though?"

"Yes?" The question marks were piling up on both sides of the conversation.

"Mr. Pease knows him? I typed up a proposal for him a few months ago? But he didn't accept it?"

"?" Words were superfluous with this woman.

"You know, to sell his house?"

"Let me see. Jolly Johnson wanted to sell his house and Laurence Pease offered to do so. Johnson declined. Is that right?"

"Yes, that's it." Sukie sighed.

"So why wouldn't he say so? Was Pease annoyed that he didn't get the listing?"

"Probably but he never said. Mr. Pease doesn't know that his name is Jolly. I mean, that's not his real name?"

"Which is?"

"Oh dear, I don't remember. I'm getting as bad as my mother? I could look it up and call you back?"

I figured I'd caused enough commotion in the poor woman's life. "That's okay, I can take it from here. By the way, I thought you were a temp. How long have you been in Pease's office?"

Another hysterical giggle. "A little over a year?"

"You've worked for him that long and he still calls you a temp?"

"All his people are temps? Because then he doesn't have to pay their health insurance and unemployment and stuff?"

God, not only was the man a gossip and a snob, he was a cheapskate too. Greedy bastard. I thanked Sukie Grimes for her help, considering all the stress she was under. She said goodbye with a question mark.

So. Jolly Johnson in Windmill Village. That's a giant trailer park, acres and acres of metal homes, neatly lined up across from a golf course. Before I had a chance to think whether Windmill Village would tell me if they had a Johnson whose name really wasn't Jolly among what had to be hundreds and hundreds of full-time and snowbird residents, the phone rang again.

"Too Good to be Threw, good afternoon, thanks for calling," I said.

"You are most heartily welcome, if this is Wendy Sue."

"It is," I said, "and you are?"

"Henri Pousse, we met this afternoon at my shop. I was wondering if I might buy you a drink. I might have an idea to help you with your problem. "

"What a coincidence," I said. "I was just finishing up here." Susan and Annie exchanged looks and motioned, grinning, at the full rack of clothes I still had to go through. I turned my back on them and Henri and I agreed to meet for a drink at Ruth's Chris, a cooly elegant restaurant with a chic little lounge. It was close to my shop, which would give me an extra twenty or more minutes to get ready while he drove down the Trail. Thank God I always keep a few changes of clothes at the shop.

I was in the dressing room, slipping into my simple basic black and debating between a wine jacket for air-conditioning defense or a hand-painted silk shawl as Susan and Annie started joshing me.

"Date, huh? Haven't been on one of those in a while," said Susan.

"Neither have you," I retorted.

"Huh, I have a date every night. Drew and the kids."

"Me too," added Annie. "Mine are just surprises."

I didn't want to reply to that one. Anything I could say about Annie's penchant for pick-ups would be the wrong thing.

"Well, maybe this one'll be a surprise to me," I said. "I might even want a second date with him."

91

Henri must keep a change of clothes at his shop, too. He was in black now, so he was a bit hard to see in the dark lounge, but I managed. And I managed to put one hip on the bar stool without tripping on my fringe (I'd decided on the silk shawl) just as he said "How about the couch back there?" So I slipped off again, rather gracefully I thought.

Sliding across the couch was another proposition. Why do classy joints always have velvet? You can't slide worth a dang. My little black dress was revealing my large white thighs by the time I settled in, so a twitch and there goes the shawl off my shoulder. Now I remember why I don't date more often.

"Sherry again?" asked Henri.

"Umm, it really isn't my favorite," I said.

"Good. It isn't mine, either. I keep it at the shop for the condo crowd. What would you like, then?"

The waitress was a customer of mine, and she had to tell me how much she loved the outfit she bought last time before we could order.

"I must come see your shop sometime," Henri said when she left.

"Anytime. But call before you come. I've been out a lot recently."

"Ah yes, looking into Ilene's life. May I ask just why you are doing this?"

The question seemed a bit pointed for date chat. My defenses went up. I'd planned on asking him about the list, and the other names on it, but all of a sudden that didn't seem like a wise thing to do.

"Just trying to clear things up. Her mother's in a nursing home in California." Let him think I was doing an old lady a favor. I wouldn't say anything about my suspicions about how Ilene died.

"Clear things up. Yes, that's what I wanted to talk to you about." Our drinks came. We clicked glasses. Delicious, even more so because it was the middle of the afternoon. I could be a hedonist if I just let myself go. And Henri might be just the

92

person with whom to let go. Hmm.

"Hey, Harry, how's it going?" A brash ruddy-faced man had come into the lounge, a man with broken blood vessels in his nose and a potbelly. The type of man you'd expect to see in a sports bar on a Monday night.

"Bob, what a surprise." Henri had gotten to his feet.

"Yeh, same here. Imagine seeing you here. What's it been, four, five years? You down here now? I always said if anyone'd manage the easy life, it'd be Harry Grass."

"Actually, Bob, I own an antique shop now. If you'll excuse us... "

Bob twisted around Henri to wink at me. "Antiques huh? That what we're calling them nowadays? 'S okay, I can tell the two of ya wanna be alone. See ya Harry. Good luck. And you, pretty lady, watch your little behind around this one." With a hearty slap on Henri's elegantly-clad shoulder, the man was gone.

"Pardon him," Henri said as he sat down again next to me. "An acquaintance from Up North."

Up North is what we use when we really don't want to bring up specifics about our lives Before. It's kind of a code phrase, and it would be the height of bad Florida manners to ask *Where Up North?* or exhibit any curiosity. I took another sip of my martini.

"Lovely room," I said. "Are these Greek olives?"

"Probably. Listen, Wendy Sam, I've been thinking about the items Ilene brought in, that last time, when I didn't buy anything from her." He played with the napkin beneath his drink.

"Oh?" I asked in what I hoped was a leading way.

"Several were quite good, and Ilene wasn't asking nearly enough for them. They weren't my type of thing. I suggested that she try some other dealers, said she'd get more from them. She said she was in a hurry for the money, and tried to get me to buy them, then I could resell to the dealers at a profit."

"Did you?"

"No."

"Why not?"

I took another drink. He'd barely touched his. He looked away, then back at me. "I was afraid they were hot."

"Because she was trying to sell them fast and cheap?"

"Yes, and they weren't her normal things. They were more, well, up-to-date. Usually the things Ilene brought me, they were pieces people had brought down, family heirloom stuff."

"And these? What were they?"

"More decorative. Newer. The kind of thing new money buys. Porcelain platters and crystal pieces. A small oil or two."

"What are you talking about?"

"Small things," Henri said meaningfully.

I was confused. "As opposed to big things?"

"Things easily carried. Or concealed."

I got the drift. "Things that could easily have been burgled."

"Yes," he sighed. "I'm afraid so. That's why I'm wondering why you are, shall we say, stirring things up. I believe there could be some unpleasant aspects of your friend's life. Things that you wouldn't want exposed. You were friends, right?"

I nodded, miserable. I hadn't thought about that, about possibly uncovering things Ilene wouldn't have wanted known.

Henri put a well-manicured hand over mine. "Just think about it," he said. "You don't want to sully her name."

I had been so sure that someone had pushed Ilene to her death and that whoever it was should be punished. Now, thinking about the possibility of finding out that my friend was less than moral and of letting others find that out as well, I hesitated. Was I so sure that Ilene hadn't simply fallen? Even a graceful dancer could trip. Was I simply being nosey, poking around in a life cut short in the middle of living? Was I right to risk exposing something less than upright just on a feeling, a feeling that my friend didn't die in a freak accident?

The elegant man opposite me looked at me as though he understood my conundrum. "You are a good woman to have on one's side, I think. You jump right in to defend her."

"Yeh," I said. "Jump right in. That's my middle name."

21

We parted after one drink. Henri had somewhere to be. That was okay. I wanted to be alone, after hearing that my friend might have been dealing in stolen goods. I couldn't see Ilene as a cat burglar. What worried me was that I *could* see her as a fence. After all, she knew folks who might be on the edge of honesty, who might have something stolen to sell. She also knew which dealers would buy what. The perfect go-between.

God, am I terrible or what? First I think Ilene's dealing drugs. Then there's Gary the Vegetable whom her mother thought she was afraid of. Now I think she's a fence. Why am I so sure something was fishy in her life?

Because she was murdered because of something flashed across my brain. *Whatever she might have done, she didn't deserve to die. But would her mother, her friends, would I want to have our last knowledge of Ilene be that she was involved in something wrong?* I rolled my window down, needing the brisk rush of tropical air across my face to keep me real. Henri Pousse and his elegant lifestyle had lulled me into thinking things were better left unsaid. That if there was anything dishonest going on in Ilene's life, it should be left unremarked. But *Ilene's murderer must be punished.* If I found out something unsavory about her life, I'd keep it to myself if I could. *But she was murdered. Murdered. Murdered.*

I shook my head to clear it. Henri's position was seductive. Let the dead rest. That was okay, but I was damned if I'd let a murderer get away with it. Maybe Chloe could help me figure out what Ilene was worried about. *I have to get in touch with her.*

By now, I was driving across the Causeway on my way

home. It was still early enough that the wind surfers were out on the Bay, and as I drove towards St. Armand's Circle, I decided to do the full circle, enjoying the summer crowds at the cafes and the shops. Usually, I turn off to avoid the Circle, but a drive through out of season is fun. During season, it's impossible. The traffic and the tourists who can't keep their minds on the road when presented with such a tempting group of interesting shops, not to mention the omnipresent pedestrian crossings, make for a nightmare.

Outside Cha Cha Cocoanuts, on a sidewalk table beneath an umbrella, sat Tom Litwin, in a navy windbreaker this time. I don't know how I spotted him but I did. From what I could see, he was alone, sipping a beer and reading. I pulled into the next parking space I could find, draped my shawl fetchingly, and strolled nonchalantly back to the bar. I had a sudden craving for their specialty, cocoanut shrimp.

"Why, hi Tom," I said, trying to act like I was surprised to see him there. "No son tonight?" Damn, what was the kid's name? Justin? Jeremy? Couldn't be Jerome, could it?

Cop that he was, he spotted the clue. "Not tonight. Joshua's mother's a little, well, casual about my visitation rights." Belatedly, he put down his book, stood up and pulled out a chair. "Join me?"

"Why thanks," I said. What's with the whys? Surely I could come up with better conversation than that. Must be that South Trail martini coming home to roost.

The server came over, took my order for the coconut shrimp and a mai tai (what else do you drink with coconut shrimp?) and disappeared.

Tom looked good with palm frond shadows. Hell, he probably looked good in the dark. Jeez, there I was again with the double entendres. I fiddled with the fancy-drinks placard and concentrated on not blushing. I don't think it helped.

"I understand you were asking Laurence Pease about some list of Ilene's," Tom began. "Is there something I should know... like where you got this list?"

I explained about Mrs. Brown, that she gave me permission to see after Ilene's apartment. I told him I had a key, even dug it out of my purse to show him, that Ilene'd sent a note asking me to feed her fish. I did not, of course, mention that the list was in Ilene's record book which I removed from the scene. Nor Ilene's concerns in the note she sent with her key. I didn't think it was necessary, since the official position was that there was no crime.

"A note? You didn't mention a note," Tom said.

"Just a, umm, thank-you note for a party I gave. Mentioning that she'd be away for a few days and would I see after her fish."

"Where was she going?"

"She didn't say. I assumed to some sale or something. She traveled a lot, you know, to buy her stock." My mai tai arrived. I resisted twirling the little paper umbrella, but did look up at him through my eyelashes as I sipped through the tiny straw.

"So this list. What is it?" Tom said.

"I don't know, but since it was on the back of Pease's card, I thought maybe he might. You know him?" I wondered why he and Pease had been talking. I hoped I wasn't in trouble, like for interfering with an investigation. But that was just the point, wasn't it? There was no investigation. No murder. So Tom and the rest of the police thought.

"Sold us our house." He winced. "Her house, now."

I wondered how long he'd been divorced. From brain to mouth, that's me. I asked.

"Three years."

Oh good, long enough to be recovered and not counting in fractions like three and a quarter years. I judged him over it. I hoped it was true.

"So," he said, as my shrimp arrived and his salad did. Damn, I hate a man who eats healthier than I do. Dressing on the side too.

"I have to tell you, Wendy Sam, Pease called to complain actually. Said you were questioning him like a cop."

97

I stared at him. "I was just asking him about the list."
Inside, I was thrilled. *Questioning him like a cop. Or a private eye. Maybe I'd become a private eye, like Patty wanted to be.*

Tom shook his head. "Maybe you came on a bit strong. I've noticed that about you."

"Strong is good."

"Strong is fine." He nodded. "But sometimes, a little tact goes a long way. Pease felt like he was being grilled."

"He didn't have to answer. As a matter of fact, he wasn't much help at all."

"This list. Laurence mentioned a Jolly Johnson?"

"Yes, but it's a nickname, it's really Walter. Apparently Johnson lives at Windmill Village now."

"Nope."

"Nope?" I said, dropping a shrimp. How did Tom know?

"I checked it out. Walter Johnson lives at Dunroamin. Easy mistake to make, both big trailer parks."

"Why would you do that?" I asked, check it out I meant.

He shrugged. "Had a few moments, managers answer questions from cops a lot easier than from civilians."

"Thanks," I said. "I was going to try."

"I figured." He looked like he doubted I would have succeeded. "So, who else is on this list?"

"It's not all who's. A couple names, an address or two, even some groceries. . ." I was torn between wanting to figure it out myself, and wanting to have a reason to keep talking to him.

"Groceries?"

"Liverwurst and papayas."

He waited for a moment, then said very quietly, like I imagine a detective would to a suspect, "May I see the list please?"

"So you think there is something to investigate?" I asked.

"No, I don't, but I am thorough."

"And opinionated."

"There's that too. Not to mention nosey."

So I dug in my purse and pulled out the card with Ilene's list. Dang, I realized. Could have told him it was at my place, then he'd come back with me, then...

"*Jolly Johnson, Sandpiper, Ugly Court, Wm from Wisc, Liverwurst, Blowfish Bayou?, Epazote/ St. J? AM! Loquat.*" Tom looked up at me. "Loquat, not papayas."

"Same thing, almost." So loquats are small and orange and papayas are big and green. They're both fruit.

He shook his head and looked back at the paper. "Strange list."

"Exactly what Laurence Pease said. I did find out some things, though."

He raised his eyebrows. So I told him about Ugly being Ugli and Mrs. Amberson and Charlotte Penzar who'd moved to a nursing home. And that Ilene had been there. At that point, Tom frowned and got out a small notebook from his inner jacket pocket. As he reached, I noticed a strap over his shoulder and realized, with a start, that he was wearing a gun. It had never occurred to me that he would, but of course he was a cop. And I thought the wind breakers just meant he was the chilly type.

He asked for details as he pulled a pen out from the spiraled wire. I decided God was giving me a second chance, and told him that my notes were at my house, which is just down a few blocks, and it was a lovely night, and would he care to walk me down there? I didn't mention my car, hastily parked just off the Circle. I could always get it tomorrow morning.

So that's how we ended up at my place, where I had to pretend to get my notes from the bedroom when they were really in my purse the whole time. Over coffee and Kahlua, I told him about the two AMs, Amelia's Memories and Henri Pousse's suggestions of stolen items, and Blowfish Bayou. And about Ilene at a bar with a druggie. As I recited all this, I realized that I'd learned a lot. I was impressed with myself. Maybe Tom would be too.

"So how does this all connect?" he asked after a while.

"You're the detective. You tell me."

"You have drugs, you have hot goods, you have a couple of addresses."

99

"Not for sure hot goods. Just maybe. And there's something else," I said.

So I told him about how Mrs. Brown had asked if there was anyone in Ilene's life that might have scared her, someone with a name like Gary Somethingvegetably. I told Tom I thought that was a clue too but I had no idea what to do about it.

Tom put his hand to his face. Either he was trying to decide whether he needed to shave or he was hiding a smile.

"What? What? That's something worth looking into," I said. "And if you were half a cop..."

"I'm sorry. It's just, I can't see myself looking around for someone with the last name Somethingvegetably. On the other hand, I can see you asking around. In your own bumbling way."

"So then, I will. And see if I ask you for any help. You still don't think there's been a crime committed, do you?"

"No, I don't. I'd say, though, if I were you, that your next step might be looking around Blowfish Bayou, I mean Vamo. Have you done that yet?"

I didn't want to admit I didn't have the foggiest idea of what to look for. I shook my head.

"Well," he said, getting up off my couch, "We could do that tomorrow. If you're free, I mean."

"You'd help me?" I asked. "Does that mean you think there's something to investigate?"

"Not particularly. It means I would like to spend some time with you."

Did he really say that? I tried for nonchalant, flipping my hand casually and looking over his shoulder at nothing. "Why, thanks, I could use the help."

He grinned. Guess nonchalant doesn't play well with detectives.

22

I was too excited to sleep after Tom left. Not only was I getting to play like Nancy Drew, I even had a beau! Who wanted to *spend some time with me.* Cool. I wondered what my chances were of finding a roadster to drive. I wondered what in blazes a roadster really was, anyway.

It was too late to call Chloe to see whether she knew what Ilene was asking around about so I sat down and looked carefully, page by page, through Ilene's book again. No Kumquat, no Liverwurst, no Sandpiper. Wait a minute, Sandpiper. Wasn't that the name of the development on the sign I saw last week? One of those obnoxious *Another Sunshine Improvement* developer's signs? I got up to get a map, to see if Sandpiper was a street. I keep my maps in a bottom drawer in the kitchen, since I don't have a lot of culinary gadgets to store there, so I was leaning over, protected by the breakfast bar, when my front window exploded.

23

Glass flew everywhere. I could hear it hitting the floor, the walls, the glass table. Then there was silence. After a while I raised my head from the shelter of my arms and looked. My front window, all eight feet of it, was shattered. My sheer curtains billowed over a tile floor glittering in shards of glass. The couch where I had sat only a minute ago was carpeted in glass as well.

I went to the door and opened it. There wasn't a sound. Not a car motor, not running footsteps, nothing. It was as though a meteorite had landed in my living room. But it was no meteorite. It was a paper-wrapped rock on a couch cushion. Just about where I had been sitting before I got up to find a map.

"Wendy Sam, what happened? Are you all right? Sacred Mother of Jesus," said Dom. He must have been watching television when he heard the explosion; he was still clutching a TV Guide and had on heavy-rimmed glasses I'd never seen.

"Fine, Dom, fine." The paper was taped around and around. What a nincompoop. If I was meant to read the damn note, why would it be taped so tightly I had to rip it to get it off? And this is too lumpy for a rock or a brick. I pushed past poor Dom, who stood looking stunned at the mess, and ran out onto my driveway.

"I'll be damned," I said. "They used my own damn conch shell," pointing to a blank spot in my edging. "Damn nerve of them." That's when I started to cry.

Dom, bless his gentle Italian signore heart, is at his best with weeping women. Before I knew it, I was in his place, with a glass of grappa in front of me listening to Dom on the phone telling James and Michael that they were needed, here, now.

My ex-cop friends must have broken the speed limit and

run every red light. They were there in no time. Dom had insisted I wait until "the boys" arrived to go back into my place. That was okay by me. A little fortification with a second glass of grappa was a wise avenue.

We went back to my place, my three guys and me. James had a gun in his waistband. Michael went for a broom and dustpan. Dom brushed glass off of the dining table. I pulled the sheer curtains closed and found clothes pins to clip them tightly shut. For all the good it would do.

"The glass repair company will be here any time," James said. "We called them from the car."

We sat around the table and I spread out the note. It was tattered from the throw and my efforts to get it away from the shell, but it was still readable. It said *Mind your own business. It was an accident* in block letters in blue marker.

It took me twenty minutes and another glass of the rough brandy to tell all three of them what I'd been up to. James decided it was Henri Pousse, the antique dealer, while Michael figured it had to be Pease the realtor. I think Dom was leaning towards the unknown drug dealer, Mark Four, from the bar. "I haven't even tracked him down yet," I said.

"Don't," all three men said. "At least not alone," James continued. I agreed that I'd take at least one of them with me if I went to the Sand Box. I hoped that wouldn't be necessary. I really hate noisy bars, especially bars where I'm older than the patrons' parents.

"What?" I said. "No one thinks the thrower could be Biddy Amberson, the gardener with the awful lemonade?"

They made me go to bed then. I guess I wasn't used to grappa and speeding conch shells. I fell asleep just as I heard the glass repair van pull onto my shell driveway and James and Michael greeting the driver.

24

When I got up the next morning, I forgot the window until I almost stepped on a missed piece of glass. I picked it up carefully. After I'd started the coffee, I wiped the whole floor down with damp paper towels to pick up any moreslivers. Michael's mother must have forgotten to teach him that trick.

I decided not to say anything to Tom about the note. With his help I could solve the murder before anything else happened.

I had to retrieve my car from its parking place on the Circle, make a picnic lunch, and ready myself. What does one wear for scouting around Vamo? Lying on the couch with cucumber slices on my eyes, to get rid of puffy morning-eye (it comes with being forty-plus, nothing to get alarmed about. Usually I just ignore it.), I settled on linen walking shorts, a striped seersucker shirt, and sneakers instead of my usual sandals. When I got the outfit all together though, it looked too safari-ish. For heaven's sake, this was Vamo, not the heart of Africa. I switched to a tropical-print shirt. I thought I looked pretty good, but Tom didn't say anything besides *Get in* when he drove up. He did smile at the picnic basket, though.

On the way down to Vamo, we passed Dunroamin Estates, where Jolly Johnson lived. Tom signaled for a turn before I could draw a breath to ask if we could talk to Johnson. I like a decisive man.

It was handy being with a cop. The manager directed us to Johnson's double-wide without hesitation. It was neat and well-kept, but you could tell no woman lived there. No flowers, no ruffled curtains, no cutesy yard ornaments. Car parts in the carport and a recycling bin full of glass and tin cans right at the

104

front door. I knocked, then panicked. What was I going to ask the man? I wanted to find out why his name was on Ilene's list, but chances are he'd have no idea.

Goodness, the man looked like Santa Claus, at least Santa on vacation, in a pair of faded red cutoffs, flip flops and an open red-striped shirt, from which a pot belly whorled with snow-white hair protruded. His cheeks were rosy, his eyes twinkled, and he was smiling.

"Mr. Johnson? My name is Wendy Sam Miller, and this is. . ."

"A friend, Tom Litwin." Tom stepped forward and offered his hand. Well. There must be a reason Tom wasn't telling Mr. Johnson that he was a cop, so I'd play it cool and ask later.

"Come on in, nice to see some young folks for a change. This here's what they call an over-55 community but I swear it's really over 75. If I'd known before I moved here..."

His sentence was lost as he turned away from us, gathered up a pile of papers he'd been working on, and gestured for us to sit in his little dinette. "Coffee? Iced tea?"

"No," I said as Tom said "Yes, thanks, coffee'd be great."

So we three had coffee. After it had been made (instant, microwave, if you call that made) and the low-fat milk and artificial sweetener had been doled out, Mr. Johnson looked at us and raised those bushy white eyebrows.

"Mr. Johnson, I'm a friend of Ilene Brown. She died a few days ago and I'm trying to figure out a note she left," I said.

"Call me Jolly, please, everyone does. It's because they think I look like Santa Claus, you see."

"Why yes, now that you mention it I can see a resemblance," I said. "Did you know Ilene?"

"Not really," he said. "She did come by though and asked me about some of my flock."

Flock? I was lost. Did this Santa-look-alike raise sheep? Or geese? Oh, geese came in gaggles, not flocks. Flocks of reindeer? No, that was probably herds. Or blizzards. Blizzards of reindeer, that'd be good.

"Flock?" said Tom. He must have been lost, too, but he didn't seem to go off on the mental tangents I did.

"Well, you see," and here Jolly leaned back and laced his fingers across that snowy belly, "I always wanted to be a minister, but my dealership was always going so well, I never had time. So when I retired, I traded in my interest in Chevrolets for an interest in my fellow man. Got me a mail-order divinity degree," here he waved towards some gold-sealed document framed over the couch, "and started helping mankind."

"And you do this by?" Tom asked.

"Volunteer here and there, deliver Meals for Seniors every day, organize activities down at the Friendship Forum most Saturdays, and seeing after some folk who aren't doin' so well."

"That's very kind of you," I said. "And Ilene found you how?" Tom wasn't the only one who could move a conversation forward.

"Let's see, she said she got my name from someone. Mrs. Timmons, probably. She was my most talkative home-aloner."

"Home-aloner?"

"The oldsters, the ones who live alone. We worry about them a lot, afraid they'll need help in the night or something. So I leave my name and number on all my flock's refrigerators, big and bold. Maybe Ilene just read my name somewhere."

"You didn't ask Mrs. Timmons if she'd talked to Ilene?" I asked, which was kind of off-course since I was trying to get to why Jolly was on Ilene's list, and I didn't know Mrs. Timmons from a hole in the ground.

"Can't," Jolly stroked his beard. "She died."

"Oh." I didn't know what to say.

"Took a fall. At ninety-six, that's not a good idea. She was dead long before the crew got there. Told me she'd probably been on the floor like that since the evening before. Couldn't reach the phone to call, me or anyone else."

"You were there?"

"The EMTs called me, from the flyer you see. It was a

shame. She'd been having dizzy spells. I'd told her to get one of those beeper things you wear around your neck, but she said they cost too much. Her house sold as soon as her son down from Chicago put it on the market. For more than half a million. But she couldn't afford a beeper." He shook his head. "Come to think of it, Mrs. Timmons was dead before that Ilene visited. That's right, I remember. That young girl helped clean out Mrs. Timmon's house. So she must have read my name from the refrigerator."

He bustled up and got a flyer from the stack of papers he'd moved before we sat down. It was neon green and said *If help is needed, call Every Little Sparrow, Rev. Jolly Johnson, Dunroamin Estates, 324-9994 day or night.*

"We're sorry for your loss," Tom said. "What did Ilene ask you?" There he goes again, getting back on course.

"Hmmm. She wanted to know who else I was watching over. I didn't think that was a real good question to answer, seeing's how I didn't know her. I was afraid she was just looking for business, you know, clearing out people's houses. That's what her card said she did. Then she asked if anyone else I knew was dizzy all of a sudden, and I had to tell her most everyone over seventy or so usually is. It's all the medications old folks take. Me," he patted his belly like it was a pet, "me, I'm done taking medicines. I've been feeling just fine. This may be a trailer, but I like it just fine here. Feelin' better than I have in ages."

Well, I still didn't know why Jolly was on Ilene's list, unless she'd planned to come back and talk to him further. Why was she worried about the health of people she didn't know? I didn't think Ilene was so crass as to be the secondhand trade's equivalent of an ambulance chaser, but how well had I really known her?

Tom and I didn't talk much as we continued on down to Vamo. I was mulling over what Jolly had said about Mrs. Timmon's dizziness, and remembering Amy's story about the customer she'd had who slugged down some medicine when she felt faint. Was that what I had to look forward to when I got old? Would I die alone? I looked out of the corner of my sunglasses at Tom Litwin. What would he be like to grow old along with? He must have sensed me looking, because he turned his head momentarily towards me and said, "We're going to have to work on your questioning skills."

"What? What skills?"

"Exactly. If you're going to ask strangers nosey questions, you have to learn how."

I was hurt. After all, I'd been talking all my life and no one ever complained before. I decided not to share my old age with this oh-so-superior man. I pressed my lips together.

"What?" he said. "What? Don't you want to learn something new?" A smile flickered around his eyes.

"I do too know how to ask questions."

"Sure you do. Just not necessarily the right ones."

"Hmmpf."

"And how to get people to open up. Like with Johnson back there. If they offer refreshments, say yes. If they offer coffee, even better. Takes a while to make. People keep talking, just to fill the air. You can learn a lot that way."

I was silent. One thing we hadn't learned was exactly when Ilene had visited Jolly. I would call him back. Without Tom at my elbow. I did too know how to ask questions. I just didn't know exactly which ones to ask.

Tom glanced over at me again, but I stayed silent. Finally he said in a quiet voice, "Next time, watch me."

By then we were at the turn for Vamo. We cruised through the neighborhood, looking for any trace of Blowfish Bayou that was left thirty-some years after Dot 'n Ot and their friends visited, and for any clue as to why that name would be on Ilene's list. If I'd known the right questions to ask, and who to ask them of, I could have. Really, I could have. But there was no one and nothing to ask. Why Ilene had Blowfish Bayou on her list seemed destined to remain a mystery.

At the end of several streets there were docks, some even with county park signs (and no parking, which meant of course no one could use those docks unless they lived within hauling-your-boat-by-hand distance), but no hint of a bait shop. One minuscule park did have a few parking spaces. We parked, and I got out of the car, sniffing the salt breeze and smiling, despite myself, at the sight of mangrove islets and herons and egrets. I looked south, and there was an old house standing alone on its little point of land. The house looked as though it had sheltered people one hundred years ago from the sun and storms of a vastly-different Vamo. Funny. This area would not even have been called Vamo when that house was built. Names change, but the land looks the same.

Tom stepped out of the car and stretched. I could hear his spine crack. "Pretty spot," he said.

The flat bayscape stretched out in front of us. You can keep your mountains and your mesas, give me sea level any day. "Yes," I said.

There was a canoe barely beached on the thin strand of sand. I reached down to pull it more firmly on land when a determined child in an old-fashioned kapok life vest marched towards us from the street.

"Hey," the child said. I had to look closely to determine whether this was a boychild or a girlchild. Girl, I decided once I'd seen the barrettes. "That's my canoe."

"Jasmine, slow down!" A grey-haired woman came puffing up. "And mind your manners, young lady. Say excuse me."

"Excuse me, that's my canoe," the child said, and elbowed past me.

"My granddaughter," said the woman, and brushed a strand of hair out of her eyes. The wind was picking up. She held out her hand. "Jeanne Lockerbie. Jasmine's real possessive, please pardon her matters."

"Wendy Sam Miller, and Tom Litwin," I said, mindful that Tom hadn't wanted to be identified as a policeman at Jolly's.

"I just wanna pull it up," the child said, at the same moment Tom said, "Here, let me help you."

As Tom and Jasmine struggled with the boat, Jeanne and I made two-women-talking noises. Turns out, Jeanne lived in the first house up from the park, a small stucco bungalow with a big ear tree shading it.

"I tried to tell Grandma we needed to pull it up," Jasmine said between puffs of breath. "But she had to tinkle."

Jeanne winced. "Jasmine, you don't need to be telling folks all our business."

Tom manhandled the canoe up onto dry land and told Jasmine we'd carry it around the fence if she'd like. She did. We did, which took a few hot minutes. When we'd gotten the canoe high and dry in the parched grass, Jeanne offered us a cool drink. I glanced at Tom and said yes.

We sat on Jeanne's front porch drinking lemonade. Jasmine had untied her life vest and cast it aside before she'd disappeared into the backyard.

"My son's raising Jasmine alone. Seems manners aren't always a priority there. I do what I can. I even redid Joey's room, that's my son, for Jasmine, so she wants to stay here more. It's a good house to raise kids in."

"Sounds like you've lived here a while," I said. The lemonade was a lot better than the stuff Mrs. Amberson had served me on Ugli Court. "I heard somewhere around here used to be called Blowfish Bayou. Do you know anything about that?"

Jeanne looked over her glass at me. "Haven't heard that name in a coon's age," she said. "Blowfish Bayou. Yes. There were them that called this that, but oh my, that was a long time ago. Joey was about Jasmine's age then. So, what, thirty years or more?"

"So what exactly was Blowfish Bayou?" I asked. Tom stirred in his seat.

"A silly name," Jeanne said. "I mean, this isn't a bayou," she continued, waving her lemonade glass towards the water. The contents of her glass seemed paler than mine or Tom's, and with a whiff of the onshore breeze, I realized why. Her drink had been liberally laced with gin.

Another trip into her kitchen for refills, and I realized Jeanne remembered the bait shop as Blowfish Bayou, not the area. "Folks would stop in there for Cokes and bait shrimp and the like," Jeanne said. "No Circle K's back then, leastway's not around here," she said. We both sighed, nostalgic for the days when convenience franchises didn't disfigure every intersection in Florida. I mean, I didn't live here then of course, but I still felt entitled to long for the good old days.

"So what was special about Blowfish Bayou?" I asked.

"Special? Nothing. Just a bait shop, like any other. The young man that run it, though, he was, well, quite a man," Jeanne said, winking at me. The gin must have been going straight to her head in the heat. Tom stirred again.

Jasmine reappeared with two paddles. "I need help," she said. "I'm just a kid, I can't manage this myself." Tom went off to help with whatever the little vixen had in mind. Just in time. I'd show Tom a thing or two about letting people fill empty air.

"Say, you got anything to put in this lemonade?" I said. Jeanne grinned and led the way into her kitchen. She poured gin with a heavy hand into my watered-down lemonade and got an old-fashioned ice cube tray out of her refrigerator. "Quite a man, you said? How so?" Now that was a leading question. *Good for you Wendy Sam.*

Slapping the aluminum tray down on the counter, she yanked on the lever and ice cubes skittered over the red linoleum counter. "Bartram," she said. "Ladies' man, you know. Anything with tits, he was interested in." She plopped a handful of ice cubes into my drink and didn't notice that the counter was now sticky with spilled lemonade.

I took a sip of my doctored drink. No wonder she was so talkative. Three more sips, and I'd be out like a light in this heat.

"So this Bartram, he ran Blowfish Bayou?"

She nodded, licking her fingers. "Those were the days. Party-time!" And with that, she trundled into the living room and

111

sat down heavily in the striped velveteen recliner in front of the television.

By the time Tom came back from his errand of mercy for a six-year-old, Jeanne was snoring softly. I could hear her through the screen as I sat on the porch drinking my electric lemonade. No sense wasting it, I'd decided when Jeanne fell asleep. I'd tucked my business card under her glass at her elbow with a scribbled "thanks for the drink!" on it.

Jasmine peered in at her grandmother, sighed, and said, "I'm going next door to play with Margaret." We watched as a dark-haired woman with a baby on her hip answered the door, let Jasmine in, and waved to us.

Tom and I waved back and got into his car, me very carefully since I could feel the gin. "I thought I handled that pretty well," I said. Tom sighed.

"What? *What?*" I asked. "She told me what Blowfish Bayou was. Besides," I continued, "I thought you were going to teach me how to ask questions. I didn't hear you asking many."

"You seemed to be doing okay yourself. So. Does any of what you learned tell you why your dead friend had the name on her list?"

"Oh," I said, very small and somewhat sobered. I guess not. I wasn't making very good headway.

25

Tom was making eyes at the picnic basket I'd loaded in his back seat, so I suggested that we have lunch at Historic Spanish Point. It's my favorite place for a picnic. I go there so often, in fact, that I bought a membership. It's acres and acres of old Florida right on Little Sarasota Bay. You drive off Tamiami with its SUVs and pool service pickups, its sports cars and landscapers' trailers and instantly, you're in heaven.

You can sit on a deck high on a shell midden from thousands of years ago, overlooking Little Sarasota Bay, and gaze across to Casey Key, where the rich and famous live. At least the rich, famous, and private. The ones who *want* you to know they are rich and famous tend to live on Longboat, two keys north.

"Much better than the food court," Tom said around his sandwich as he watched high-schoolers practice their sculling and ospreys soaring and pelicans diving. Behind us was Mrs. Palmer's Pergola, where she took tea in the 1910's. We could see the boat dock where the homesteaders who settled here loaded their sailboat with the oranges they grew.

We gathered up the remains of our picnic and walked down the midden past bamboo and citrus trees. We peeked into the display of the layers of shell which made up the midden. We made a vague date to bring Joshua back to enjoy the full display of prehistoric artifacts. Kids like that kind of stuff.

As we strolled across the boardwalk over Webb's Cove, I told Tom what Jeanne had said about Bartram being a ladies' man. He didn't see the connection. Come to think of it, neither did I. We leaned on the railing to admire the historic reproductions of old sail boats. From where we stood, only the tops of two condos on the south end of Siesta Key reminded us that we were in the twenty-first century, not the nineteenth.

Tom was counting mullet jumps when something occurred to me.

"Tom, you said Laurence Pease mentioned Jolly Johnson to you."

"Twelve. Wow, that was a big one! What?"

"Pease knew Jolly Johnson, knew his real name was Walter, right?"

"Yeh? So?"

"He told me he didn't know anyone by that name. The only reason I knew it was his secretary called me. She knew him."

"So maybe she reminded him. No big deal. We found the man and he told us everything he knew about Ilene. Which wasn't a lot."

Not everything, not yet. But I'd call Jolly and find out more, and then I'd show Tom how good a detective I could be. But meanwhile we'd better get out of the sun. I could feel the sun burning from above and below thanks to the mirror-like water.

"So why do mullet jump?" Tom asked as I dragged him away from the boardwalk. I told him I'd ask my friend Polter and get back to him on that.

We headed back towards my place. "So we know Jolly watches out over seniors and Ilene visited him. That Blowfish Bayou was a bait shop. That either Amelia's Memories or the antique shop in Herald Square is the AM on the list, but I don't know why. And that Pease didn't remember Jolly Johnson. I can't figure out how all this fits together."

"It doesn't," said Tom. "All you're proving is that anyone's life has inconsistencies, odd bits and pieces. Life is not a detective novel, Wendy Sam, where everything means something."

"Speaking of which, why didn't you want me to tell Jolly you were a cop?"

Tom glanced over at me. "You caught that. If I'm not on

police business, it's not such a good idea. People get leery. You have to pick and choose what you tell people."

"But you are on police business," I said.

"Wendy Sam. Please. For the last time. There is no case. Ilene Brown fell to her death. No one wanted her dead."

"But she is."

"Yes, she is. And I'm sorry, for her, for you. But death happens. That doesn't mean someone murdered her."

Was I totally wrong? What if Tom was right, that no one wanted Ilene dead? What if I really was, like Henri suggested, just raking up parts of Ilene's life that didn't need to be seen?

No. There were too many things going on. Ilene had been asking people things, Biddie Amberson and Jolly and Laurence Pease. Ilene had said *Something's not right, it's gone beyond greed* and *Chloe thinks she knows what's going on but she doesn't.* I had to talk to Chloe, to figure out what she thought was happening, and then figure out what Ilene knew different. There had to be a solution. There had to be a murderer.

We were silent for a while. I was thinking. I don't know what Tom was doing, although I did see his head swivel once or twice, first for a deep red sports car weaving through traffic in the opposite direction, then for a sleek black convertible waiting to pull onto the Trail. "Boxster," he said when he saw me watching him. "What I wouldn't give for one of them."

What is it with men and cars? Maybe it's because it rhymes with Mars? There goes my Venus brain again. Gotta get back on track.

"Henri Pousse said I would just be raking up muck about Ilene's life," I said. "Do you think I might be?"

"Who? Pousse? Henri Pousse? You didn't mention that name before." All of a sudden, I had Tom's full attention.

"Of course I did. He's the second AM, his shop is I mean. Anciennes Modernes."

"What's that mean?"

"I don't know, something like Old Moderns I guess. Why?"

115

"His last place," Tom said grimly, "was called Meubles. In Naples." Naples is south of Sarasota two hours or so. Even bigger bucks than Sarasota.

"Marbles?"

"No. Meubles. I'm probably not pronouncing it right. Means furniture in French."

"Oh. And you know this because?"

"The Naples Police sent us a heads-up. Pousse left town under a shadow, as they say. They'd figured he'd stay in Florida, maybe end up in Sarasota."

"What kind of shadow?"

"There were stolen items in his shop, and wadda ya know, all those people missing things? He'd been at parties at their houses. Of course, so had dozens of other people. Nothing was ever proven, but Pousse is on our list."

"You have a list?"

"Well, so to speak. Names to keep an ear out for. You never mentioned his name before."

Maybe I didn't. If Pousse was a burglar, though, or a suspected burglar, then what about him warning me off from investigating Ilene's life? Was Pousse Ilene's fence, or vice versa? Something to think about, but I decided I'd think, for once, before talking. I wouldn't say anything to Tom until I had it figured out. We drove on. Tamiami Trail sometimes seems unending. Problem is, it's mostly the only way to get from here to there. At least it wasn't tourist season, so traffic was moving.

We were passing Ilene's. Tom said, "Don't you have to feed her fish?"

"Oh Jeez, I forgot all about them. How often do you have to feed fish, anyway?"

"I think it depends on what kind of fish they are. Salt-water or fresh?"

"I don't know," I said. "Fresh I guess. I think they're just goldfish."

116

Which is exactly what they were. I felt strange, being in Ilene's place without her, and then sad, remembering every place was without her now. After finding and sprinkling the fish food in their tank ("Not too much!" Tom said. I rolled my eyes and gave them another sprinkle. This was no time to be on a diet, I figured), I looked around, trying to decide where I'd start cleaning out the place as I'd promised Mrs. Brown. I poked around in Ilene's closets a bit looking for the train case Mrs. Brown had mentioned and collected Ilene's jewelry cases, but then I decided we ought to leave and made some comments about what a full day it had been and how I needed to get home.

Why? I didn't want to go through Ilene's things while Tom was with me. After all, I half-expected to find something that would link to drugs and that man named after a car, or maybe something that wasn't Ilene's to have, like stolen things. Didn't think Tom would be too pleased to see anything like this, and I wasn't terribly sure that even if I found something incriminating, I'd show him. I'd come back without Tom and his nosey eyes.

So I contented myself with gathering up Ilene's photo albums. Those, I knew, were a definite yes to send to Mrs. Brown. As I piled them onto the kitchen table, one slipped and fell to the floor, open. Tom leaned down and picked it up, handing it to me. He wandered off in the direction of Ilene's glassed-in sun porch, where we'd seen boxes in a storage closet. I went to flip the open album shut and gasped. Tucked into the page was a picture of three women in swimsuits, standing in front of a shack with a sign reading Blowfish Bayou hanging from the roof edge. I flipped the loose photo over. There was no notation on it.

What was one of Otto's pictures doing in Ilene's family album? It had to be from the same roll of film as the picture I'd seen at Otto's; I recognized the striped capris and silly sunhat on one of the women. All of a sudden, it seemed important to me to know which woman was which: Dot, Mehitabel, and the third one. Inge or Ingrid? I was beginning to sound like Mr. Bruniger. I wondered if old age was catching.

117

Well duh. Sooner or later, we all come down with it. If we're lucky. I smiled, until I remembered Ilene would never be so lucky.

With smarting eyes, I slammed the album closed so Tom wouldn't see the photo. Not that he'd seen the first, but I wasn't up to trying to explain to a logical man my illogical thoughts. I wasn't real sure I could explain the matching photographs to myself, even. Maybe Otto could.

Tom came back and we put the albums into a box. "Let me just get a glass of water," he said, and went into the kitchen. I heard the water running, then Tom said, "This vine needs water," and I remembered the rootings Ilene had been nurturing. No sense letting them die. I'd take them home with me. I went in to pack them up and gasped. There was only one bottle still upright, the leaves of a philodendron curled around the curtain rod. The rest of the bottles were in the sink. Their greenery had spilled out and died.

They had been all neatly aligned last Wednesday when I was here. Someone had swept them aside. Who had been in Ilene's apartment? Who messed with her bottles? I looked around. Nothing else seemed disturbed.

"No, wait, that cupboard's ajar," I said. Tom looked puzzled as I leaned past him and looked in the cabinet. It was full of glassware.

"I just took a glass out for water," Tom said, holding up a Flintstones tumbler. "What's the matter?"

"Those bottles weren't in the sink last week," I said. "I know because... well, because I noticed." I didn't want to mention that I'd taken the blue bottle from the sill without permission the day Ilene died. I doubted Mrs. Brown would mind, but Tom seemed like a real stickler for rules.

He looked down at the dying plants in the sink. "I just figured she was a messy housekeeper."

Maybe I needed to keep this to myself for the time being. The jewelry cases seemed untampered with, so whoever had been in the apartment had not taken the only things remotely valuable

118

in the place. And if the breaker-inner had something to do with drugs, I definitely didn't want Tom around.

"Yeh," I said. "I'm probably not remembering it right."

But why mess with the windowsill? Maybe whoever it was just wanted to see out the window. I leaned past Tom. I didn't mean to brush his arm with a breast. Really, I didn't.

The only view out Ilene's kitchen window was the back of the marina office. I saw Jerry Beeton down there, sitting in a cheap plastic chair, his feet on the porch railing, smoking a cigar and scratching his belly. He must have seen my movement, because he looked up, squinting into the low sun as he did so. He stood up and started towards the apartment. I moved away from Tom who seemed frozen in place.

There was the sound of leather sandals on the steps, and Beeton yanked the wooden screen door open. "What are you doing here?" he snarled.

The man was so rude. For heaven's sake, he'd seen me before at Ilene's. He'd even been there when I discovered her body. He'd brought me coffee while I sat in the police car. What was making him so rude today?

"Her mother asked me, see, I have a key," I was holding up my key ring as though he could tell one of them was Ilene's. "And her fish..."

"Beeton, isn't it?" Tom stepped forward. "Detective Litwin, we met last week. Ms. Miller here is simply gathering up some of her friend's items at the mother's instruction. I am accompanying her. What is your connection here?"

Could it have been Beeton who'd been in the apartment and disturbed the bottles? Had he stolen something? Could it have been drugs?

"Caretaker," Beeton muttered, head down. He'd gone from belligerent to penitent in record time. "I took care of Ilene. This place, I mean. Kept an eye on her. Young girl like that, shouldn't be livin' alone. Came home all hours."

"You don't live here, do you?" I asked. How could he have known when Ilene came home?

Beeton's chin came up and he glowered at me. "Nah, down Nokomis. With my sister and her kids. What's it to you?"

"How would you know Ilene came home at all hours? Unless you were here late?"

"Kids."

"Kids?"

"Yeh, my sister's brood. Damn noisy brats. I come back evenings, after she gives me my supper, just sit on the dock and think. Quiet here. Don't go home till the kids are asleep." *And until the six-pack is all gone*, I thought, looking at his beer belly.

"And you would watch Ilene?" I got the creeps, thinking of this boat rat guzzling and looking in her windows.

"Not like that," he said. "Just like, noticing . I'm not some prevert, lady. I was watching out after her."

Well, prevert or pervert, I'm sure Ilene wouldn't have cared to know she was of such interest to Beeton. Ugh.

He sniffled and hitched up his shorts. They were filthy. "Gotta get this place cleaned out for the next tenant now." For someone who watched out for Ilene, the man seemed remarkably unfazed that she was dead.

Maybe he's the one who had knocked the bottles off the window sill. "Have you been in here since Ilene died?" I asked.

"Course not. Crime scene, right? I'm a law-abiding citizen, I am."

I looked at Tom. He didn't seem likely to correct Beeton's mistake, to tell him this wasn't a crime scene because according to the police there was no crime. I figured Tom knew what he was doing so I would keep my mouth shut. I was proud of that decision; it's one I seldom make.

Tom picked up the box with Ilene's photo albums. "You'll need to stay out of here until Ms. Miller has completed her inventory. She'll probably be back several times. She'll let you know when you can come in."

"Yezzir." Tom herded Beeton out the door and down the steps. They had a few more words that I couldn't hear, then Beeton walked away. Tom motioned *come on* to me. I picked up the jewelry cases and made my way carefully down the steps which had cost Ilene her life. The empty wrought-iron hanger, where the cranesbill had hung, reached out like the claw of a monster.

"One thing I'm wondering," Tom said, his eyes firmly on the road now. He missed a new Thunderbird in the right lane but I didn't figure he wanted to hear about that. "You haven't been in Ilene's apartment since Wednesday?"

The day she died, the day I found her body. "No," I said.

"So this list, the one we're working on now, it wasn't in her apartment?"

Oh hell. "Not exactly," I said.

He still didn't look at me, but he rolled his eyes. I could see that, behind his sunglasses. Next to his very appealing crows-feet. Oh Lordy, is that a sign of aging? That crows-feet are appealing?

"So. Where."

A man who got to the point.

"Well, I kinda maybe sorta like rescued, yeh rescued, her record book from a puddle."

"Kind maybe sorta like? You sound like one of my prostitute arrests."

"Ex-cuse me? What a sexist thing to say."

"Not sexist. Men can be dumb too. So?"

"So what?"

"Wendy Sam," he said, and even I could tell that he was really trying to be patient, "you took her book from a crime scene?"

"There!"

He almost ran into the car in front of him, which for some reason had decided to stop at a yellow light. That's simply not done in Florida. Must be a damn tourist. "You should think in August we'd be safe," I said.

"What are you talking about?" he said.

"Tourists," I said, waving at the inert vehicle in front of

121

us. "Oh, yeh, and crime scene."

He didn't say a word, just clutched the steering wheel tighter. His knuckles were white against his tan.

"You said," I began patiently and calmly, "that I took something from a crime scene. But according to the police, of which you are one, Ilene's death was an accident. Ergo, no murder. Ergo, no crime. Ergo, no crime scene."

"Of which I am one?"

"Well, you are."

"I mean, who talks like that?"

My feelings were hurt. "My feelings are hurt. I do. Besides, you've avoiding the issue."

"Oh, we have issues now?" We were rounding the curve on 41, and the marina sprung into view. My heart leaped as it always did. God, this was a beautiful place.

"No," I said, looking at the new man beside me. "We do not have issues. You just can't admit that I'm right, that there's a murderer to catch."

"Believe me, Wendy Sam, there's lots of murderers out there to catch. I just don't think that one of the bad guys murdered Ilene."

Well, turned out he was right. If I'd have known that then, we could have had a much more satisfying relationship.

We just couldn't seem to agree on anything, and our goodbyes ten minutes later at my door were muted. Tom said he'd call, but I thought it was just empty noise, like "we must get together soon." As he turned to leave, I put my hand on his arm.

"Sorry." I said. "I'm kind of distracted."

"Wendy Sam," he said. "Believe me, it was an accident. No one killed Ilene. There was no reason to. Please, believe me. If there had been a reason, we would have found it."

I had no idea whether the "we" Tom was using meant "we the police" or "we" as in "you and me." I didn't care, I thought wearily. There was no "we," just me. I had to find out who killed Ilene. Tom was not going to be a magic genie. It was up to me. Not we.

122

26

Tom hadn't noticed the new window and I wasn't planning on telling him about the conch shell incident. I pulled the curtain shut which I seldom do in summertime, since the street is almost deserted, all the snowbirds back up North. Weekend days can get busy, with locals headed to Lido Beach, but at night, it gets mighty deserted around here. To be honest, I was a little nervous. I had no idea who threw the shell and no idea why they were trying to scare me off. But if I told Tom, he'd have me arrested or something. For proving him wrong, maybe. Nice guy, but strong-headed. There was a murder and I would prove it.

I opened one of Ilene's albums that evening over a cold supper, the one with the photo of the three women in it. The Blowfish Bayou sign had been hand-painted by an amateur. The letters were enthusiastically painted but unevenly spaced. Over the capris woman's shoulder there were mangrove islands. Impossible to identify where this dock was and anyway it was long-since gone. Mehitabel Madison Frazier had told me it was Vamo and Jeanne of the electric lemonade had said it was somewhere near her place but hadn't pinpointed it. I didn't even know if the location was important, and I sure as hell didn't understand why Ilene and Otto had photographs from the same day in their respective family albums. And I still didn't know which woman was which. I could call Otto and ask, but he didn't seem the type to remember which woman wore what over thirty years ago if I described the clothes over the phone. I could go ask him tomorrow in person. Or better still, I could call Mehitabel. She's a woman, she'd remember.

I looked at the time: not too late to call, late enough that

123

Mehitabel had probably had her evening beer or two and might be talkative. She was. "Hey, Wendy Sam, I called Otto and he's coming to see me real soon. Nice to make contact after all these years. Dunno why I never thought of it. So, you find Blowfish Bayou?"

"Guess it's gone now, Mrs. Frazier, but I have another question."

"Lemme get my cigarettes, hon, won't be a minute."

When she got back on the line, I described the picture I'd seen at Otto's, the one with all three couples in it, Dot 'n Ot, Mehitabel and the late Mr. Madison, and Inge Johannsen and Olaf. I didn't mention the version in front of me, Ilene's. I'm not sure why.

"I was wondering which woman was which."

Mehitabel laughed so hard, she started coughing. She really ought to quit smoking, I thought. "Bless you, honey, that's easy enough to tell. I'm the fat one."

I looked more closely at the photo. In twenty-first century terms, all three women were quite curvy. "I don't see a fat one."

She laughed again. "Go on, flattery'll get cha everywhere. Long dark hair. I usually wore it in a braid. I longed to be a hippie but I was too old."

The braid must have been lying down her back, but now that I concentrated, I could see that one woman's hair was much darker than the other two's. "Oh yes," I said. "You have on a floral swimsuit with a skirt."

"See, those skirts work. You didn't even notice how fat I was!" She was enjoying this. Then she paused. "You have the picture in front of you?"

"No, no. I just have a really good memory," I lied. If she only knew. Ilene and I used to laugh about our mental quirks: she usually got names wrong, I couldn't remember them for five minutes. We both made absurd connections between thoughts and ideas. That's probably what had made us friends.

"I remember one of you had capris on, and a silly straw hat, one that tied under the chin," I said. "Who would that have been?"

"Wait a minute. Why are you asking all these questions? What's it to do with you? Otto said you have a consignment shop. You sound like a detective. Why do you need to know all that?"

Panic: she might not answer me. But at least I knew that the woman with the hat had to be Dorothy or Inge. That was progress.

Pride: she said I sounded like a detective! That means my questioning was improving. *Fie on Tom. I'll show him*, I thought, *and I'll solve this murder.*

I back-pedaled and decided that maybe a bit of the truth might help. So I told Mehitabel about my murdered friend and that she'd had another photo of that long-ago Blowfish Bayou day in her apartment.

"Murder?" She lit another cigarette. "If it's murder, why aren't the police asking these questions?"

So I had to admit that I was the only one who thought it was murder, that everyone else seemed to accept it as an accident and that it was up to me to prove them wrong and catch the murderer.

"Sounds like you read too many detective stories," Mehitabel said. "You sound like a young woman. You ought to get out more. Go dancing. Oh, the fun we had when we were young. Do it now, honey, before the arturitis sets in."

Just what I needed. Another mother. "I get out," I told her. "And I met two nice men just this week." Granted, one might be a thief a la Cary Grant in that movie, and the other one was a mule-headed policeman, but that was more men than I'd met in the last year. Great, here I sit, mentally defending my social life to a woman I'd never met. "So anyway, about this photograph."

"Maybe your friend, Ilene did you say? just bought it from Otto," Mehitabel said. I knew she hadn't, it was in her family album after all. But wait a minute. It was just stuck between two pages, it wasn't glued down or anything. Could it be that Mehitabel had figured something out on the damn phone that I hadn't observed with it in my lap? Maybe I wasn't such a hot-shot detective after all.

"Yes, maybe that's it," I said. "You might be right. Maybe she did just buy it. But not from Otto. He never mentioned meeting Ilene."

Mehitabel seemed a little mollified. "Well, hon, I wish you luck. That silly hat? Did it have pom poms around the brim?"

It did. I hadn't noticed before. Was I an idiot to think I could be a detective when I couldn't even notice pom poms? I mean, jeez, I was a consignment shop owner. Even a consignment shop owner ought to notice pom poms, yet alone a detective.

"That was Inge's," she said. "It had been her mother's. Inge thought it was funny. She wore it all the time."

We said our goodbyes as Mehitabel popped open another beer. Beer sounded good to me, so I hung up and went to my refrigerator to see if there was one left from my party. As I pulled the door open, I thought about why Ilene would have tucked a stranger's snapshot in her album. I poured and went out in the back yard with my beer and the leatherette book. I felt safer there than in my front room, even with the curtains drawn.

I could hear Dom in his yard even though I couldn't see him over the six-foot fence. Actually it wasn't Dom I heard but his music. Some Italian opera. Someday I'd have to get him to teach me about opera. All I know is that there's always some fat lady in them, like Mehitabel in her skirted swimsuit and me. I sighed and took a big swig of beer and opened the album one more time.

Okay, say the photo had nothing to do with Ilene and she had just stuck it in her album. Maybe it was simply a safe place to keep it until Ilene found a frame. Idly, I looked at the pictures mounted on the pages near where I'd found the Bayou one. Pictures of a little baby, then a toddler Ilene. Her hair was flaxen and fine. I looked at Ilene's mother holding her infant daughter over her shoulder to show the baby a Christmas tree. Could that mother have imagined outliving her daughter?

That was all I could take for one evening. I closed the album and finished my beer. Dom was singing along now, some

126

part of the opera even a Philistine like me recognized, the barber song I think. I climbed up on my wooden bench and peered over at Dom. He was singing lustily, waving the hose around, and grinned lopsidedly when he saw me spying on him.

"Sorry!" he hollered, and turned the volume down on his boom box. "The wife always said I played it too loud."

"No, it was the singing. You're really good."

He ducked his head. Mumbled something about lessons.

"You used to take singing lessons?"

"Yes," he said. "But once the babies came along, there was no time. No time, no money."

"You should take them now. Now you have time and money."

"I'm too old. Who'm I kidding? Old man, old voice. Speaking of which, who was that man that picked you up and dropped you off today?"

It's nice to have neighbors who care about you. Sometimes though it's nicer than other times.

"That's right, you haven't met him. Tom Litwin. He's with the police. I'll introduce you next time he's over." *If he comes over*, I thought. That wasn't a given for sure, seeing as how we'd parted.

"The police? Was he investigating who threw the shell? Did you show him the note? What did he say?"

"Umm, Dom, we need to keep that under our hats for a bit," I started. Dom interrupted.

"Now Wendy Sam, you mean you didn't call the police? I can't believe you. That was a threatening note. Wait a minute. If you didn't report it, why was a policeman there? Hey, and wait another minute. Wasn't that a picnic basket you were carrying?"

Sharp old man. Doesn't miss a trick. "Friend, Dom, he's a friend. He just happens to be with the police."

Dom looked like he didn't believe me but that he was willing to drop it. For now. It was late, almost dark, so we said good night and retreated into our separate homes. I pulled the conch shell note out of the drawer where I'd stuffed it this

127

morning and sat down to look at it.

Mind your own business. It was an accident. Well, what did they think I was, stupid? Someone throws your own conch shell threw your window and says *Mind your own business?* Pul-eeze. If they really wanted me to mind my own business, wouldn't it have been much smarter to ignore me? Therefore, it wasn't an accident. Therefore, it was a murder. Now all I had to do was figure out who I was bothering enough that I had to be warned off. Obviously, an amateur.

I needed a plan here. I still had to talk to Chloe, and see about Annie's drug dealer, the guy with the name like a car. Ford Fairlane? No. Mark Four. And figure out the photograph, and call Jolly back, try to figure out what Ilene knew when. Maybe that way I could figure out who got scared, scared enough to kill her.

Oh yeh, I had a business to run too. The next day was Monday, always a big incoming day in consignment shops. I'd better get some sleep. I made the rounds of the house more carefully than I ordinarily do, still spooked by the incident last night. I turned off the lights before I peered out the new window. There was a figure in a parked car across the street, just sitting there. I watched for a few minutes, trying to decide whether to call my own private cop, and jumped when the phone rang.

It was James. "Wendy Sam, go out to the car and tell Michael to turn the damn cell on. He's always forgetting it. I don't know why, it was his idea in the first place that we needed them."

It was Michael in that car. I groaned. "James, for heaven's sake, I don't need watching. I'm not a baby."

"Just go tell Michael to turn the phone on, honey, and go to bed. At least you'll be able to sleep like a baby. Polter said he'd take the last shift, so you probably should make him breakfast."

"Good night, James." I hung up, made Michael a cup of herbal tea, and took it out to him. We talked some, I yawned, he told me to go in. "All under control, Princess. Sleep tight."

So I did. But not before I remembered that I had planned to go back to Ilene's apartment tonight. Maybe I could, early tomorrow, before I went in to the shop.

128

27

I woke up early. Getting groggily out of bed, I finger-combed my hair and pulled on an oversized tee, then started the coffee. While it perked, I would get the newspaper from the front yard.

In Sarasota, the paper is delivered not by some adorable kid on a bike draped in a canvas bag but by guys in vans who toss the paper in the general vicinity of the abode of the subscriber. My paper has a tendency to end up in the prickly pear cactus on the other side of my shell drive. This requires a certain amount of bodily protection.

Accordingly, at the front door, I attired myself in heavy canvas work gloves and yellow flower-sprigged gardening clogs (from Too Good to be Threw of course) to retrieve the paper from its likely landing spot.

I opened the door and almost tripped over Polter, sitting on the stoop reading the sports section. "Oops," I said, backing up so as not to give him a crotch shot.

"Pancakes," he said.

"And a good morning to you, too."

"I've been dreaming of pancakes for the last two hours."

"I think I can manage that." I retrieved the rest of the paper while Polter followed the scent of coffee into my kitchen. I disgloved and unshod myself, made a detour into the bedroom for a proper robe, and joined my night guard. He'd poured us both big mugs, and I sipped mine while I rummaged for the Bisquick in the pantry. Pancakes involve Bisquick, right? I was peering at the side panel, hoping I had whatever other ingredients might be needed, when I noticed Polter's frown.

"Sit," he said, and aligned the newspaper neatly in front of

129

one of my breakfast bar stools. So I did. He was assembling bowls, measuring cups, other arcane kitchen utensils I didn't remember owning. I don't cook a lot, I believe I've mentioned.

"Got any cottage cheese?" he said, as he opened the refrigerator.

"Any self-respecting woman always does," I said. "It makes us think we're on a diet."

He retrieved it from the back left corner of the bottom shelf and congratulated me on the fact that it was mold-free. I was enjoying the compliment, backhanded as it was, when he came up with another request I could easily fulfill. Sour cream. That's something that I always have.

Within a few minutes, he had a pancake batter mixed up, and was looking for the griddle. All I had was a frying pan. There's nothing to be ashamed of in that; many women don't have griddles in their kitchens. Do they?

Then Polter was aghast that I did not have maple syrup in the house. I redeemed myself by whipping up a little gourmet treat of strawberry butter, and we settled down companionably to breakfast. I told him what I'd learned so far while we ate. About Ilene's visit to Pease the day before she died, and about Jolly Johnson whose name was on the list Ilene wrote after her visit with Pease, and how he dealt with seniors. And the mystery about a nickname like Blowfish Bayou being on that list too.

When our tummies were full enough, Polter asked to see the note that had arrived via conch shell. I dug it out of the drawer and he moved the newspaper aside to study the note.

I watched him. If anyone could deduce anything from a note written in blue marker on a common sheet of paper, it would be my friend Polter, master of trivia. He licked a finger and rubbed it over the -*ent* in *Mind your own business. It was an accident.* The ink smeared.

"Overhead projector pen," he said.

"Why? Any washable marker will smear. Here," I said, opening my junk drawer and pulling out two markers, one washable and one not. I made a squiggle on the margin of the note in each, then rubbed a licked finger of my own over them. As I thought: the permanent marker didn't budge, the washable one did.

Polter shook his head. "See the washable marker? The ink can be moved," and he gestured to my mark, "but not diluted," and he pointed to the original smear.

"I'll be damned," I said. The ink on the note had actually lightened, like watercolor paints do when you add more water.

"Overhead projector pen," Polter declared with conviction, and finished the last few bites of his cottage cheese pancakes.

"Using your conch shell, from your yard, argues a person who came unprepared, or a person who decided at the last minute that throwing a note through your front window would be a good idea." He was leaning back in his seat now, preparing to lecture me. "And who would that person be?"

"That's the big question," I said, clearing the dishes and running water into the batter bowl he'd left in the sink.

"Who carries around overhead projector pens with them?" he said. "Think, Wendy Sam."

I scowled. "Someone with a briefcase. A business person."

He nodded. "Someone who runs meetings, gives motivational seminars, rallies his troops with pie charts and graphs, who scribbles on them to prove his point."

Boy, he's good. "Someone like, say, a real estate agent? Laurence Pease?"

Polter smiled at me. "Good, good. There's hope for you yet."

"I don't understand why Pease would do it. He wasn't too happy about my questions, but I kinda felt that was because I was interrupting his work day." *Except*, I thought, *he told me he didn't know Jolly when he did.*

"You said he sold like ten houses a week, right? Why does someone work that hard?"

"For money?"

131

"Yes, Wendy Sam, for money. Greed. You've already found out that Ilene went to Pease right before she died. Then you go and ask about what they talked about, and he bluffs his way through your visit, then he throws a rock through your window with a threatening note wrapped around it."

"Conch shell."

"Huh?"

"Conch shell, it was my conch shell. And the note didn't *threaten* anything."

Polter sighed. "Don't you watch old movies, Wendy Sam. Standard shtick: rock through window means *or else*."

What an idiot I was. I really hadn't seen the note as a threat. More as a suggestion. A suggestion I hadn't given the first thought to taking. It arrived Saturday night and I spent all of Sunday most specifically *not* minding my own business. Only way to continue at this point was to not mind my own business faster, and figure out who killed Ilene and why.

I was sure glad I hadn't told Tom about the conch shell et cetera. With any luck, I never would have to. I'd solve this case, Tom would arrest a murderer, and we'd live happily ever after. Maybe I'd name my first child Ilene. Ilene Litwin, daughter of Tom and Wendy Sam Litwin.

Oops. I forgot. I'm too old to have these fantasies.

Polter noticed the dreamy look in my eyes. He knew me well enough to know I was no longer on his wave length. He told me to be careful and left before I could properly thank him for guarding over me as I slept. He's a good friend.

Even with pancakes and crime-solving, it was still early enough that if I hurried, I could go to Ilene's and pick up the train case and the statuette Mrs. Brown wanted. When I pulled into the parking lot of the marina, I looked around for that slimy Beeton guy. I didn't want to see him and I didn't, thank God. I scurried up the steps and opened Ilene's door quickly just in case he was around.

The brass figurine of a old man with a dog was right on

Ilene's night stand. I picked it up and looked at it. It was really wonderful. The patina of the old brass seemed to accent the sad look of the man as he clutched the scruffy mutt to his chest. Was the dog sick? Did the old man have to give up his dog because he was going into an old folks' home? Was the old man homeless and his dog his only companion? I sighed and went into the kitchen to find a bag to put it in, before I started searching for the monogrammed case.

While I was there, I gathered the dead vines together. Opening the cabinet below to put them in the trash, I started to toss them in but stopped. The last thing thrown away was a flurry of tiny white scraps.

Going through the trash was a detective-y sort of thing to do, right? So I did, laying it all out on the counter. Besides the scraps of paper, there was the usual: used tea bags dried in contorted postures, a Styrofoam take-out container with what looked like Chinese food bits clinging to it, a cheese wrapper and a barely-smoked cigarette butt.

Wait a minute. Ilene didn't smoke, did she? No, she hated being around smoke. I looked closely at the butt and wondered if I should save it for DNA evidence or something. It was brown, as though it had been extinguished under the tap instead of being stubbed out. I could imagine Ilene snatching the cigarette from a visitor and dousing it with water. I wonder who the smoker was and how he would have reacted. Smokers can be touchy about their filthy habit, but even I didn't think drowning a cancer stick would be cause for murder.

I put the cigarette aside and tried to fit the paper scraps together. It was a business card. Plain white with black lettering. It read Barry Cobb, President/ Sunshine Improvement/ A Division of BB Construction and gave an address and about four telephone numbers.

This must have been the card Ilene picked up, the one Chloe had dropped at Marina Jack's on our Girls' Night Out two weeks ago. Barry had thrust the card into Chloe's hand since she didn't seem to want to take it. After Ilene picked up the card, she got mad. Very strange. What was so emotional about a business card?

Maybe it had something written on the back. Carefully, I turned it over piece by piece. Yes, there was something. Written in strong masculine handwriting was the name and address of my new consignor, Otto Bruniger.

I picked up Ilene's phone and called Susan at the shop.

"Yes, I know I said I'd be in to help, but there's something I have to see after. Come on, Susan, you're my manager. Manage."

"It's not that," Susan said in her *I-am-a-reasonable-Mommy* voice. I'd heard her use it on the phone to her kids, so I could imagine the rolled eyes and impatient toe-tapping going on. "I think you are getting carried away with all this. You're not an investigator, for heaven's sake. Let the police do it. It's their job."

"They don't think anything happened."

"Tell me again why you do?"

I wasn't about to tell Reasonable Mommy Susan about the conch shell incident. She'd probably send me to my room or take away my TV privileges. The incident, I now noted to myself with a wry smile, had done the opposite of what was intended: it had made me positive that there was something going on, that someone had indeed caused Ilene's death. So, did I really think Laurence Pease had thrown it? Would such a canny guy be so dumb as to, in effect, encourage me to keep hunting?

So I told Susan about Ugli Court and Jolly Johnson and Blowfish Bayou. She remained unconvinced and didn't think the list had anything to do with the death. "All right, Wendy Sam, you go ahead. But I'm going to have to call Annie or Elsie in to help. Markdowns are getting behind, I've got a fistful of return-at-requests to pull, and the window washer managed to wreck your display."

I swallowed hard, visions of payroll getting out of hand, and told her to do what she had to do. Maybe, without the shell through my window, I would have given up at that point. This investigation was eating into my income. But the conch-thrower had encouraged me. I hoped whoever it was, he was just as stupid about something else, something I would find out about. Soon. Before I went bankrupt.

Otto Bruniger was home and would be delighted to see me. I'd called ahead and asked, like the well-brought-up woman I was, if there was anything I could bring.

"If you're going past Geier's, would you pick me up $2 worth of liverwurst? The kind with onions? I'll pay you back. It's such a waste to spend taxi money going there." The German butcher shop was on Tamiami, so of course it was on the way. I'd only have to backtrack a mile or so.

"Be happy to. Anything else? Their chicken salad is terrific," I said. He declined.

The requested liverwurst stowed beside me on the car seat, I headed for Otto's. I needed to figure out why his name was on Barry's business card that had been handed to a reluctant Chloe, then read by a mad Ilene, then ripped up into the smallest pieces possible and thrown away. By Ilene? By whomever was in Ilene's and messed with the window sill?

And on top of that, I had to figure out why a photograph like Otto's was in Ilene's family album. Could Ilene be Otto's granddaughter? But she never mentioned any family except for her mother, and Mrs. Brown lived in California.

He was as happy to see the sausage as he was me. Happier maybe even. He wanted to make me coffee. Remembering Tom's advice, I said yes and followed him in to the kitchen.

Surprise. He got out a bag of whole coffee beans and a small electric grinder and a Krups machine. Who'd have thought? Especially after the lukewarm Lipton last visit. He must have seen my look.

"Nice, isn't it? I remember Dot used to have a hand grinder for coffee when we were first married. The wooden kind,

135

where the grounds fell into a little drawer?" I nodded, remembering them. "Then we got so's we'd buy Maxwell House, you know, good to the last drop?"

I smiled. "Lots has changed in a lifetime," I said. "But you look up to date," waving my hand at his Starbucks. "All the latest. Maybe you should get a cappuccino machine," I teased.

"Well, now, that's what he wanted to get me, but I said no, don't want to be fiddling with that hot steam and such at my age. I told you about my eyesight, didn't I?"

"Who, a son?"

"Don't have a son, no kids. Dot couldn't."

There goes my Ilene-as-Otto's-granddaughter theory.

"I'm sorry. Who wanted to give you a cappuccino machine?"

"That man, the one who wanted to buy my house. Thought giving me a present would soften me up, but no sirree. Nice coffee machine, but that doesn't mean I'm ready to sell Dot's place. Did I tell you she loved this place?"

"Yes, you did. I can see why. Who was this man? A real estate agent?" Didn't Otto mention something about an agent who told him he could afford an apartment with what he'd get out of his house? Hell, if I knew even a little about the price of bayside land, I thought as I looked out at Siesta Key across the bay from Otto's yard, Otto should be able to afford an apartment complex with what he'd get for this place. An inland apartment complex, of course.

"No, not him. He didn't offer me a coffee machine. He didn't even seem to want to offer me a contract to sell the house. Unenthusiastic guy, he was. Strange that an agent would be so low-key. You'd think they'd be real go-getters. In my time, they were. This guy, I wouldn't even have hired as a sales clerk in my hardware store Back Home. Nah, the guy who gave me the machine wants to buy my house, himself, no agents or lawyers. He said he'd even forget a house inspection. Said he loved the old place."

"No inspection?" Where else had I heard about skipping

136

the inspection, a standard part of any house sale?

"That's what made me figure he was looking to tear it down." Otto patted the worn Formica counter of his kitchen fondly. "He said he wouldn't, but we all know how people lie." He winked at me. "No one putting anything over on this old man. Kinda fun, to con a con man." He fiddled with the assortment of prescription bottles lined up near the sink and smiled a foxy little smile.

So that was Otto's game. Sure, he loved his house for the memories of his wife it held, but basically, he was getting his last licks in. He poured coffee for us, and I toasted his attitude silently.

After a bit more chatting, mostly about his kidneys and how they weren't functioning as well as they did once upon a time, the cost of prescription drugs and how you had to be real careful about taking them all together, I asked to see the pictures in his sun room again. This took a while, a discourse on fishing, another refill of our cups, and a few tummy growls from Otto. He was thinking of the liverwurst, so I decided to get to the point, before he got too hungry to be chatty.

"A friend of mine has a photograph that looks like it came from the same roll as this one," I said, standing in front of his Blowfish Bayou shot. The three happy couples continued to smile out at me.

"That's Ilene, is Ilene a friend of yours?"

I was surprised. "You know her?"

"Well, not really. I called her, you know, from the ads? I wanted her to do a house sale for me, clean out some of this junk." He indicated the entire house. "But it wasn't a good idea, she said, I didn't want to sell enough stuff for her to have a sale. She did buy a few things from me though. She really likes old photographs, did you know that?"

I didn't know whether to tell him Ilene was dead. Such a statement would dry up the tale he was telling me, but it seemed cruel just to let him go on. I let him go on.

"She saw this picture and said she really liked it. I found a shoe box full of snapshots that I guess Dot thought weren't good enough to frame or put in the album, so I let her buy them. She took a couple other things, too, a planter and some old wine glasses I never use nomore. Gave me $100 for them." He looked proud at having made a good deal.

Actually, he did. I'd been junking with Ilene a couple of times and she didn't give $100, usually, for anything less than her Jeep full. And Jeeps hold a lot.

"Sounds like you got the better end of the deal."

"I did, sugar, I did. And I will from this other fella, too. We'll see what he pays me for this place. I know it's worth more than that real estate idiot told me. I plan on just stringin' this guy on."

He smiled triumphantly and my estimation of his acuity went up a couple of notches.

"Excuse me, dear, just need to take another pill." He winced as he got up. He was gone a long time.

I was admiring the view of the water from his jalousie windows when he returned. The over-achieving monstrosities on Siesta were softened by distance and didn't, really, look *too* bad.

"Damn kidneys," he said. "Doctors say they're doing all they can."

"Have you tried any natural medicines?" I asked, thinking of the story Amy told me of the lady with her tonic.

"These things I'm taking, from the doctors? They don't mix well with herbs and things like that. Guess I just have to go on making the drug cartels rich. Richer, I'd guess you'd say."

Well, I was done here. And I still wanted to call Jolly, figure out the *Wm from Wisc* clue, and what did Loquat have to do with anything? I'd found out that Ilene had indeed, as Mehitabel had suggested, bought the photograph from Otto. It had nothing to do with her and nothing to do with her death. I couldn't very well ask Otto why Barry Cobb had written his name and this address on one of his own cards and handed it to Chloe, could I? That's when I felt like smacking my own forehead.

"Otto, you didn't tell me the name of the man who gave

you the Krups, the one who wants to buy your house."

"Doesn't matter. He'll be back."

Okay, I can be subtle. I can take a hint. I'm not totally rude. Otto didn't remember the man's name. Simple as that. I thought maybe I'd help him, though.

"Did he leave you his card?"

"Wouldn't take it. Take a man's card, that obligates you. No sirree, young lady, let me tell you this. Don't take a man's card unless you're willing to deal with him. I wasn't and I didn't. I don't need to get in touch with him, and he knows where to find me. Good enough."

Well, yeh, good enough, except I needed to know if by some chance it was Barry Cobb, Sunshine Improvement, who had been here. I suppose I could have asked Otto for a description of the man, but it was obvious even to dense me that Otto considered the conversation ended. The liverwurst was calling him. I made *I should go* noises and Otto let me.

"I'm sorry about your friend," he said as I gathered my purse.

He knew all along Ilene was dead. "Thank you," I said. Otto smiled the defiant smile of an old person thinking of someone recently dead. A *I've learned to accept it but damn if I like it* smile. I thought of the pain it took to perfect that smile and pressed his hand. "Thank you," I said again.

"And thank you for the Braunschweiger," Otto said, as he pulled himself up from his chair slowly and carefully. "Oh, let me get you your money," and he started towards his bedroom.

"No, no," I called after him. "You know, my mother used to call liverwurst Braunschweiger. Hey, Braunschweiger for Mr. Bruniger! That's kinda funny." By now Otto was back, pulling two singles out of a worn leather wallet.

He smiled. "You young girls," he said. "That's what Ilene said too, that my name sounded like Braunschweiger. That she was going to call me Mr. Liverwurst from now on." He pressed the bills into my hand; wouldn't take no for an answer.

28

I managed not to gape and got out of there fast. So Ilene had written Liverwurst to indicate Otto Bruniger. I was making progress and I rotated the puzzle pieces around in my brain, trying to see if any of them fit. So far I had an old nickname for a place that no longer existed. A street with a giant new house going up. An old man who refused to sell his bayside home. One mail-order trailer-park minister who oversaw his elderly flock. One or maybe two shops with the initials AM which bought things from Ilene, or maybe the reference was to their owners, Picture-Hat Amy or Suave Henri AKA Harry Grass. Talk about a motley crew.

Then there was the rest of the list. I still had no idea who *Wm from Wisc* was or even if it was a person or a place. *Sandpiper* and *Epazote/St J?* were mysteries still. And *Loquat?* All I associated with that are those weird little fruits in heavy syrup Chinese restaurants try to foist off on you as dessert. What is it with Chinese restaurants? Preserved fruit or fortune cookies, what a choice. I made it a habit to head for the closest Big Olaf's after a Chinese meal, for a nice sweet gooey hot fudge sundae. Just the thing after vegetable lo mein. Or am I thinking of litchee? I need to look that up in a dictionary.

Otto was on Ilene's list and on the card in the trash. I hadn't figured out a way to ask Otto about that, not that he'd necessarily know why his name would be on a card that might have been the card Cobb handed Chloe, that was maybe the card Ilene picked up off the restaurant floor, and then possibly ripped up and threw away? This was way too confusing.

I couldn't help but worry that I was in over my head. The fact that the card had been ripped up in such little pieces probably meant the ripping was done in anger. So was Otto in danger? Or was I reading into this more than there was?

It seemed like such an obvious clue. Would a murderer have left it in Ilene's trash? In all the murder mysteries I read, the bad guy is way too smart to do something so stupid. And those heroines are even smarter. I was feeling like I was bumbling about tripping over clues and hints right and left. It was almost as though I was being led by the nose. I didn't like the feeling, and it gave me the creeps to think there was someone out there who not only could throw Ilene down the steps to her death, but who was playing with me. Maybe it was time to try to talk Tom into taking this case over.

When I got back to the shop, I smiled apologetically at Susan and Elsie who were up to their necks in clothing and scurried into my tiny office. I picked up the phone and called Tom's cell.

Don't you hate calling people on their cell phones? Either they are really busy people with important jobs that you don't want to interrupt, or they're people who like to imagine they're important and busy but they're really getting a pedicure or standing in the grocery line. Or they're trying to merge onto Interstate 75 and a semi full of household effects from New Jersey, bound for Punta Gorda, is bearing down on them. I live in fear that I'll say *Hi?* and hear the squealing of brakes and a metallic crash.

"Litwin."

"Tom, it's Wendy Sam. Can I buy you dinner tonight? And ask you some questions?"

"Sure, but it'll have to be late. Do I get to critique your questioning skills again?" He sounded relaxed, even merry. What was so amusing? It better not be the thought of my ineptness at asking questions. Boy, did I have a lot of tell him, everything I was finding out.

"Actually, what I need is for you to help me draw it all together," I said rather frostily. "I have answers."

"Ah, but are they answers to the right questions, is that

it?"

"You're good," I said.

"We'll see about that." He was being awfully blithe for an officer of the law who was overlooking a murder. Blithe and (was I imagining it?) rather suggestive. Mentally, I reselected what I'd wear to dinner.

"Yes we will," I said, and suggested a place rather more romantic than I'd planned on. "Eight?" That was fine with him. Now I really needed to get busy and see if I could solve another clue or two before then.

I hung up the phone and stared at the map of Sarasota taped over my desk. Map! I was looking for a map when the conch shell exploded my window. I was going to look up Sandpiper, see if there was a street by that name. Ilene had Ugly written on her list and there was one of her hated gorilla houses going up there, so maybe Sandpiper was another construction site. It could be that Ilene's list was just potential clients. But I thought she wrote it after her visit to Pease. And Pease was really uneasy when I talked about it, so I had to think the list meant something more than just daily business.

If I could find a Sandpiper Street or Lane, that might help me figure out what was going on that connected the names on the list. Or Court. Or...Close! That's why the name was familiar to me. The sign I saw last week when I was driving Chloe to my place. Sandpiper Close, Another Sunshine Improvement. And another item on the list connected to Barry Cobb.

When I opened my office door I practically bowled little Elsie down. "The pants needed marking down," she said, waving the markdown sheet at me. She had a ways to go since she was still in the size 4s. *Good, that will keep her busy.* Susan was busy with a customer so I could slip out before she gave me what-for. I waved a jaunty *See you later* and got out while the getting was good. I ignored her look of dismay and Elsie's *Wait I...*

Behind the oversized *Sandpiper Close Coming Soon/*

Presales Open August 15 was an overgrown plot of land, almost a jungle. I could see the bay peeking between the oaks and myrtles. I drove down the rutted road past two mailboxes. There were giant vines growing over the trees and squirrels and birds all over. In the middle of all this nature there were two neat little houses, mirror images. Identical, except one was blue and one was—could it be?—yes, it was definitely pink. Both, despite or maybe in spite of the sign, were still inhabited, judging from the crisp café curtains and full hummingbird feeders. They looked loved and cared-for, not like they were going to be demolished any day now.

I paused as I got out of my car. It was a fairy tale. I loved the place instantly. But I was here on detective business, so, let's get serious here. Which house should I approach, and come to think of it what was I going to say?

I was ready to get back in my car and head for home to ponder what to do next when a little round woman scurried out the front door of Blue, making a bee-line for Pink. She was wearing blue, too, from her playsuit to her sandals, and concentrating so hard on balancing a cookie sheet she didn't look up at me. As she stepped onto the porch of Pink, her clone opened the door. It would have been a perfect fairy tale if the Pink lady was wearing pink, but she wasn't. She had on a big white apron, one of those bibbed ones professional chefs wear. Except it was daubed with bright colors, mostly red and green. She looked up, noticed me and waved in a friendly manner. Blue looked around to see. As she did, her cookie sheet tilted and spilled its contents.

Both ladies tossed slender arms in dismay and bent their round little bodies over thin legs, trying to gather up what had spilled. I decided they needed help.

I stepped onto the wooden porch. "Here, let me," I said, and started to pick up the Christmas cookies scattered about. Christmas cookies in August?

"Oh thank you dear," said one.

"Be careful dear, they're still warm," said the other. My head was down so I didn't see who said what. Or maybe both sentences came from one and the other was mute.

"EeeOw!" Those cookies weren't just warm, they were hot. Hot enough to burn. I let a snowflake fall and stuck the affected finger in my mouth.

"Oh dear, she must have touched a paper clip," said one.

"Come in dear, let's get an ice cube for that," said the other.

This was getting old. I introduced myself so I could get their names. Leona was the woman in blue, Noela the aproned woman whose home we were now in. They were delighted to meet me, and loved the name of my shop, and were great fans of shopping used, and really should stop in sometime, but you see, and here Noela whipped her big apron off her compact little body, "We dress alike except she" waving at her neighbor "always wears blue and I always wear pink. So we probably couldn't find the right outfits in your little shop."

Remind me to tell you some day how much I hate people calling my business "little."

"Now Noela, you exaggerate," said Leona. "Remember those purple dresses we have."

"Leona, those were bridesmaid dresses, and you know Mabel has zero taste." She turned to me and noticed I was still sucking my finger.

"Oh dear, ice, the ice," and we all three ended up in her tiny kitchen.

Once the two women fussed over my finger, I asked why there were hot paper clips in their Christmas cookies. Both women clasped their hands to their bosoms and beamed at me.

"Bless you, dear," said Noela. "They're not for eating."

"They're decorations! But they're supposed to look like Christmas cookies," said Leona. "I baked them."

"And I paint them," added Noela.

"Except every other day."

"Then we switch."

I hated to ask the obvious, but I wanted to be sure. "You're identical twins, aren't you?"

144

"Well, no," Noela said. "Leona's older than I am."

Leona made a mock hand-slap motion. "That's getting really old," she said to her sister and turned to me. "Of course we're identical. I'm ten minutes older."

"All our lives we'd wished Mama had us around midnight so we could each have our own birthday."

"But really we love being twins."

"We even married brothers. Would have married identical twins if we could have found them."

"Of course now with the internet maybe we could."

I was tired of keeping track of who said what and it didn't seem to matter to them, so I figured it didn't to me either.

"Oh dear, what are we thinking. Can we offer you some refreshment?"

Ah, another chance to apply my lesson from Tom. "Coffee would be terrific."

"I'll just run next door and get some cookies," said Leona. "Some real ones this time dear."

Noela got busy making coffee. I tried to think of a way to ask her if she knew Ilene. I couldn't, so I just plain asked. "Do you know a woman by the name of Ilene Brown? She buys and sells things at garage sales and the like?"

"Oh, my, yes, such a pleasant girl," Noela said. "We called her about selling some of our things. You know, her ad in the paper?" I'd forgotten about her ad. *Buying Always: Old things, junk you don't want, precious family heirlooms.* Ilene always said those three categories covered it all. "We made her coffee and cookies, too," she went on happily. "She said she'd get back with us."

Once again, do I tell about Ilene's death? I decided not to. The twins were such happy little women. I looked around the rosy kitchen. In the corner where there would normally be a kitchen table, an easel and painting supplies were set up. On the easel sat a watercolor of a beach over-run with sandpipers. Aha! Sandpipers!

"Great sandpipers," I said, going right up to it.

145

"Thank you, dear. We love sandpipers. That's why I named it Sandpiper Close," Noela said just as the coffee started to perk in the old-fashioned aluminum pot on the stove. "I got *that* written into the contract. Leona," and here she lowered her voice, as though her sister was still in the room, "Leona wanted NoLee Park, you know, for our names. Well, actually, she wanted LeeNo, since she's the oldest, but I persuaded her that NoLee sounded classier." I was lost. But Tom told me to just let people keep talking so I did. Noela reached up into the cabinet for some mugs. They had sandpipers on them.

"Well, we just couldn't see eye to eye, and we're not used to that, so we decided to just let the whole thing rest for a while. He got really upset that we couldn't decide."

Her head was in the fridge now, hunting the milk. "Oh?" I said to her pink bottom.

Leona was back and sure enough, home-baked cookies. On a blue dish of course. "Sorry it took so long, there was a message on my phone."

Noela raised her eyebrows.

"Yes. He's sounding more and more upset. You don't think we're going too far, do you?"

"You didn't call him back, did you?" Noela frowned as she poured the milk into a tiny pink pitcher.

"Of course not! We agreed."

Not only was I totally lost, I was at sea. Lost in the woods. Wandering around caves looking for a ray of sunlight to guide me. The feeling was so uncomfortable, I had to do something.

"That coffee smells wonderful," I said to Noela. "And the cookies look great," to Leona.

Well, we settled in the living room and chatted. They really were as alike as two peas in a pastel pod. "So, you married brothers?" I asked.

"Yes, John and Don. Leona got first choice of course, she always does, even since we were born."

"But Noela ended up with the nicer brother."

"He just seemed that way to you. John was a dear too,

146

dear."

They beamed, well-pleased obviously with each other and their lives.

"Of course the boys are gone now," Leona said happily. I must have looked surprised at her tone of voice because she added without apology, "Well, it's been a while. And they were old."

"And it's time for us to be moving on. We're getting a place together," said Noela.

"In Denver," they said together.

"Denver?" I said. "It's cold in Denver. And there are, like, mountains." I shuddered. I don't care for heights.

"Right!"

"We've going to learn to ski!"

"Or at least sled."

"And hike."

"And climb."

With their little round bodies and thin limbs, I wondered whether they would or could. "So you're leaving Sarasota?" I asked. "Selling your homes?"

"Well," said Noela, curling up her little tea napkin. Her glance was as coy as anyone over eighty could make it. "As soon as a few details are ironed out."

Leona said to her sister, "He went for the name, he'll go for the rest."

"Name?" I said. I was determined to battle my way out of that cave, land my boat, whatever you want to say.

"Sandpiper Close," Noela said, waving her hand in the direction of the sign in their front yards. "We named it!"

"Well, actually," Leona said, "our friends did."

They giggled in stereo. "We've always been called the Sandpiper Twins."

"Because we bustle about."

"And because we have skinny little legs." Here both women stuck their legs straight out from their armchairs and did a little thing with their feet, both right, both left, toes in, toes out.

147

Some sister act.

I had to laugh. "You two are something else."

They said, together, "Ain't we though!"

And Leona said, "And we're going to be beloved something elses, too."

"A legacy," Noela said. "We're leaving Sarasota a legacy."

"A beach," Leona said. "DonJon Beach Park. We had no problem naming *that*."

"A beach? Where?"

"Why right here, dear. At the end of our road. The bay is there, you know. It won't be big, but it will be as big as we can talk him into."

That was it. I was tired of being lost. "Who?"

"Why, the developer, of course."

Barry Cobb again.

"We won't agree to the sale until we have a beach, a public beach, on the water."

"Of course he keeps insisting that he needs to have the waterfront to build homes on so he can afford to buy this land from us, but we know he's just being greedy."

They nodded. "We used to have all the kids for miles around down on our beach when we were younger," Noela said.

"We didn't have children of our own so we welcomed any of them that wanted to come. Sometimes we'd have, oh just piles of bikes at the end of the road, oh it was wonderful."

"So we can't just sell up and let them fill our land with those outrageous big things, and wall the children out."

"Of course we haven't had many children lately."

"They're all indoors playing video games."

"But a beach, a proper beach."

"That will get them out again."

"But we do need to sell, of course," Noela said. "Leona's not well."

Leona glared in what seemed to me to be a perfectly healthy manner. "And I suppose your dizzy spells are less than mine? It's just age. All that work, cleaning out, figuring what to sell so that nice girl, Elaine? Ilene, that's it, Ilene, could come give us an offer."

"Well, Leona dear, you *are* older than me," said Noela triumphantly. "And you take more tonic, too. Besides, I worked just as hard. That girl," she said to me, "Ilene? She gave us a good price. Why, our houses are practically bare now!" She waved a hand around. If this is what the sisters considered bare, I'd hate to have seen it before. *So Ilene knew them. Well, of course, idiot,* I said to myself. *That's why they're on the list. Now all I have to do is figure out why.*

"I need that tonic," Leona said. "Besides, it's in a blue bottle. Blue's my color," she said to me.

A tonic in a blue bottle? Like the one Ilene had that now sat in the sun at my house? Like the bottle Amy mentioned a lady taking a nip from, that Ilene had called her back about, asking the color, which was blue? I remembered the strange smell of Ilene's bottle as I rinsed it out.

"Do you have a bottle of this tonic handy?" I asked.

"Why, certainly dear. Perhaps you might want to take some. Seems to be good for what ails you. Wait a min, I'll go get it."

Noela came back promptly with a tablespoon and a blue bottle. Identical to the one I had. "It doesn't smell too good. You might want to hold your nose while you take it. That's what this one over here does," Noela said, indicating her sister.

"May I?" I sniffed. Same smell as in mine. Had Ilene been taking a tonic? And given the twins some because they had the same symptoms? Maybe Ilene had dizzy spells and maybe she did really just fall on her steps.

"Please, have some," Leona said. "Don't be shy. Chloe should be here today with more. At least she said she would," and looked worried.

"Leona, you worry too much. Just because Chloe missed us last Wednesday's no reason to worry. When I called, she said she'd just forgotten and she'd be here today." Noela looked at her watch. "Any time now, actually."

149

"Chloe? The Thymely Lady?" I asked.

"Yes, that's her. Thymely Remedies and Essential Essences, that's her business. Isn't that cute? Thymely Remedies and Essential Essences. Do you know her? You'd like her."

"Oh dear, it is late," I said. "I've taken up far too much of your time. Must run." I had to get out of there before I ran into Chloe. I needed to think. I couldn't figure out a way to ask the Sandpiper Twins not to mention my visit, so I didn't. I'd just have to hope they didn't tell Chloe that I was asking about her.

"No tonic, dear? It's all natural. It can't hurt you," said one or the other of the twins as I practically ran to my car.

29

Thoughts buzzed through my head as I pulled things out of my closet and tossed them in every direction. I wanted to get my information straight even as I messed up my bedroom. I wanted to have something to present to Tom and it had to be logical. But most of all, I wanted to look good for our date.

Well, maybe "date" was too big a word. Meeting, perhaps. But I was leaning towards the slinky red Carol Horn number, which was awfully sexy for a "meeting."

Stockings? I hate pantyhose. And it's August in Sarasota. In my drawer were gossamer-sheer stockings with tiny rhinestones at the ankles. I'd bought them in a weak moment. I scrounged around in the bottom drawer and stood up triumphant. A red and black garter belt and bra given to me as a going-away present back in Ohio. I never had the nerve (or, to be truthful) the occasion to wear it. Perfect. I tried it all on, push-up bra, garter belt, slinky red number. Oops, no room for panties.

Hey, I'm a grown woman. If I wanna go to dinner panty-less ain't no one's business if I do. Humming the tune, I took it all off, headed for the tub, and sloshed an extra dollop of Joy in the bath water.

I pinned up my hair and got in the scented tub. Heavenly. I got out again, pulled on my *It takes a woman* t-shirt, and padded into the kitchen, leaving wet footprints on the tile as I went. There was a bottle of cold white wine. I reached down a crystal wine glass, one of two that had come into the shop, and poured myself a drink. Back to the tub.

Ahh. Now, to organize my thoughts about bottles, tonics, stolen merchandise, old photographs, megamansions. I sipped and thought. Then I just sipped. Tom would help me organize my thoughts. As long as I didn't focus on my panty-less state, I'd be just fine.

It took an hour to get my hair and make-up just so. Normally, that's a five-minute job. So you can understand just how gorgeous I felt when Tom came by to pick me up. I looked good, I smelled good, and I was about to ask a hunk to help me. How more feminine can you get? He even opened the car door for me.

As we drove to Ophelia's we chit-chatted. I was waiting to sit face-to-face before I tried to put it all together for him. Besides, he was holding my hand.

"Aren't you supposed to have two hands on the wheel? I mean, as a policeman."

"I'm a detective, not a state trooper," he said. "Besides, I'm lucky to have one hand free. You are looking very, er, very pretty tonight."

Pretty, hell. I was dynamite. Might as well go whole-hog.

"Thank you," I said. "I'm feeling pretty too."

"Er, new dress?"

"Excuse me? You ask if a resaler has on a new dress? It's new to me."

Across the bridge to Siesta. Around the curve where you can't see the houses for the tropical foliage. "I had a case over there a few years back," Tom said, indicating a private road. "Gorgeous place."

I sighed. "There are a lot of gorgeous places," I said.

He looked over at me. "Do you ever want one?"

"I have a gorgeous place. And it's one that I can afford, and I can take care of, and I can afford to take care of."

He grinned, trying to be subtle about it, but it's hard to do a subtle grin.

"What?" I said.

"Unusual to find a woman who doesn't always want more more more."

"Or a man," I said. "Let's not be sexist here."

"Or a man," he nodded. "Seems like folks just constantly

want bigger and better."

"Better in their minds. What's better about a giant TV than a normal-sized one I don't get."

Well, conversation went on like this as we happily cruised through downtown Siesta Key. It was almost time for the sun to set, so we decided to make a stop at the beach and see it safely off. Because of my stockings and heels, we stayed on the patio of the pavilion. No hardship there: the native plantings recently added around the building glowed in the low-angled sun. I longed for my watercolors and tried to memorize the hues, the textures, the feeling.

Once again, no green flash. I've watched a thousand sunsets, probably, since I moved to Sarasota, and nary a green flash. Folks think they're a myth, but they're real, all right. I'd seen one once, years ago, and been looking ever since. We turned into the velvet violet evening and headed for the waterfront restaurant.

Ophelia's was gorgeous and the head waiter couldn't do enough for us. Apparently Tom had solved something or other for the man. Neither offered to illuminate me.

"Seems like you were able to help him," I said. "Now how about me?"

"So what did you find out today?"

"What makes you think I found anything out?"

"Well, Wendy Sam." He paused as he placed his napkin in his lap. "Yesterday afternoon, you dismiss me. This afternoon, you ask me out on a date. Therefore, there's something you found out that you think I can help you with. So let's hear it."

I tried not to sputter. "A date? Dismissed you? You can help me?"

"Yup. Speak."

"This is not a date." He made a show of looking over my slinky getup. I raised my eyebrows at his elegant tie and new haircut.

"And I did not dismiss you. I just had things on my mind." He smiled.

"And yes, you can help me. You're the detective. That's

153

your job." We both smiled.

He leaned back, twisted the wine glass stem in his wonderful strong and slender fingers, and waited for me to begin.

"Okay." I took a deep breath. I remembered, barely in time, not to mention the discovery Poltergeist and I had made about the note-writer. Tom didn't know about the whole conch-toss incident and I had no plans to include that in my report.

"I found out who Liverwurst is. And Sandpiper (2) too." I told him about Otto's name on the business card in Ilene's trash. I didn't mention the matching photographs since as it turned out Ilene had simply bought hers from him. Then I told him about the Sandpiper Twins. And that Otto and the ladies knew Ilene. And that the twins had tonic from Chloe in the same type of bottle and smelling the same as the bottle in my breakfast nook.

"And Ilene gave you this bottle?"

"Yes." I decided anything else was too complicated to explain.

"So Chloe gave the twins a tonic, and probably she gave it to Ilene as well. What does that prove? After all, she's in that business, right? Herbal stuff?" He shook his head, as though he couldn't believe me and my friends weren't more average people like secretaries and teachers and lawyers.

I frowned and took a sip of my wine. "It seemed a lot more sinister when it was happening."

He put his hand over mine. "You say the ladies are moving, and Mr. Braunschweiger, I mean Mr. Bruniger, wanted to clear out. So it was natural for them to have known Ilene. That's what she did for a living, right? She was a—selector, did you say?"

"A picker." We paused to order. I chose something light, something I could eat without making a mess. Don't all women on their first date? This is not a date, I reminded myself severely. A meeting. Albeit a panty-less meeting. Damn, I swore to myself that I wouldn't think about that.

"Okay, let's review. You have Johnson, who watches out over his whachmacallems."

"Home-aloners," I said. "That's what he called them."

"Right." Tom shook his head as though to clear it. "Then you have Mr. Bruniger and the twin old ladies and Blowfish Bayou which no longer exists."

"And Gary Vegetably," I said. "Don't forget him."

"If he exists," Tom said. "Mrs. Brown didn't seem to me to be too, well, alert. Could be she's mixed up. Saw something on a soap opera maybe."

"No, this was something to do with her one and only daughter," I said. "Mothers don't mix up their daughters with soap operas. And then there's Henri Pousse that you say may be a thief, the AM on Ilene's list."

"Unless AM is that place in Osprey, what, Annabelle's Memorial?"

"Amelia's Memories," I said. "You're as bad with names as I am. And then there's Mark Four."

"Mark Four?" He was looking totally flummoxed. At least I think that's what that expression meant. I mean, tell me, who really knows what flummoxed looks like?

"Oh, I forgot to tell you about him. At the Sand Box. The night before she died. He's a drug dealer."

"He is?" Well, if not flummoxed, nonplused. Come to think of it, I have no idea what that looks like either. Shall we go with puzzled?

"Well, that's what Annie says. Not that she should know, it's not that she's into drugs, she's just young and a little, how can I say this, enthusiastic about the opposite sex?"

"And Annie is?" Tom was straightening his tie although it wasn't crooked.

"Oh, sorry, my part-timer. She's twenty-one, kinda wild but very good-hearted. She saw Ilene at the Sand Box talking to this Mark Four guy and she just let it slip that he's a drug dealer."

"She says."

"Yes. I don't know why she'd lie about something like that."

"I could probably find out for you," Tom said.

"Oh, that'd be great. I'm a little nervous about going to talk to him."

"You better not," Tom said. "At least let me find out about him first. Give me his real name," he said, pulling his little spiral notebook out like he had on Saturday. Again, I glimpsed the leather belt of his holster. Wearing his gun? On a date? Sorry, a meeting. I had to giggle. Visions of him strapping on his gun and me deciding against nether garments at the same moment really were laughable. Gotta keep a sense of humor.

"His name? What's so funny about that?" Tom had to move his notebook aside as our entrees appeared, borne aloft and flourished genteelly by two servers.

It looked wonderful. They both looked wonderful. We decided to eat and let the case rest.

After dinner, Tom drove us home. "So, you never answered me."

"I didn't?" I asked dreamily. Chocolate mousse for dessert does that to me.

"This drug dealer's real name. I assume it isn't Mark Four."

"Oh. Him." I was trying to put him out of my mind. I really didn't want to go to that bar. "Annie said he was named after his car."

"Do me a favor. Find out for me. Before you talk to him. No, better yet, I'll do that. You stay away from him. I have to hit the bar scene anyway a few nights this week. Some other stuff I'm looking into. That reminds me. Can you do me a like, real, favor?"

Tom had parked the car and we were walking on the pedestrian way up the Ringling Bridge. It's a beautiful view at night, if you just ignore the cars whizzing past.

"Sure," I said. "Favors I do. Taking orders, I don't. Mark Four's my lead. Leave him to me. But a favor, sure. What?"

"It's kind of a big favor, I wouldn't ask except..."

156

"So ask."

"Could Joshua spend Friday evening with you? Like from the time school's out until around ten or so? He's usually with me, but I have this investigation, and his mother's going to be out of town."

I hesitated. It's not that I didn't want to do him a favor, but what could I do with a kid for six or seven hours? Ah, what the heck. "Sure," I said. "What do I feed him?"

Tom laughed. "He's not a goldfish, Wendy Sam. You could ask him. Although our usual Friday night supper is pizza."

"Pizza I can do. No problem."

Then he put his arm around me and walked me back to the car. And kissed me very gently. Many times. And headed the car to my bed. I mean house.

As we turned onto my street, I was puzzled. There was a big old car in my driveway. All my lights were on and Willie Nelson was singing. I took my hand out of Tom's lap.

My front door opened and Dom peered out. "There you are!"

"Hi Dom," I said as I got out. It really is a drag sometimes having neighbors who are *too* friendly. Tom got out his side and adjusted his trousers. *Oh God,* I prayed, *don't let this chance go by,* and faced the music.

Elsie and her new beau, Bill, were sitting on my couch, hand-in-hand. Elsie wouldn't look directly at Tom, preferring to linger over my attire.

"Oh, that looks perfect on you," she said. "But it's awfully dressy, isn't it?"

I was puzzled. Sure, she'd seen me try it on the day it came in the shop, but why was it all of a sudden too dressy? Figuring she meant for a Monday, I just thanked her.

Dom fussed around, getting Tom and me ginger ale out of my refrigerator. He plopped two of my maraschino cherries in each and added my palm-tree topped swizzle sticks. Dom sure knows how to throw a party.

Then I attempted to figure out why these three were in my living room. Not that they are not all fine old friends, even my newest old friend Bill, but I kinda had different plans for the evening. I didn't say any of this out loud of course. My mama raised me right.

Eventually it came out. Elsie had heard me talking about Jolly Johnson, then Bill had a golf date and when she asked him who he played with, the answer was Jolly. Turned out, the same Jolly. So she brought him on over tonight to tell me, but we weren't here, and Dom said I'd be back soon, and she suggested they could all wait in my house. I wondered how Dom knew when I'd be back. No sense thinking about it. It's Old Man ESP.

"You know Jolly?" I asked Bill.

"Heck yes. We play golf every Tuesday. Old buds. I even helped him move, twice. Once out of his house, then later into Dunroamin. In between he was staying at an apartment. You know, until he found a place? That apartment? He shoulda kept it. Right on the eleventh fairway. Sweet place. Wouldn't have minded it myself. Of course, never would have met my little Milchcow here then." He squeezed Elsie's waist.

"So Jolly moved out of his house before he was really ready?"

"Guess so. He had a nice place, on the water. Said repairs were piling, he didn't trust himself on a ladder, so a smaller place would do. Sold his place before the agent even got the contract filled out. He was real pleased, didn't even have to clean it."

"What happened to the house Jolly sold?" I asked. Waterfront, the lot could have been cleared and sold three times by now.

Bill shrugged. "Never thought to ask. He never mentioned. I could call him though. Tomorrow," he added, looking at his watch.

Elsie was still studiously avoiding looking at Tom. She's a sharpie, probably figured out why my lipstick was smeared. She excused herself to go to the bathroom, and Dom and Tom were talking about something quietly in the corner. I moved over and took Elsie's spot on the couch by Bill. He was awfully nice, and I wanted to know him better.

"You called Elsie a milk cow. That's not very nice." I shook my finger at him. "She's my favorite employee, so you'd better be nice to here."

He laughed, a big, hearty, nice granddaddy laugh. "Not milk cow, Milchcow. It's a term of endearment. You've never seen a calf still sucking? Big brown eyes, calm temperament? Just like Elsie?"

And after all, Mr. Borden did name his spokescow that. "Okay," I conceded. "I guess it's okay by me if it's okay with Elsie."

"Well, truth be told, I did have to explain it to her, too. Cows in Florida aren't nearly as pretty as cows in Illinois."

"You're from Illinois?"

"Yup. Waukegan. Of course that's not farmland anymore, but it was when I was a boy."

"I thought Waukegan was in Minnesota," I said.

"Nope. Just over the line from Wisconsin. You young ladies, didn't you have a map of the states in front of you in grammar school?"

"Musta been absent that day," I said. "I always mean to study up on it." Ilene and I used to joke about how we should enroll for Remedial Geography.

Trying to eavesdrop on what Dom was telling Tom—it better not be about the conch shell—I missed Bill's next comment. He repeated it when I asked.

"Funny. Ilene thought it was in Wisconsin."

"Ah well," I said. What else could I say? My throat got tight. Ilene didn't need to know the states now.

Elsie bustled back in and said, "Well, boys, it's getting late. Shall we all leave Wendy Sam alone to get her beauty rest?"

Tom had stood up when she re-entered the room (don't you love a gentleman?) and now Dom got to his feet as well. Bill looked like he'd rather stay. I stood up and held my hand out to

159

him. Nice guy or not, I wanted him, and Elsie, and Dom, gone. Tom could stay. Tom better stay or I'll slit my wrists.

"William my love, come on! We're all going so Wendy Sam can get to bed, I mean, go to sleep." Elsie seemed to be using the word "all" a lot.

Oh my God. William. That's what Bill is short for. Ilene thought Bill was from Wisconsin. *Wm from Wisc.* Bill was on Ilene's list too. Calmly I said, "So, you and Jolly golf together. Did you sell a house recently too, so you could like give him tips or whatever?" I thought that was a rather smooth question, but both he and Elsie stared at me like I'd sprouted horns.

"Well," Bill said. "I did help him move. But no, I didn't sell my house. Well I was going to, had it appraised and all. But then I started feeling poorly and my son came down from Up North to check on me. Liked it so much he decided to stay, so I signed my house over to him and moved to Fun n Sun. Sure am glad I did," he said, patting Elsie on her bottom. "Met this fine lady. And I'm feeling so much better, I'm back to golfing with Jolly."

"Oh," I said, more to keep him talking than anything else. "Had you stopped?"

"For quite a while," Bill said with a nod. "First I didn't feel good, then Jolly didn't. But we're both back in the pink. I think it's because we have interests. Jolly with his mission of old folks, and me with this little filly here."

Tom said, "Well, good night all," and went to the door as a host would. Elsie glared at him when she realized he wasn't leaving with the rest. But Bill took her arm, Dom followed them, and Tom shut the door behind the trio.

He stood with his back to the front door, hands in pockets, and looked at me. He didn't know what to say to bring back our earlier mood, and neither did I. But boy did I want to.

"What were you and Dom talking about?" I asked.

"You."

"That's flattering."

"Apparently, he's arranged for some friends of yours take

160

you to the Sand Box, since you're so determined to speak to this character. James and Michael?"

I groaned. "Yes, James and Michael. Isn't that just like Dom. Nice but just a touch interfering. I don't need babysitters."

"Oh, Wendy Sam, don't look at it that way." Tom came towards me and put his hands lightly on my shoulders. "Think of them as your bodyguards."

I tensed, thinking the boys had told him about the conch toss and their overnight vigil.

His hands slid down my bare arms and around my waist. "And it's a fine body to be guarding."

Guess Dom didn't tell him about the shell. Thank God. I reached up and encircled his neck and was determined to forget everything that had happened since that fateful Wednesday. Forget everything except that I had met this man.

"I dunno," I said. "Seems like these lips are overexposed. They could use..."

Well, they were covered very nicely. And things progressed smoothly from there on in, things covered and uncovered and so on. I don't need to draw you a picture, do I? Well, just one little snapshot. His breathing got real ragged when he discovered my lack of panties. Then mine did. Apparently, the garter belt was appreciated as well.

30

All good things must come to an end. Tom had left early with kisses and the traditional Murmured Endearments, and my fingertips and other parts still tingled as I headed over the bridge back to the shop.

Susan was doing some mother thing, so I was working alone until Elsie came in at one. Between the customers, the consignors, and daydreaming about last night and nights to come, I kept busy. Too busy, really, to think of Ilene.

A woman called asking to make an appointment to bring in some clothing. I explained that she could stop by anytime, that she didn't need an appointment, but she insisted upon one, saying that's how her shop Back North did it. Rather than explain I told her I could squeeze her in around 11:45, and she hung up happy. I'd forgotten to ask her the spelling of her name, so I wrote it down phonetically. Mrs. Karate.

That Back North remark reminded me of the guy who had called Henri Harry. Henri must have reinvented himself in Florida, too, like so many. I sighed. I could have been the only stick-in-the-mud in the state, doing the same thing here that I did back in Ohio.

Henri had seemed awfully keen on getting me to stop poking into Ilene's business. Was he trying to keep something hidden? Interesting. Who could I ask about his reputation?

Evil Thalia. As much as I hated being in her debt, Thalia with her vintage shop might well know. I looked at my watch. After eleven, so Thalia should be open. If the spirit had moved her. She was wealthy enough that if she didn't feel like opening her shop, she just didn't.

"Kackle kackle, the Witch is out on her broom, leave a

message."

"Thalia, this is Wendy Sam. Call me when you..."

"Hi Wendy Sam." God I hate people who screen their calls.

I asked her about Henri Pousse and his shop. Where did he get most of his stock? How long had he been in business? Was he honest?

"Good-looking guy, isn't he?" Thalia was fishing. "I'm not at all sure he's in the market, though, Wendy Sam. I wouldn't get your hopes up if I were you."

"Not interested in him, just his business." I was damned if I would let Thalia give me love-life advice.

"He hasn't been around too long. From Chicago or somewhere like that. Gets a lot of his stock from there still. I met his brother one night at Madfish. He'd driven a truck full down for Henri. The brother's last name was different, though. Spears. I remember I asked him if they were stepbrothers or something. He laughed and said no, that his brother had changed his name to French to make it sound more expensive. Said that Henri Pousse could charge a lot more for his junk than Harry Spears could."

Harry. That's what the man in Ruth's Chris had called Henri. So, not only a reinvention, but a new name. Interesting.

"So," Thalia said. "You fall for the French, too?"

My cheeks burned. Thankfully, I was alone in my shop. "Not at all. Just keeping track of the competition."

"I doubt his shoppers are yours or vice versa, dear. Just like yours and mine. My customers wouldn't be caught dead buying *used* clothes."

Not for me to dissuade her. But two insults in a row was all I could take, even for the sake of investigation. "Gotta go, Thalia. Customers coming in. And my, they look like spenders."

I couldn't resist, I thought as I put the phone down. Even though the person coming in was hidden behind a towering stack of folded clothes. I sighed. Must be the "Up North" Mrs. Karate. Apparently I'd forgotten to tell her things needed to be on hangers or more likely, she had chosen not to hear it. The stack

163

she plopped on my counter went tumbling to the floor.

Well, we got them all picked up, and I handed Mrs. Karate a copy of the consignment agreement to read and sign as I started to look through her items and hang up the acceptables. She signed, then printed her name and address in the boxes at the bottom.

"Oh, It's spelled almost like Carrot," I said as I typed her name into the computer. Karrote.

She grinned ruefully. "Actually, it is Carrot. But my boy had such a time in school back up North, I decided to change it when we moved down here after the divorce. I say Karate now, even though Gerry's grown up."

Another reinvention. I finished getting her account set up, printed her out a receipt, sold her a pair of green sandals and a white linen jacket, and by then, it was time for lunch.

Oops. I'd forgotten that I was alone until one, when Elsie was due in. Maybe Patty was in her office upstairs and would grab me something from Mocha Mama's when she went. She was, she would, she picked up veggie wraps for both of us.

Watching Patty balance on a stool beside my counter could be quite entertaining under other circumstances, but I wasn't in a whimsical mood that day. I was totally puzzled and ready to give up. Maybe Ilene really had just fallen. Maybe I didn't want to peer any closer into her life for fear of what I'd find.

"How many secrets do you think people have, on average?" I took a teeny bite of my sandwich: vegetarian wasn't my style, and wasn't usually Patty's either. She must be on a diet again. I took another nibble. Not bad.

"Oh Lordy, Wendy Sam, you don't want to know. Lots. Most really silly but some are really icky. That guy I was following around the other day, the one who is suing the grocery and the grape growers? The one I was gonna get a shot of on the golf course, bending over with the greatest of ease?"

"Yeh?"

"Not golf. Sex. In the open, at a park, where, like, kids could see them."

"Ugh, get a room time, huh?"

"Nah, I think they got off on maybe being seen. Like that was the whole point."

"So, did you get pictures?"

"Nope, got out of there fast."

We chomped in silence for a while. "So, do you need to know someone's secrets? I can Google for you."

"What?"

"Look them up in all the search engines. The first one you use is Google."

"So Google is a verb now?"

"Amongst us investigators, yes. And kids, they Google too. In fact," and she grinned, "we probably got the term from them." She may be serious about wanting to be a private investigator, but she has a sense of humor too.

"I don't really know who I'd want you to Google," I said. "Let me think about it."

We munched companionably for a little bit. I wondered where all my customers were.

Patty poked at the end of her wrap. "What's this?" she said, pulling out a long green strand. "Looks like grass."

"It is," I said. "Something new and healthy supposedly. Chloe was telling me about it. Lemon grass? Something like that."

"I don't believe I'm eating grass." Patty said grumpily. Boy, am I a good detective or what? She *was* on a diet.

"Wait a minute," I said. "Grass. That was what that man called Henri. Harry Grass. But Thalia said his name was Spears."

Patty looked at me skeptically. "See what eating too many greens will do to you. Cause incoherent babbling."

"No, no," I said. "I'm making sense. Some guy called Henri Pousse Harry Grass. Then Thalia told me his name is Spears, Harry Spears. So which is it?"

Patty tossed the remains of her sandwich in the trash, told a last slurp of her milk shake, and took a piece of scrap paper from my stash behind the desk. "Spell it," she said. "My first Google, coming up."

165

She went away happy, promising to "get right on it," just like a PI would. PI the PI. I'd have to keep an eye out for a trench coat, size 24, for her at this rate.

When Elsie came in at one, I excused myself from the sales floor to make a call in the privacy of my office. Just a word or two of appreciation, I figured, was the modern woman's answer of *but will he call me tomorrow?* I was determined to be a modern woman but I wanted to know if I'd been on his mind for the five hours since we'd parted.

I don't need to tell you all the inane things we said to each other, either, do I. We've all said and heard them at some point in our lives. Suffice it to say I was feeling very loved and somewhat oozy. That out of the way, I needed to pick Tom's detective brains once more.

"You said Henri Pousse might be a thief," I said. "Could Pousse be an alias? Could he really be, say, Harry Grass?"

Tom burst out in laughter. "What?" I said. "What's so funny?"

When he could, between sputters, he said, "That's Harry *the* Grass to you, ma'am."

Well, that clarified things. "You mean it's a nickname, like Eric the Red?"

He started laughing again. "Eric the Red? Your mind works in mysterious ways, Wendy Sam Miller. More like Joey the Snitch."

"Like the Mafia? Henri Pousse is in the Mafia?" I was beginning to think that not only was I over my head, I was in severe danger of drowning.

"Doubt it," Tom said. "But criminals have dreams of glory just like regular folks. They use scarey-sounding nicknames. To grass is Cockney slang for ratting on your criminal buddies to the police."

"Did he do that?"

I could hear the shrug in Tom's voice. "Not that I know of. We don't even know if he's for sure a thief. His background just looks suspicious. Could be some rival of his somewhere gave

166

him that name, mainly to keep him from being trusted by other lowlifes. But it is interesting that someone called him Harry the Grass."

I had enough to think about, what with Ilene's murder and Otto's photograph and so on, so I decided, in a very grown-up way I thought, to leave the honesty of an antique dealer to Tom and his cronies. A few more kissy sounds and a date for Wednesday evening since tonight I was being escorted by my bodyguards to talk to a drug dealer, and we hung up. Slowly and lovingly.

Elsie was content to be left alone for the afternoon as long as I promised to come back to close up. She didn't like being responsible for the till balancing, and truth be told, I always had to redo it all anyway when it was her turn. I told her I was going to Barry Cobb's office, and she frowned. "Alone?"

"Why not? He's a well-known, perfectly-respected business man," I said. "Chances are he's not even there, but I can't think of what else to do on the case just now." I had to wait for Patty's Google of Henri, although I doubted it would tell me anything I needed to know.

"I don't think you should," Elsie fretted. "And I don't see why you can't just let poor Ilene rest in peace."

I patted her hand. "I'm not disturbing her peace, Elsie. But don't you think, if she was murdered, the murderer should be caught and punished?"

"Not by you," she said. I sighed. I'd explained over and over to all my friends that the police had decided it was an accident and they wouldn't be looking for a killer. I just couldn't explain again.

"Don't worry," I said. "I'll be careful." She still wasn't happy, but I couldn't help that.

167

31

On the way to Sunshine Improvements I tried to figure out just what it was that I'd ask Barry Cobb, and why he would bother to answer any questions I posed.

What were he and Chloe putting their heads together about? First at Marina Jack's and then when James and Michael saw them together?

Why did he (if it was him) write Otto's name and address on the back of one of his cards and hand it to Chloe, if the ripped-up card I found at Ilene's was the same card?

Was he the man who gave Otto the Krups machine in an attempt to get Otto to sell? That seemed like a laughable bribe to me for waterfront property, but what did I know?

And Noela and Leona: was he going to let them have their beach as a memorial to their husbands and a gift to Sarasota?

Not a single bit of which was any of my business, really.

So what is a legitimate reason for me to get to Cobb one-on-one?

I was halfway to the office building where the offices of Sunshine Improvements were located when I got a brilliant idea. Sarina, Cobb's wife, was a consignor of mine, right? And she'd brought in, from time to time, a few pieces of his clothing, along with hers. How about I could say I'd found something in a pocket of his that I'd rather not tell his wife about. Chloe's phone number on a matchbook? Way too corny, and besides, Chloe didn't smoke. But maybe he did.

It'd have to do. I was almost there. Now, to find a matchbook. I pulled over onto Hillview Street and searched my purse. I had a matchbook there somewhere, for emergencies, like

168

if I got lost in the wilderness and had to light a signal fire. Aha! Success! Oops, the matches had been in my purse so long that they advertised a restaurant in Columbus Ohio, Paul's Pantry. I needed matches you could pick up in Sarasota, preferably somewhere chic and suave, somewhere Barry Cobb would be likely to go.

Fortunately, Hillview Street and its cross-street, Osprey Avenue, are chock-a-block with elegant little restaurants, all perfect for some sexy tete-a-tete that Barry might have had with Chloe. A few restaurants later, I had my choice of matchbooks. I wrote Chloe's number in one and stashed it in my pocket.

Doing a good deed, not telling the wife, returning the evidence to him, would be my entree into Cobb's office. Flimsy excuse, but then, I was willing to let Cobb think I was an idiot as long as I could get a better feel for how he was connected to Ilene's list.

Doctored matchbook tucked carefully in my purse, I got out of my car and headed for Cobb's office. His secretary was on the phone. She smiled and held a finger up *be right with you.* Her desk was piled so high with files and papers and pink message slips I couldn't see a name plate. Funny, she didn't look disorganized and the rest of the office was neat and clean. I looked around. One wall was filled with the same sort of plaques that I'd seen in Laurence Pease's office. Only instead of Top Salesperson, Cobb's plaques were civic honors, thanking the development company for support, contributions, and so on. I remembered the Cobb Foundation and its massive contributions throughout the area, but all these plaques were for Sunshine Improvements. You'd think some grateful recipient would spring a few bucks to thank the Cobb Foundation, wouldn't you?

Another wall was covered up almost entirely by photographs in brushed-steel frames. Mostly black-and-white, they all seemed to be of boats, docks, marinas. Some of the oldest showed Sarasota in its infancy, including the old steamboat that operated between here and Tampa, mullet smokers tended by men with handlebar moustaches, and kids in sailboats. A nice collection. I was enjoying them thoroughly when the secretary behind me hung up the phone and said, "May I help you?"

I turned around just as one of her piles started to slip. I lunged forward just as she did, and between the two of us, we got the papers herded back together. She grimaced and said, "It's almost not worth going on vacation, is it, knowing you have something like this growing while you're gone."

Cobb was out at the moment, but I was welcome to wait. "He doesn't have a meeting or anything this afternoon," she said. "At least I think that's right. Where's the date book?" and another pile shifted. I grabbed, she grabbed, but it was no good. They slid onto the floor in a graceful swoop of manila. We both started picking them up, but I couldn't see where I could unload my armful without the same thing happening again.

"Over on that chair would be great," the woman said, motioning with her chin. I stacked the files on an office chair directly next to Cobb's inner office door, under the dozens of maritime photos.

I'll be damned. There's another Blowfish Bayou photograph. This was getting spooky.

The version on Barry Cobb's wall showed the pom-pom hat lady alone on the dock in front of an old cabin cruiser. She was turned towards the boat as if admiring it. The only reason I could recognize her in the picture was the hat.

"Interesting photo, isn't it?" the secretary said. "That's an old Chris Craft, unrestored of course, but boy, if you had one of those today..."

"Yes, of course, the boat," I said inanely. "It looks as though Mr. Cobb really likes boats." I made a quick inventory of the wall full of cold metal frames, but no other had a Blowfish Bayou picture in it.

"Yes, he collects pictures of old Sarasota boats," she said. "But the one in front of you, the Chris Craft? That must be his favorite. He always touches it for luck before he does his deals. And my, does he do deals!" She laughed. "As you can see by my desk."

The phone rang and she answered. "Yes, yes, certainly. Oh, and there's a woman here to see you." She covered the mouthpiece and asked my name. I shook my head *never mind* and got out of that office. I could hear her saying to her boss "Never mind, she changed her mind" as I plowed directly into a man talking into his cell phone.

Damn. It was Barry Cobb. I couldn't think of a thing to ask him now, now that I'd seen Otto's picture on his wall. "Oh," I said. "It's you."

"And you are?"

You may have gathered by now that I'm not the world's best liar. I know that too, so I tend to go with the truth. "Wendy Sam Miller. I own Too Good to be Threw, the consignment shop your wife uses?" Okay, so under stress I too use too many question marks. I never said I was perfect.

"Oh?" He was looking at his watch now, the phone stowed away in his suit jacket, his hand on the door knob to his suite.

"Umm, it's okay, I can talk to Sarina next time she's in." I had no idea what I was talking about, and neither did he, but he didn't look like he cared. Thank God.

He nodded and went in his office. I left the building.

32

Okay, so Barry has a photo of the woman in Otto's group, Inge. But actually, the photo was of the old cabin cruiser, and Barry collected pictures of old boats. So how had he come across that picture, and when? The secretary said he "always" touched it for good luck, which made it sound like he'd had it a long time, and that it meant something special to him. Something more than just a lust for an old wooden boat? I wondered. I wasn't ready to let Barry Cobb know I was nosing around his life. Mostly because I could be wrong. Just because his business card had been torn up in Ilene's apartment and because his company was developing Sandpiper Close, was that any reason to drag him into a murder investigation? And if Barry Cobb and Chloe were fooling around, it was none of my business. I was sure Ilene would have agreed with me.

I hadn't been back at the shop very long when I got a call from Thalia. "You were asking about Henri's honesty, weren't you? You hung up so fast I forgot to ask you if it wasn't Ilene's honesty you should be asking about since you seem so keen on finding out everything about her."

"What do you mean?" Thalia was always witchy, but she sounded especially cold and evil.

"Your great friend, oh-so-perfect Ilene? Rumor has it she wasn't particularly above a little nefarious action. I just thought you might like to know, since you seem so intent on digging up dirt."

"Meaning?"

"Come on Wendy Sam, don't be naive. There's deals to be made out there, money to be had, and no one the wiser. Hell, if people don't know what they have and you do, you can, shall we say, *steal* it?"

"Are you saying Ilene was doing something illegal?"

"Get off your high horse. Everyone is looking for the most for the least. Everyone does illegal things if they get the chance. The only thing that keeps people honest is they're scared someone will find out."

Ugh. I could feel the slime from Thalia's attitude dripping through the phone wires. Or rather the airwaves, since it sounded like she was in her car. What kind of idiot makes a phone call while she's driving, just to cast aspersions on a dead woman?

"Unless you have something specific to say, Thalia, forget it. Ilene was as honest as I am."

I could hear her wicked laugh as I slammed down the phone.

It was time to close, which I was glad of. Too much information today, none of which fitted together. Elsie rang up the last customer, a woman who'd listened avidly to my half of the conversation with Thalia, and I turned the sign to *Sorry we missed you/ See you next time.*

Elsie counted the cash while I totaled out the drawer, submitted the charges, added the checks. I was done before she was. She seemed to be fiddling with the money rather than counting it.

She squared her tiny shoulders and turned to me. "You may think this is none of my business, Wendy Sam, but it is. Did Tom Litwin, err, spend the night with you last night?"

So. Tom's staying while they left didn't go unnoticed. Not that we had anything to hide, I mean Tom and I were both single adults, right?

"Why is that your business?" I asked her.

She stuck her chin up, defiant. "Because it is."

"Why," I said, trying to inject some humor into the tenseness, "is he your son or something?"

"You know he isn't." Elsie's two kids lived in Atlanta.

"So? Why do you care what I do with my nights and with whom?"

173

"It's my fault," Elsie said. "You are not supposed to, you know..."

"I don't know what you are talking about."

"He was only supposed to watch you, to guard over you. That's what I'd asked him to do. That's what he *said* he'd do."

What was going on? "Elsie, sit down. Tell me what you are talking about."

She sat and drew a shaky breath, as if trying to gather courage. Then that chin went back up, and the glint in her eye reminded me of the photographs of Cracker wives I'd seen in historical exhibits, the ones who dared wildfires and wild cats and yellow fever germs to touch their loved ones.

"He was going to just leave, leave you to your own devices. The police don't think it was a murder, you know that. So he didn't have any reason to stick around, to watch over you. No legal reason.

"So I went to him, and I told him how stubborn you are, and that you might do something dangerous, and I told him to stick around, to watch what you do. So that's what he was doing. Exactly what I asked him to."

The bottom fell out, literally, of my heart. I could feel shame and sorrow pooling around my ankles. I sank to the floor at Elsie's feet.

"Oh dear God what did I do? Oh Wendy Sam, please, please, don't look like that. Please."

So. Running into Tom in St. Armand's Circle wasn't a fluke. It was planned. His wanting to "spend time with me" on Sunday? A ruse. His acceptance of our dinner "date"? Just doing what this steel magnolia in front of me requested of him. And the rest? Just another way to keep me in line. I was humiliated. I was furious. I was crushed. I was heart-broken.

He was just obeying the wishes of his citizenry. He was a public servant. I thought of the night before and wanted to crawl in a hole.

Elsie was back, holding a paper cup of water out to me. I accepted it, smiled at her, told her I'd be fine, to go home, I'd be fine. After a while, she did. I finished up the bank deposit and went home myself.

33

James and Michael picked me up at ten. We had decided that later was better, to see if we could find Mark Four at the bar. They were a little puzzled, I think, at my low-key demeanor, and must have figured that I was scared of going into the bar.

They decided to be extra-jolly. Not a pretty picture. Two overly-cheerful fifty-some gay men and one depressed forty-some chubby woman. I'm surprised the bouncer let us in.

The music and the heat pouring out of the door had to be dived into, head-first. All I could see, coming from the parking-lot lights, were neon beer signs behind a long bar. People were standing in front of a stage, listening to a musical group. No one was dancing. I could see why. How were you supposed to dance to that?

There were a few tables empty, and Michael claimed one while James went to get drinks. Michael held out the only chair to me and went off to find a couple more. I sat there, alone, drinkless, a lump at a table for one. Fortunately, an invisible one. Not a single patron, all of whom were half my age and weight, looked at me.

Well, James and Michael sat a drink in front of me, found one other chair, and took turns sitting with me and cruising the bar, looking for Mark Four. When James was with me, he was all bluster and bonhomie. "Hey, girl, we'll find this guy, we'll talk to him, you'll see, it'll be fine." When Michael was the one keeping me company, he leaned one shoulder in to mine and said "No way, hon, no way, Ilene and drugs. There's some perfectly innocent explanation."

I wasn't sure I even cared any more. I'd been threatened via conch shell, I'd been warned that I was turning over rocks just to see the bugs scurry, and I'd been, you should pardon the expression, well and truly screwed. Ilene was dead and there was nothing I could do about it. I should just pack up the mementoes her mother wanted, release the apartment to that oily Beeton character, and get on with my life. No more private investigating, no more cops. Definitely no more cops. The Slimeball. Well, except for my ex-cops, James and Michael. They really were just trying to help me.

"There, over there," James said, coming back to the table. He indicated a slender boy-man with a wispy goatee, slouched by himself over a Bud Lite. Even in this light I could see the acne scars and the cheapness of the leather vest. What, a discount-store drug dealer? Well, maybe he was a very bad drug dealer. I mean, they can't all be successful, can they?

I must have sat up with some purpose, because Michael said quietly, "You go, Tiger" to me, and James offered me his arm. "I'll walk you over, I'll stay out of sight."

I did. I did feel better. I could do this. Even with a broken heart, I could do this.

"So," I said, sitting down on the stool next to Mark Four, "I understand you're called Mark Four."

The callow youth looked me over, top to toe. I probably reminded him of his mother because he said "Yes, ma'am."

"Named after your car, I hear?" I signaled to the bar tender for a drink.

"Yeh." He took a last gulp of his beer and banged the bottle on the bar. I caught the bar tender's eye again and waved at the empty bottle.

"Can I call you Mark?"

"Why not. Everyone does."

The drinks came. He drank, staring into the back mirror at himself, ignoring me.

Bull by the horns. "Last week you were here talking to a woman named Ilene Brown. Do you remember?"

He looked at me in the mirror, not directly. "Ain't senile," he said, as though he suspected I was.

177

"You know Ilene Brown?" He really hadn't answered my question.

"Knew. I knew her. She's dead," Mark said.

I could see James and Michael in the background.

"Yes, she is. What did you two talk about?"

"You cops?"

"Do I look like a cop?"

"I dunno. All old people look alike to me."

Charming. "No, I'm not a cop. I was her best friend. What did you talk about?"

"Best friend, huh? Like on *Friends*? So how come you don't know what we woulda talked about?"

"Sex, drugs, rock-and-roll." Maybe a little levity would help here.

"Huh?"

Oh God, he was too young to get that reference. "Never mind. Did you talk about drugs?"

"Hey, lady, drugs are illegal."

"Right. Have been for decades. Ilene tell you she was at Woodstock?"

"Where?"

This was hopeless. Time for the big guns. I signaled to my two hovering angels. They came over and flanked the boy and me.

"You were the last person to see her alive," said James on his left.

I had to admire the kid's coolness. "Yeh," he said, waving a hand around the room. "Me and couple hundred other people."

"Well, the last person except for the murderer," said Michael on my right, leaning over me.

"She wasn't murdered," said the kid. "They said she fell."

"Who did?" I asked.

He looked at me like not only was I senile, I was from another planet. "The tee-vee," he said, as if that were the only form of communication in the world.

178

"Well they were wrong," from the left.

"She was pushed," from the right.

"So we need to know what you were talking about the night she died," I contributed.

The routine worked. The kid's head swivelled to and fro and finally sank to his chest.

"M'truck," he said into his cheap leather vest.

"Your truck?"

"It's not runnin'."

"Oh," I said. "And this mattered to Ilene because?"

"Missed her deliveries. She was pissed. Said she relied on me."

"You deliver furniture for her?" asked James.

The kid winced. "Pipe down. Ya want people to think I'm a mover? Jeez."

"So that's what you do, deliver and pick up things. Nothing wrong with that," I said.

"Girls." He was speaking to his vest again.

"Huh?"

"He means, Wendy Sam, that the girls would rather be with a drug dealer than a delivery guy. It's sexier," said Michael.

"Oh." I guess when you think about it it makes sense. I guess. When you're twenty-whatever.

So Ilene's conversation, the one that Annie saw, didn't seem to mean a thing. It was just something she was taking care of, not knowing that that night was her last on earth. And I'd been laid by a mercenary. Life sucks. I turned away. So this is what "world-weary" felt like.

My guys moved in to flank me. James said, "Tell me, Truckdriver. Ilene your only client?"

"Hell no," the kid said. "I do it for a lotta people. Antique shops, people movin', that weird broad that makes herbal stuff. I do her deliveries too. Course, not this week."

I turned back to him. "Chloe? The Thymely Lady?"

"Yeh," the kid said. "So what's it to you?"

"Why not this week?" Michael asked.

179

The kid whined. "I *told* you. The truck's *broken*. Duh. Hard of hearing too, are you?"

We turned to leave this example of America's youth.

His whining got louder. "I thought you were buying, lady." James tossed a bill in the general direction, and the kid hopped off his stool to pick it up before it disappeared under the cowboy boots of the musicians, who had finally stopped and were crowding the bar for a drink.

34

The boys agreed with me. The conversation with Mark Four was simply something Ilene had done before her death, nothing that was connected to it.

But even if most of the kid's surliness was due to being interrogated in his social milieu, such as it was, by three old fogies, still he struck me as someone not to be trusted, someone who would be delighted to be underhanded. James and Michael agreed, they said as they took me home. And they were adamant that I stop this investigation right now.

"There's nothing to be gained," James began.

"And we don't like that conch shell bit," Michael added, twisting around in the front seat to look at me in the back.

The street lights played over his kind, concerned face. "Guys, Ilene died," I said.

"That doesn't mean it was murder."

"I think maybe you've just stirred up a hornet's nest of greed."

"And that's what the shell was about. Someone doesn't want you to know all their business."

"Which is probably true of most people."

I interrupted their repartee. "But most people don't throw notes into most other people's living rooms," I said.

"God, you're stubborn."

"At least promise us you'll let this rest for a few days. Michael and I are going on a tour to Fairchild Gardens, and we won't be back until late Sunday. Leave it, Wendy Sam, until we're back. In case you need us."

"Again," Michael said. Like tonight with Mark Four.

"Have a good time in Miami. Take lots of pictures," I

said as I got out at my place.

"Promise," they said in unison.

I waved my hand good-night and went inside. I couldn't promise. I fell asleep thinking of Ilene. It was sad but at least it kept my mind off of That Traitor Tom Litwin, who never even called.

At two in the morning the phone rang. My "Hello?" must have sounded cross because whoever was on the other end sucked in a deep breath.

"Oh dear. Is this Wendy Sam?" The voice was elderly and female and sounded a long way off. I mumbled encouragement.

"It's Ingrid Brown." It took me a moment to think *Ilene's mother*, and I realized I hadn't known her first name until now.

"Yes, Mrs. Brown, hello."

"I know it's terribly late, but I have been feeling so guilty, I had to call. I've been keeping a secret, and it's been a secret for so long, it didn't occur to me that you might need to know it now."

I hate secrets. I especially hate secrets that people need to tell me. Especially at two in the morning. "Do I?"

"It maybe might make a difference. You said you'd try to figure out who that man was, that man I told you about. Maybe this will help. You haven't found him yet, have you? You said you'd call, but you haven't, and Gary Bean, that just doesn't sound right, so I guess I need to tell you what I told Ilene." She sounded like she was talking fast to keep tears away.

"No, I haven't run across that name yet." No sense telling her I'd been trying. That would involve my telling her that I thought her daughter had been murdered. I *really* didn't want to tell her that. At least not until I knew for sure who and why.

"I'm so ashamed. I let her think all along her father was Olaf."

Olaf? Wait a minute. Olaf and Inge. The missing couple from the Blowfish Bayou photographs. Inge, that's short for

182

Ingrid. Mrs. Brown was Inge? Ilene was Inge's daughter? That's why Otto's photo was in Ilene's family album. But Ilene had never mentioned to me that she'd been born in Sarasota. And how come Otto or Mehitabel hadn't told me this? "Olaf?"

"My first husband, Olaf Johannsen. I remarried when Ilene was just two, and my husband adopted her. That's why she's Ilene Brown, not Ilene Johannsen. But we thought it best, Buster and me, that was my husband, Buster, we always told her her real father was Olaf, that he'd died when she was a baby, but that wasn't true."

"It wasn't?" I was confused.

"Well, he died, but later. You see, Olaf divorced me. When he found out Ilene wasn't his."

"So she was Buster's?" I was confused.

"No, no, I'm telling this all wrong. I never met Buster until Ilene and me moved to Indiana. After the divorce."

Wait a minute. Otto had told me the Johannsens both "passed." And Mehitabel Madison Frazier hadn't mentioned a baby or a divorce. In fact, now that I thought of it, Mehitabel hadn't mentioned Inge and Olaf at all.

"You lived in Indiana?" That was all I could think of to say.

"Yes, I had family there. Buster and me moved to California just a few years ago, when he retired. We were going to have the good life, but then he took sick and died and I got the sugar and had to have my foot off. That's why I'm here, in this place. Otherwise, I'd be on my own."

"When did you tell Ilene this?"

"Well, I didn't so much tell her as kind of confirm what she'd found out. It was right before she, she, she..."

Died. I took a breath. "Mrs. Brown, I know this has been terrible for you. But why do you feel guilty?"

"Because I wouldn't tell Ilene who her real father was. I didn't think it mattered. I never even bothered to tell him. He was just a boy, you know, and I'm sure he moved on long since. All I told her was that he was a college kid who ran a bait shop that summer. I wouldn't tell her his name. Oh, and she was so mad. She was so mad, and she hung up on me. My last conversation with my daughter, and she hung up on me." She sounded infinitely sad.

Oh God. The kid who owned the bait shop at Blowfish Bayou. The photo in Barry Cobb's office. It wasn't there just because it was a picture of an old Chris Craft like the secretary said. It was there because it was a picture of Inge, the blonde older woman he'd loved when he was twenty. Barry was short for Bartram.. Barry Cobb, the developer of Godzilla houses that Ilene so hated. Barry Cobb was Ilene's father. And Ilene had found this out just before she died.

"Mrs. Brown," I said as calmly as I could. "Will you tell me the name of Ilene's father?"

"I guess I will. It couldn't possibly matter anymore. And who knows where he is now? It was Bartram. Bartram Crawford."

35

It was all I could do to turn off the damn alarm. Getting up was out of the question. Mrs. Brown had thrown me for a loop. I thought I'd had it all worked out during the course of our conversation: Barry Cobb was Ilene's father, which she uncovered in the course of trying to figure out whatever it was that linked all these people and places together. But it turned out to be just a coincidence that Barry had a similar first name to her mother's bait-boy impregnator: Barry might be a nickname for Bartram, but men don't change their last names. The name Mrs. Brown had given me was Crawford, not Cobb.

I stumbled up and started the coffee. What I wouldn't give for a man. A nice man, a sexy man, a man I could trust. Unlike that SOB Tom Litwin, who had (I blushed even alone) taken his public duty to such a (you should pardon the expression but I was pissed) Fucking Extreme. Anyway, what I wouldn't give for a man around the house, the kind that would start the coffee while I lolled in bed.

It didn't happen. I drank the coffee, and so on, and headed into work. Birdie was at the pond again. I tossed out the remains of my peanut-butter toast.

Susan and I were working together. Shortly after we opened, Lucy Goodman stopped in to pick up her no-thank-you's, the things we couldn't accept. She still looked like a camp counselor in her uniform and I felt vaguely illegal reminding her that she'd told us we should donate to charity whatever we couldn't use. Like she was going to give me a ticket for DUI. Donating Uglies Immediately.

"Oh, that's all right," she said. "As long as they're out of

185

my closet."

"They went to a good cause," I said, "the free clothing pantry for women who are reentering the work force."

She hitched up her equipment belt. Don't you hate women who have a hard time keeping things on their non-existent hips?

"I understand you've been looking into some of the low lifes in our fair county," she said.

I saw red. That damn Litwin had been talking to her. About my business. This sixteen-year-old cop was privy to my personal life.

"Oh?" My tone was as icy as I could make it.

She was oblivious. And skinny too. And, damn it all, she could talk to Litwin, when all I could do was wish he were dead. Oh God, speaking of dead, I'd promised The Rotter I'd baby-sit his son Friday night. I made a mental note to call him and tell him I still would, even though I wasn't talking to him. I believe in honoring my commitments. And besides, the kid had nothing to do with anything. He just needed to have someone seeing after him for an evening. I could do that, even if I hated his father.

"Mark Four?" the skinny young woman said. " Didn't he mention you were going to see him?"

"Did he?"

"Well, yes. See, the thing is, Detective Litwin is kind of old, I mean, kind of not clued in to the younger scene?"

"Yes," I said with gritted teeth, delighted to agree but not willing to occupy the same passè age group.

"So, Mark Four's like an alias, right? In case you didn't find out? His real name is Gerrry Karrote."

She pronounced it Carrot, just like Mrs. Karate, err, Karrote, had told me.

Gerry Carrot? As in Gary Somethingvegetably, like Mrs. Brown had said? That Ilene was afraid of this man *because he doesn't care about anyone except his own wallet... anyone, not anything. Like he was hurting people somehow.*

I couldn't imagine Ilene getting worked up over a wispy-bearded punk like Mark Four, but even a punk can push a woman to her death. And I could see him valuing money above all else. Had Mark Four, the sleazy bum, killed my friend? And I'd gone and bought him a beer? Well, technically James had, but same difference. I must have shuddered, because Lucy Goodman looked at me closely.

"Did I say something wrong?"

"No Lucy, no problem. I was just thinking I have a customer Mrs. Karrote. Wondering if it was the same family."

"Probably. But don't worry. The guy's just a wannabe. No worse than any other toughie his age."

Which wasn't, I couldn't help but think, that different from Lucy's age.

"That's what I told Detective Litwin, too, when he was crabbing on about you wanting to talk to Karrote." And with those parting words, Lucy Goodman clanked her gear out of the shop.

So. She told Detective Litwin. Ha. See if I care. I called him, yes, on his cell phone. I hoped he was negotiating the Gulfstream Boulevard intersection with 41, the worse place to take a call.

"I just wanted to let you know I will honor my commitment to see after Joshua Friday night," I said without a hello.

He sounded amused, damn his hide. "Well, great, I'll tell the school you can pick him up," and gave me the details of how one retrieves a strange child from an elementary school in this scare-crazy world. Then he hung up with barely a thank-you.

I am so superior to this man.

Hell with him. I'll solve this on my own.

I'd scheduled Elsie to work this afternoon so I could see after things. Bill drove her in from Sun n Fun a half-hour early. Bless the hearts of the older generation. They realize that if they

187

want to shop, they ought to do it before their work shift starts, not while I was paying them. I'd had the dickens of a time teaching young Annie that. But to give her credit, once it was pointed out to her, Annie understood. Now if I could just persuade her that her cell phone switch should be in the off position while she was on the clock. Always something, isn't it.

Bill came in, didn't just drop Elsie off. Heck, he even trotted around the car to open the door for her. And she sat there waiting, like it was expected. When was the last time that happened to you?

He was looking pretty spiffy, and I told him so.

"Lands' End," he said. "Elsie's got me revamping my wardrobe."

"From that twinkle in your eye that's not all she's revamping," I said. I love to tease older men.

Bill grinned so wide, his dentures almost popped out. "Now Wendy Sam, is that any way to talk to your elders?"

"Well, you're the one told me you were feeling better."

"That's right. I finished that whole bottle of tonic. Did the trick. Feeling like a million, now, I am."

"Five hundred thousand," Elsie called from the vicinity of the lingerie.

"What. He's only half as good as he thinks he is?" I asked.

"No, he's ever bit as good. Just takes my five hundred thousand to make a million," she giggled, holding up a solid lace peignoir set in front of her tiny body.

Bill had to turn his head from me at that. I think between Elsie and me, we were embarrassing him. Ain't it fun?

"Wait a minute," I said. "Tonic? You were taking a tonic?"

"So? Natural remedies, they're good for you. Just like she said, take the whole bottle, you'll be a new man. Have to admit, though, it took me a few months to get the stuff down. Kept telling myself I'd take my dose later. Stuff tasted awful. Still, the worse it tastes, the better it works, right?"

That tonic was popping up everywhere. Is that the connection on the list? A foul-smelling tonic? "This tonic," I said. "Where'd you get it?"

"Now that's quite a story," he began, and started settling in on the stool.

"He got it from Chloe," Elsie shouted from the dressing room. She came out in the lace nightwear. Didn't have the same effect, being tried on over her floral shirt and with her little Keds sticking out from under, but still, Bill's eyes lit up.

"Now Elsie, you gotta let me tell my own stories. I tell pretty good ones."

"Yes you do, dear," Elsie said, her back to us now. She was searching the racks for more goodies. "Just, I start work in ten minutes, and your stories take, oh, at least half an hour."

"I can be brief." He stuck his chin out. "Watch."

He turned to me. "Met her before my sale. Remember, I was going to sell my place? So I had a sale and she came, first thing in the morning. Nice lady, that Chloe. Why, she even stayed and helped me, when the lines got too long. Who'd think that so many people wanted my old tools and things. Even sold a box of doorknobs, of all things, for $30. Chloe told me that's how much I should ask. I had $5 on 'em. Nice girl."

"See?" Elsie hollered from the shoe department. Now she had on the floral blouse, the lace ensemble, and lipstick red high heels that brought her up to, oh, say five feet one? "He met her at the sale, she gave him this medicine, he took it, it's gone. End of story." She leaned down, wobbling on the red heels, to adjust the ankle strap.

"Ha. Lot you know, woman. She called me a couple days ago. Wanted the bottle back, so's she could recycle. Fine young woman," Bill said to me. "Concerned about our eckology."

"It's ee-cology," Elsie said.

"Elsie hasn't known me long enough to know all my jokes," he said in a confident tone to me. "I call it eck-ology because it's about ecky stuff."

"That's icky," Elsie said. "Which? The red or the

aubergine?" She was modeling two different shoes now.

"This bottle," I asked. "Did you give it back? What color was it?"

"I like the purple ones," Bill said. Both Elsie and I wrinkled our noses at him. They were aubergine.

He looked at me. "Yes, she picked it up a few days ago. It was blue, a real nice blue."

Around eleven, Tom called back. "Got it all arranged about Joshua," he said cheerfully. "I really appreciate this. Sorry I couldn't talk earlier, traffic was a mess."

"Nothing to talk about," I said.

"So how'd your visit to the local den of iniquity go? Find anything out?"

"Yes."

"Oh I get it, now you're busy. Didn't mean to interrupt your day, hon. You can tell me all about it tonight. How about that new place on Longboat? I'm in the mood for some red meat."

Is the man crazy? Has he no idea of how humiliated I am? Then I realized that he didn't know Elsie had told me. He thought he was still doing his civic duty.

"None of this is necessary," I said. "You don't need to watch after me any more. As a matter of fact, you don't need to do anything. Except stay away from me."

"What are you talking about?"

"Stay away from me. I don't need babysitting, and I sure as hell don't need your version of keeping me in line."

"Wendy Sam, what is it? Oh God, hang on, please, hang on a moment."

His hand went over his phone, and I could hear another male voice telling him something, and his muffled "Yes!" as though he'd won the Florida Lottery. Then he came back on the line.

"Listen, babe, this is really good, Henri Pousse? He's..."

190

"I am not your babe, I never want to see you again, stay out of my life." I hung up.

Elsie, of course, had been listening in, as well as the three or four customers who were feigning great interest in the jewelry counter, which happened to be right next to where I was staying, hand still on phone, shaking with emotion.

"Good for you, Wendy Sam, the cad. Taking advantage of...."

I motioned with my eyeballs to our audience. For once, Elsie picked up on my silent signal and changed the subject to one the customers would love. "So, boss, shall I mark down the designer rack?"

The customers followed her and her red pen over there, and I completed my shaking in privacy. Then I took the phone off the hook, just in case That Cad wanted to call me back.

Susan was back from lunch now with sandwich in hand. Sounds strange, unless you're a mother. Mothers, I've learned, spend their lunch hours running errands and grab a bite to eat on the way back to work. Elsie and Susan decided that the tee shirts should be where the blouses are, the blouses should be where the shorts are, and I forget the rest. I wished them luck and beat it out of there. I needed to go see Jolly, ask him about this dizziness of his that Bill had told me about. And, too, I didn't have quite clear in my mind when Ilene had visited him. Would that make a difference? It could.

Jolly was tinkering in his carport when I drove up. Shade helps some in Sarasota in midsummer, but not enough. His white beard was sticking out in all directions and his face was red and wet beneath it. For all that, Jolly was, well, jolly.

He waved a wrench at me as I got out of the car. "Hey little lady, you back?" he yelled. I could see the curtains in the next trailer over twitch. So could Jolly. "Come gimmee a great big

191

hug!" he boomed. I came forward but not within hugging range. He winked and said quietly, "I gotta give the ladies something to talk about."

"Great. Now they think I'm your girlfriend."

"Prob'ly. Gives me a little break. Ain't pretty, being one of the few men my age hale and hearty."

"Actually, Jolly, that's what I came to ask you about."

"My health? It's great, I'm tip-top. So?"

"When Ilene was here, did she ask you how you were?"

"What, you mean specifically?"

"Yes. You told me you'd felt dizzy in the past. Did you tell her that?"

Jolly stroked his beard to think, then looked surprised at the dampness on his hand. "Damn, it's hot," he said, sounding surprised. "Can't remember. Could have."

"Tell me about this dizziness."

Jolly frowned. "I'm not much for going on about my health. Bores folks to death."

"No, Jolly, really, I want to hear."

He wiped his hands on a red shop rag, took one last gulp out of a soda can, and tossed it in the recycling bin next to his stoop.

"Come inside, then. Too damn hot out here to stand around talking. I'll get you a cold drink."

Once we were settled in on his dinette, glasses in hand (mine said *Kentucky Derby 1988*, his said *Sarasota Offshore Grand Prix 2000*), I asked again. "So, this dizziness of yours? When did it start? When did it go away? You did say you're over it, right? Got any idea what it was?"

"Takin' a survey, are you honey?"

I laughed. "Sorry, too many questions at once. Let's start backwards. When did you stop being dizzy?"

"Lemmee think." More beard-stroking. "Moved here in May, musta been about then. Yeh, that's about right. Musta been the relief, getting settled and all."

"You'd been unsettled?"

"Well, the house sale and all. Takes a lot out of a man."

Wait a minute. The twins were selling their homes and taking tonic from Chloe, but she hadn't brought them any recently. Bill had a tonic from Chloe and she'd taken the bottle back. Otto was thinking of selling his home and taking all sorts of medicine. Maybe a tonic too? I hadn't asked him.

"So," I said slowly, dreading the answer. "Did you take anything for this dizziness?"

"Doctor said it was all in my mind. Doctors nowadays, don't get me started. Too damn young to know anything, you ask me. Got a concoction, though, did a lot of good."

Calm, Wendy Sam, calm. "Oh, a concoction? What was that?"

"Some natural stuff. From that lady, you know, the crazy concoctions lady?"

"Thymely Remedies? That lady?"

"Yeh, that's the one. Funny thing, she called me just the other day. Wanted her bottle back, said it was a family heirloom or some such. I felt real bad."

"You felt bad? From the tonic?"

"No, that did a lot of good. Anyways, I'd stopped taking it after I got moved in here. No, felt bad because I'd cleared out my cupboards just a few days before that lady called."

"So you didn't have the bottle anymore?"

"Funny thing about that. Your friend, the dead girl? She saw the bottle in my recycling bin and asked if she could have it. I dunno, maybe it was one of those collectibles they call 'em. Trash, you ask us oldsters."

"Ilene took the bottle from your bin?"

He nodded. "Said she liked the color, she collected blue. Once she had that bottle in hand, she wouldn't let go of it. I wanted to empty it out, rinse it off for her. She said that was okay, she'd do it."

I took a deep breath. I was getting somewhere. Just one more thing, something that might tie it together. "Jolly, can I ask you about your selling your house? Who'd you sell it to?"

"One of those developers, silly name. I could look it up if you like. Guy said he was gonna scrape it, so I didn't need to worry about the leaky roof or the garage door. It didn't work anymore, and I hadn't gotten around to fixing it. But he was gonna scape it, you know, knock it down? Been by there a few weeks ago. Mighty fine house they're puttin' up there. Much bigger than mine, of course, you know, with garages underneath? Big sweeping staircase? Me, I wouldn't want a place you had to walk up a flight of stairs, but I guess they have elevators now, huh?"

"That developer? Was it Sunshine Improvements?"

"Why, yes, it was? You know them? Guy thinks he's so sharp, but I dunno. I got more out of him than the appraiser had said the old place was worth. These young men nowadays, they don't know how to drive a bargain. Paid more than it was worth, didn't even do an inspection, let me stay there for months until I found this place." He patted the curved wall of his trailer fondly. "I'm happier here. Did you know my electric bill last month, now July mind you, it was only $25? Efficient living, that's what I have here. Efficient living and no big lawn to mow. Gives me more time to tend to my flock. Wouldn't trade it for a million bucks."

A million bucks. That was probably Barry Cobb's profit on the house he was building on Jolly's old lot. "You had your place appraised? By an appraiser?" I asked.

"Nah, a real-estate guy, real go-getter type. Was talking to all the neighbors. He took his time with me, went all over the house, found every damn thing that was wrong with it, gave me an idea of how much it would cost to get in shape. Plenty. More'n I wanted to spend. Then one day, comes that guy knocking on my door, offers me more, says his girls would do the paperwork, I didn't have to think about nothing. It was easy, real easy."

There. Finally, a pay phone. Maybe I did need a cell. I had two urgent phone calls to make.

"Otto? You're not taking a tonic, a tonic in a blue bottle,

are you?"

"Why, Wendy Sam, how nice to talk to you. I was just thinking about..."

"Otto, sorry, but I'm in a hurry here. Didn't you say you weren't supposed to take herbal medicines?"

"Why no, herbs don't go good with my kidney medicine. I would have, but..."

"How do you know that? That they wouldn't go with your medicine? Did your doctor tell you?"

He snorted. "Doctors don't tell you squat. No, it was the Thymely Lady told me. You know, that nice woman who sells all those things? She was going to suggest a tonic for me, but she looked up all my pills and told me it wouldn't work. She gave me a nice soothing tea, though. I like it a lot better than Lipton's."

I said goodbye and hung up. So. Chloe had been going to give Otto the tonic but saw his pills and decided not to. So she knew what interacted with what.

I drove like blazes to get to Chloe's. My second call had been to her. She'd said she was leaving to go to some seminar soon, but I begged her to wait for me, that I had to see her. She hadn't sounded too happy about it, but she said okay.

So, what have I got? Chloe and her tonic, the blue bottle at Ilene's, people who sold their homes for more than the appraisals, dizziness. Chloe asking Bill and Jolly for their bottles back. Ilene took Jolly's though. Jolly sold his place to Barry Cobb. The twins were in the midst of their deal. Bill had changed his mind about selling and gave his place to his son. Otto couldn't decide whether to sell or not.

Ha, Tom Litwin, take that! I was figuring this out all by myself. I couldn't wait to solve it all and lay it in his lap. Man, I'd flaunt my accomplishment and he'd eat his heart out. What should I wear? Something professional yet sexy. *Let him eat his heart out, the cad.*

What was I going to ask Chloe? And how, really, was she

involved? She knew Barry, in fact she lived on Barry's land. She was maybe having an affair with him. James and Michael had seen the two of them. She made lots of tonics and remedies, that was her business. Bill and Jolly and Leona and Noela had all gotten the tonic from Chloe. They'd all said they felt fine now, so her tonic must have helped. But why was she trying to get back her bottles?

Normally, speeding semis full of oranges on 72 scare the heck out of us regular folk. Wouldn't you know it, now that I was in a hurry, I got stuck behind one going 25. I couldn't get around him on the two-lane road. This was taking forever. Would Chloe wait for me? She hadn't sounded very welcoming on the phone.

Chloe's SUV wasn't there. Damn. She'd gone. Well, I could at least see if she had any stash of blue bottles, or try to figure out what was going on. She never locked her sheds, and I knew where the house key was hidden, beneath a brick on the patio.

I pulled my car behind the house and got out, closing the door carefully before I realized there wasn't a neighbor in eyeshot, yet alone earshot. I'd search.

When I'd been here a few weeks ago we'd sat in the courtyard, surrounded by the herbs Chloe raised. That time, Chloe'd given me a tour of her plantings. I'd seen it all before of course, but every time I visit, it's different. Tourists think Florida has just one season, but it doesn't. Things grow and falter and slumber and come back to life, each in its own time.

"You should come back some evening soon," Chloe had said, gesturing into the tall jacarandas. "The cereus is about to bloom."

"I'd love to. Gin and tonics all around?" That's the local tradition: gin-and-tonics after eight in the evening, stand around and watch the cactus flowers unfurl from their climbing stems in the tallest trees. The cereus blossoms are as big as a dinner plate, pale ivory, and last just one night. If you are very still, you can see the pale-winged moths that pollinate the cereus waft in on the hot humid night breeze. Booze and hot sex. As good as it gets, huh?

Her gardens were bordered in meadowsweet. "Blood thinner," she said. "Good for people with heart problems." A colorful plant, some sort of coleus, grew in the hedges' shade. "Good as, probably better than, digitalis, just like the cereus."

Manzanita, too, grew in Chloe's garden. "This can be useful, too," she said, "but you have to watch side effects. Doesn't mix well with prescription medicines.

"Knit-bone here, goosefoot behind it, the tall one there, and bugloss over there." She waved her hands around. If I hadn't been with her, I'd probably have thought this was all just over-grown weeds. Chloe's a dear, really, but she is a trifle slap-dash.

I was impressed, though, with her knowledge. "There's a lot to know about all of this," I said. "How'd you learn it all?"

"Oh, here and there. You pick it up as you go." Chloe had been off-hand about it, trying to downplay her expertise I guess. "You read a lot, you try a lot. And other people help too. The herbal-remedy community's pretty open, as long as you listen.

"Now some things, you use the leaves, some the tap root, some the seeds. And then there's teas and distillations and poultices. It's a real science."

"So," I remember having said, "Got any Love Potion #9?"

Today, I didn't even glance at the plants. I wanted to find the blue bottles. There were a variety of sheds, both old wood ones and more recent metal varieties around the yard. Maybe that's where the bottles would be, but I hoped not.

Okay, I admit it. I'm as scared of spiders and snakes as the next person. I really am not ashamed of this. It's a survival mechanism I figure, in a state with brown recluses and black widows and pygmy rattlesnakes and coral snakes. So I rationalized that the bottles could very well be in Chloe's house. It was at least worth a look before I ventured into the sheds.

The back door wasn't locked so I didn't even have to turn the brick over to get the key. I took a deep breath, relieved I wasn't actually *breaking* in. To maintain the pretense, I called out

197

as I entered the kitchen. "Chloe, you home? Yoo-hoo?" I would have fainted if anyone answered, so it was a good thing nobody did. Where would Chloe keep bottles? Near the stove, I figured, so she could decant her essences and tonics into them.

I spent the next half hour going through the pantry and the cupboards and cabinets. I learned a lot about Chloe's lack of cooking interest (the pressure cooker was cobwebbed and there wasn't a baking dish in the lot) but didn't find any blue bottles. But I did find a flashlight.

Chloe's second bedroom was set up as an office. Well, a cross between an office and a witches' den. Overhead were bundles of branches, leaves and all, drying in the hot air. Old coffee cans held handfuls of seed pods, and a restaurant-sized mayonnaise jar was full of dried beans and seeds. But mixed in with the natural debris was a computer, a color printer, and boxes of labels. There were piles of plain white envelopes for dried teas and tisanes, white pots for lotions, even the little netting bags she made into spices for cooking with. A couple of aluminum ladles and several wooden spoons mingled with a cast-off pair of earrings and a box of Triscuits. Everything was messy, like Chloe usually is. I didn't find any blue bottles, though.

Opening a file drawer, I looked in dismay at the disorganization. No blue bottles here. This drawer was completely, burstingly full of papers shoved in haphazardly. I had to shove them down just to get the drawer closed again. As I did so, I noticed the tab on one of the file folders. *Recipes.*

I pulled it out. Could I find the tonic recipe and figure out what it was? And why, off all the things Chloe made and sold, I'd never heard of this one before?

I gave up after five minutes. Her recipes were so scribbled, so erased and written over in a variety of writing instruments, even if I was looking straight at it, I'd never be able to read it. Just a couple of minutes more and I'd get back to looking for the bottles. For whatever good that would do me. I sighed, thinking *Tom would know where to go from here* before I could stop myself. I did find the recipe, though for Energizing

198

Everlasting Essence, the dark liquid Chloe had poured in our drinks when I'd been out here last time. I tried to read what had been in it, but Chloe was right: she had been trying different versions of it. Amounts and ingredients were underlined or crossed out or question-marked. How did she ever keep track of what worked and what didn't?

Enough. No blue bottles here, none in the kitchen. Ugh. The storage sheds. I went outside. Clutching Chloe's Everready I chose the newest-looking one first under the theory that the spiders and rats hadn't moved in yet. I wrestled the door open, shone the light around, and didn't notice anything moving, no glint of eyes. Good. The shed was full of old kitchen cabinets, trunks, and disintegrating cardboard cartons. I poked half-heartedly at a few, shined the flashlight at others I couldn't reach.

There. Up high on a shelf. A clear plastic tub shone an eerie blue in the dimming circle of light. I needed something to stand on. I looked around. The flashlight was flickering now, and I shook it. Not sure why we do that. I mean, shaking batteries doesn't recharge them, does it? Ah, here, something to stand on.

It was a chair which had long since parted company with its cane seat. Balancing gingerly, I reached overhead and pulled the tub off the shelf. As I lowered it to the dirt floor, it rattled. Like bottles.

Blue bottles, identical to the one I'd taken from Ilene's kitchen window sill. Back to the house, but not before I took one bottle and replaced the box on its shelf.

I stepped down off the rickety chair, replaced it in its corner, and buttoned the bottle securely in the deep cargo pocket in my shorts before dusting off my hands. Picking up the flashlight, I stepped out into the sun. There sat Chloe in her SUV, looking out of her windshield at me. I froze.

She got out of her car. "What are you doing in there?"

"Oh, hi, Chloe. You weren't home."

"Yes, Wendy Sam, obviously." She held up a large bouquet of some cheerful flower that looked like black-eyed Susans to me. "I had to run to a neighbor's, these were just ready

199

to cut."

"Flowers?"

"Well, yes," she said, looking at the bouquet with a puzzled frown. "I guess they are flowers. But what's important is they're just at the right stage for preparing. This is Echinacea."

"Oh, I've heard of that. You take it for colds."

"Well, you can. But I do a digitalis booster with it. What were you doing in the shed?"

The flower delay had given me time to think. I waved her flashlight at her. "I heard a noise, so I came out to see if there was a bobcat or something in the shed. There wasn't."

"Oh good, you found my flashlight. I wondered where it was."

She closed the shed door firmly behind me and said, "Come in the kitchen. I have to soak these."

I really wanted to get out of there, since I had the bottle clunking against my thigh, so I said, "Gosh, it's getting late, I'd better get back to town and don't you have some sort of meeting to go to? Sorry we couldn't have our little visit."

She stood and watched me back out of her yard. In my rear-view mirror I could see her burn pile, a fixture in every rural homestead. Sunlight sparkled off the ashes. Blue sunlight. I looked more carefully in the mirror, then turned around in my seat. There were shards of blue glass in Chloe's trash.

I shifted into forward and took one more look. Chloe hadn't moved a hair. The gay flowers were now dropped at her feet. She had tried to burn blue bottles. She knew that I knew. I got out of there, fleeing terrible thoughts about a friend.

36

I sat numbly by my backyard fountain. I didn't even have the energy to walk the block to the beach. I stuck my feet in the cool water and thought as hard as I could.

I kept coming back to Chloe and her tonic. She gave it to the twins, to Bill, to Jolly. Then she got Bill's bottle back and asked Jolly for his, which he had given to Ilene. Someone had been at Ilene's looking for it. Ilene asked Amy at the shop down in Osprey what color the bottle was that she'd seen.

But Chloe apparently was still delivering the tonic to Noela and Leona. They had said they expected Chloe on Monday. I went to the phone in the kitchen to call them.

As I was dialing Noela's number, I walked back out into the yard. If only I didn't have a murder to solve, and an embarrassing incident with a cad to forget, it could have been a beautiful night. Heck with that. I'd make it a beautiful night. I took a deep cleansing breath, which unfortunately I was right in the middle of when the pink Sandpiper twin answered the phone.

"Ooof! Noela, this is Wendy Sam from the other day?"

"Oh yes dear, how is your poor burnt finger? Leona and I were worried about you, going off so sudden like that. Is everything all right?"

"Yes, thank you for asking. Did you ever get a refill on your tonic?"

"Funny you should ask. Leona's so upset I had to give her what was left of mine. Chloe came by this morning and insisted, just insisted, we give her back the bottles. Well, Leona was kicking up such a fuss, it gave me time to pour what was left into a mixing bowl. When Chloe left, I put it in a pickle jar for Leona."

201

"Why did Chloe want the tonic back?"

"She said she'd mismade it, that she'd be back in a day or two with a new batch. But if she knew it was wrong, why didn't she just bring the right one with her? Such a strange young woman. She was telling me once how certain plants can only be harvested in a full moon. Maybe she's had too many moon rays. You know, of course, that's where lunatic comes from? The moon?"

So, Chloe had gotten the bottles back from the twins, just like she had from Bill and Jolly. I needed to know what it was about that tonic that Chloe was trying to hide.

"Listen, Noela, this is kind of a strange request but could I possibly have just a few drops of that tonic?"

"Oh, dear, I'm so sorry. I've already washed the bowl."

"Maybe from your sister?"

"Oh no, that's not possible. There was only a little left. Leona drank it all, the minute Chloe left. There's no more."

"Oh da—I mean dear. Now what?"

"Now what, dear? Something's bothering you. You shouldn't let things eat at you, it's very bad for the complexion."

"It's just that, well, a friend of mine died recently in a fall..."

"Oh, I know, wasn't that terrible? Ilene was such a lovely person, so lively, so interested..."

I pulled the phone from my ear and stared at it in amazement. Why hadn't I asked the twins if they knew Ilene? I had a lot to learn about being a detective. Maybe I ought to borrow Patty's *Idiot's Guide*.

I waded right back in. Dumb I may be, but tenacious. "I didn't know you knew Ilene."

Noela tinkled merrily. Yes, she did. Tinkled merrily. "My goodness, we knew her well. Why, she's the one who suggested the beach, DonJon Beach Park. She told us that Mr. Cobb would go for it. I must say, though, we haven't heard from him since last week, well except for Monday, and usually he calls us every day. Trying to convince us, you know."

"Ilene suggested the beach?"

"Why yes dear. Didn't you know she just hated those big houses? How they blocked the waterfront and locked people out? That's why we're gonna insist on DonJon Beach. Especially now. In her memory, you know. Maybe we could call it DonJon Ilene Beach? Ilene DonJon?"

So. Ilene urged the twins to stand up to Barry Cobb and his Sunshine Improvement Company. Chloe's tonic, that four people on Ilene's list were taking or had been offered, was being in effect recalled by Chloe. And she glared at me when I saw the glass shards in her burn pile. And there was, apparently, an awful lot of low-balling the value of homes going on. Homes that just happened to be waterfront.

That reminded me. The first time I heard of an appraisal being overbid was the house on Ugli Court. I couldn't remember the name of the woman who'd sold it, but I did remember she was in a retirement place now. I went searching in my handbag for my index cards. I always use index cards to make notes. Someday, I might progress to actually rereading and organizing my index cards. Until then, they were a colorful accessory in my purse.

Ah, great. I'm not as much of a dummy as I thought. Charlotte Penzar, Morning Has Broken Estates, and her apartment number. *It's too late to call her,* I thought with a glance at the clock, *but it's probably better to go see her in person. Tomorrow, first thing.* With a sigh, I picked up the phone to let Susan know I wouldn't be in. Payroll was mounting.

No problem, she said. The extra money was always welcome in her household. Well, it was welcome in mine too, but so be it. I'd just have to work harder to get this case solved faster.

I was just deciding between white wine or iced tea when the phone rang. Busy little instrument. *Maybe it's Tom* came unbidden into my brain and I snatched my hand away. If it was, I wouldn't answer. But I don't have caller ID, so the only way to find out was to pick the damn thing up.

I did. It wasn't Tom. I could feel a wave of disappointment start in my toes and slither up my legs.

Sometimes one's body is a traitor.

"Wendy Sam, this is Sarina Cobb. I need to have you pick up some clothes from me tomorrow. Ilse can't drive anymore, the Longboat police found out she hasn't got a valid licence. I just don't know what I'll do. I might have to just let her go, this is all terribly inconvenient. Say ten, ten-thirty? Don't be late, I have a game scheduled."

I was speechless. I don't offer pick-up. If I did, I'd be running the Too Good to be Threw taxi service. What made her think I'd do it for her? Then I tallied up in my mind how much money her cast-offs had made me and swallowed. The swallow of dread and the slither of disappointment met in the middle of my body and I decided wine. It would soothe my innards better.

"Sarina, I'm not sure I can do that," I began.

"Nonsense. With all the money I make you? Oh, and by the way, Henri Pousse mentioned you the other day. He seemed a little, well, smitten, with you. That rather surprises me, but then, who can understand men's appetites?"

If I was any kind of judge of human character Sarina was, as they say, dissing me. What a lovely way to try to persuade me to do her bidding. My innards needed a good dose of steely spine.

"I'd be happy to stop by your little place," I said. "After all, I do have so much more energy than, well, than older women." I smiled evilly as she stumbled through an *all right then* and hung up.

Two can play at that game. I poured an extra dollop of wine into a glass and went outside to admire the stars again. When the phone rang again, I let the machine pick up. I even stuck my fingers in my ears and hummed to myself so I couldn't hear the message.

I finally punched Play on the machine as I poured my third drink.

Wendy Sam, it's me. Umm, Tom. I don't know what's going on, but maybe we can talk Friday? When I pick Joshua up? In the meanwhile, stay out of trouble. Oh, I did find out about Pousse, but he's okay, apparently. I'll tell you about him Friday,

right? Or you can call me?
Fat chance. I finished my wine and went to bed.

37

Another beautiful day in Paradise. If I hadn't have been trying to solve Ilene's murder, erase Tom Litwin from my mind, and pass the pool-care pickup in front of me, I might even have been happy.

Traffic piled up just a bit around Bay Isles. Nothing like in season, of course, but still, when I wanted to get to Sarina's, pick up her consignment, and maybe nose around a bit about her husband, I wasn't pleased to be in bumper-to-bumper traffic.

There was a convertible in front of me, just a green Sebring, nothing fancy, guy in a ball cap driving alone. I didn't even really notice the car until I saw a cigarette butt go flying out. How trashy. What's wrong with the ashtray, idiot? Doesn't that guy know that sea birds can choke on a cigarette butt?

It crossed my mind to note down his license plate and complain to someone. Who, I wasn't sure. Maybe The Pelican Man. The plate was one of those vanity ones. It read SELL PEAS. What, the guy was a greengrocer? Then it struck me. I'd seen a green Sebring in the Salesman of the Month parking space at the real estate office. SELL PEAS must be the Übersalesman Laurence Pease. The heel, throwing his butts out like that. He turned off, probably to sell another jillion-dollar house, and I continued on to Sarina's.

Sarina was face-lifted, butt-tucked, boob-blown-up to a fare-her-well. From her pouty silicon lips to her French-manicured toes she was as perfect as any fifty-year-old woman could be. Which of course never satisfies any fifty-year-old woman, certainly not one as rich and as vain as she.

I may be scruffy around the edges and have more hips than fashion deems allowable, but I like me. Mostly. I couldn't help feeling someone who'd undergone as much elective alteration as Sarina had must hate her true self.

She was on a lounge chair when Ilse, the maid who'd lost driving privileges, ushered me poolside. Sarina turned her back to me for a second to do something, then rose and strode towards me like a high-school gymnast.

"Wendy Sam, how nice to see you outside of your little shop."

I hate people who call my shop little. It isn't, particularly, unless you're comparing it to WalMart. And since I couldn't imagine Sarina in a WalMart, her "little" was a socially-acceptable putdown of my career. I refused to scowl though. Scowls make lines I couldn't afford to have erased.

We sat. Ilse brought out icy bottles of Alpine water and crystal goblets, along with a tray of carrots and celery sticks cut into little perfect nibbles. "It's my colon-cleansing day," Sarina said, "Hope you don't mind, although I daresay my girl can find some rice cakes or something if you'd rather." She took a discreet nibble.

I couldn't answer. I'd never heard anyone use *daresay* in conversation, especially not while wearing only a $500 bikini and $400 sandals.

"I do apologize," she said, waving her hand at a briefcase sitting open on the table beside her. She moved a porcelain ashtray with one lipsticked butt in it, and started to stack files to put them in the elegant case. There were pockets in the lid of it full of varicolored pens and chromium laser pointers from the Metropolitan Museum collection and gold-plated cell phones and for all I knew H-bombs. She sighed. "Committee work is so demanding, but one must of course. Why, the Cobb Foundation alone takes me 20, 25 hours a week. Unpaid, I must add," and she smiled what was intended, I guess, as a friendly smile. It came off prissy, due to the Botox.

"But you didn't come to talk about my busy life. Come,

my things are in my husband's room." She wrapped a little skirt around herself as she got up.

"Oh, right. I need to get back to my busy life, as a matter of fact." I tried to say that calmly but doubted I sounded anything but pissed off. Oh well, pissed off is better than prissy.

Sarina smiled a little dimly and led the way across the patio. I followed. Her little skirt quivered around her tan thighs and her butt didn't jiggle. Can you tell how much I liked this woman? She parted a pair of eight-foot-tall French doors and we stepped into an austere coolness.

"We call this Barry's den," she said. "Although den is such a middle-class word, don't you think? I prefer retreat. That's what I got Barry to use on the floor plans of our homes. Owner's retreat. Sounds so much nicer doesn't it?"

"Well, more expensive," I said. "More marble and tray ceiling-ish." I meant that as a put-down. She didn't take it that way.

"You're right," she said warmly. "Tray-ceiling-ish. You have a way with words."

It was the most incredibly masculine room I'd ever seen, full of leather and glossy varnishes. Those animal horns were fake, I hoped. For sure the fishing tackle was, or at least, it had never been used. The room was a moneyed version of Otto Bruniger's homey little sun room.

"Here," Sarina said. "I piled them up here."

There was a multi-colored mass of sweaters, pants, shorts on the coffee table in front of the couch. Not on hangers, of course. I started to load my arms with Sarina's clothes. She helped, meaning she loaded my arms. I couldn't blame her. If I'd paid as much money for a manicure as she obviously had, I'd be deathly afraid a silk sweater might chip my polish too.

I was steadying the pile with my chin while Sarina swooped up the last half-dozen garments and there it was, staring me in the face. I almost dropped several thousand dollars worth of clothes on her Saltillo tile.

The coffee table was actually an old weathered sign covered in heavy glass balanced on a wrought-iron frame. The old sign said, in faded red curly letters, *Blowfish Bayou*. I must have stared.

"Oh that," Sarina said. "Isn't it hideous? But one must let one's husband have his way sometimes. You're not married, are you dear?"

I shook my head numbly. To see the sign from Otto's photo in this sanitized Godzilla house was dizzying.

"Husbands," Sarina said. "They are seldom worth the trouble. One must have one, of course, unless one is willing to develop suitable escorts. Still, they are a bother. They come with such, such *histories*. Almost makes me wish I had had children. I could have raised a son to be the perfect escort. But would the ruination of this body been worth all that?" She stroked herself lovingly. Well, yeh, she did have a lot invested in that body. I could imagine the personal trainer bills, the salons and pedicurists, the health retreats and mud baths that had gone into that scrawny body. She didn't notice my distaste.

She reached down and picked up a Hermes scarf which had slithered out of her get-rid-of-these pile. "Oh, well, too late for that. I've invested a lot in making my husband a suitable companion. And he's turned out fine, I must say. No bother, really, nowadays."

I looked at her in amazement. What was she talking about? "No bother?"

"Once we'd persuaded him, my father and me, persuaded him to take my name instead of insisting on his. His was so, well frankly, common." Names can be common? I stared at her. I guess the rich are different from you and me.

She waved her armload of castoffs at me impatiently. "Well, don't stand there. Let's get these things in your car. I've got a tennis date."

I followed Sarina through the foyer of her house and out the front door. My modest car sat apologetic at the edge of her massive circular drive behind her silver Mercedes. I managed to get the hatch open without dropping the pile of clothes, and plopped them inside. Sarina contributed her handful.

209

"Didn't you mention handbags as well?" I needed a few more minutes to figure out how I was going to ask about that Blowfish Bayou sign now serving as a coffee table.

"Did I? I'm just so busy, what with the ball and the auction coming up, I might have left some things in the dressing room...."

Back into the house in her elegant little wake, past the "retreat" and up the Tara staircase into her dressing room, larger than my house. There was an oversized Smith & Hawken box full of shoes and handbags sitting on the marble top of the center island, and a Saks shopping bag loaded with beads and bracelets. I pretended to sort through these as I thought furiously. How would Tom ask the questions I had?

"Your husband took your name when you married?" Personally, I go for the direct assault school of questioning.

"Why yes dear. If you'd lived here longer, you'd know that. Everyone does. But they choose not to remember. George Crawford was not well-liked. Very pushy man. Tried his best to be accepted, which is simply not the way. He must have always been a social climber. I mean, for some industrialist to name his son Bartram. It's just too too."

I almost dropped the Maui Jack sunglasses I was holding. "Bartram Crawford?"

"Can you see me as Mrs. Bartram Crawford?" She mock-shuddered. "When I was, after all, Sarina Jefferson Cobb, daughter of the finest parents? I told Barry I would only marry him if he took the Cobb name, and dropped that idiotic Bartram."

I held up a tourmaline necklace, pretending to examine it.

"Barry Cobb was Bartram Crawford?"

"You don't listen very well, dear, do you? Now let's get these things out of here." She looked at her diamond-daubed wristwatch. "I hate to keep my partner waiting."

"Barry Cobb is not a Cobb?"

She tapped her watch with one perfectly-manicured

finger. "Really, I must be going. Of course Barry's not a Cobb. All that money in the Cobb Foundation, that was my daddy's. That's why I'm the head of the Foundation. It's nothing to do with Barry. All his money's tied up in land. Well," and here she smiled in a greedy way, "except for what I manage to put in this house."

"And on your back."

She smiled then and touched a pinky to the corner of her mouth. "Yes, and on my back. And isn't it nice that you're here, to give me a reason to go shopping again?"

38

Something was bothering me all the way down Longboat Key, around the Circle, and across to the mainland. You know that back of the brain nag? Don't you hate it? I couldn't even get my joy in the perfect day back, not even when a sailboat with spinnaker billowing glided under the bridge.

It struck me as I passed Selby Gardens. I noticed that I was surrounded: next lane over, in front of me and behind me were silver Mercedes Benzes. Or is it Benzi? A silver Mercedes was seen leaving Ilene's early the morning she died. I'd parked next to Sarina's silver Mercedes it in her driveway this morning. Of course, like I told That Cad Tom, there are an awful lot of silver Mercedes in Sarasota. Which is what got me thinking about this in the first place. The fact that I was surrounded by them. So Sarina's car ownership probably meant nothing.

I continued on and soon lost the trio. One turned right onto Orange, another left onto Osprey, and I don't know where the third went. My brain itch was still there. Apparently, silver cars were not what I needed to ponder over. Jeez, here's another silver car. A PT Cruiser with orange and yellow flames.

Egads. That's it. Flames. Smoking. Cigarettes. So few people smoke nowadays, yet I'd seen Laurence Pease doing it (and littering. What a schmuck.) and Sarina had stamped a cigarette out as I arrived at her place. So? Ah. The cigarette at Ilene's apartment, the one I'd found in her trash along with the ripped-up business card. I'd forgotten all about it. I'd put it in a baggie. But then where did I stash it? In my purse? I rummaged around in it one-handedly, stealing little looks, until a loud honk brought my attention back to the road. I'd look for the bagged butt later.

212

I forced myself to concentrate on my driving. I counted the different types of Florida license plates to amuse myself. There's over a hundred of them now, everything from sports teams to ecological concerns. Then on top of that, there's those silly vanity plates like MOMS TAXI and IMGR8. Which led me to recall Pease's plate over on Longboat. SELL PEAS. I'd thought the driver was a greengrocer before I noticed who it was.

Egads again. PEAS. Pease. Laurence Somethingvegetably. Laurence could be Larry, right? Larry Peas could be Gary Somethingvegetably, the man Mrs. Brown had said Ilene was afraid of. I smacked my head in frustration. Why hadn't that occurred to me before? And on top of that he smoked, and could have left that drowned cigarette at Ilene's. Had he been there, threatening her, then pushed her down her steps? Pease was a real estate salesman. He could be low-balling home sellers, then Sunshine Improvements could step in, offer more, and still get bargain land to build fake castles on. That's why Ilene had been to see Pease. But how did Chloe's tonic fit in? Chloe was seen with Barry, Chloe lived on land owned by Barry. Could the three of them, Chloe, Barry, and Pease, have a scam going? My friend Chloe?

But I had Gerry Karrote, AKA Mark Four, down as my Gary Somethingvegetably. God, I wish I'd make up my mind. I had to talk this over with someone. Laying it all out might help me spot what I was missing. And what I still was missing was a good reason to kill Ilene. So she found out that some elderly folks were selling their homes for less than they were worth? Happens all the time. So Chloe was distributing a tonic? Thousands of people believe in and rely on natural medicines every hour of the day. What had Ilene found out that was so damning that someone would kill to keep it a secret?

Who'd be good to talk to? Michael and James? They were out of town. Patty? I didn't think she'd read far enough into her *Idiot's Guide* to be much help. Polter Geist. That's who. He is such a font of useless information that some of it has got to come in handy somehow. I'd call him when I got back to the shop

213

and invite him over tomorrow night, when I'd promised to entertain Joshua Litwin. Kids like Polter. Everyone likes Polter. As opposed to Joshua's father whom nobody likes. Least of me. I slammed that door in my mind. Gotta get to work, check in Sarina's clothes, earn and living. And solve a crime. No time for Dastardly Men.

I took a short detour to check out Thalia's Witch in the Wardrobe. I like to keep tabs on the competition. Plus, she does really nice displays so I can always learn something. And sometimes I get a real laugh: something I wouldn't accept at my shop because it was too dated or too ugly, will end up in hers with a hefty price tag. Good thing there's a lot of different customers out there.

I pulled up in front of her shop and got out of the car before I noticed her *Closed* sign. She is remarkably casual about keeping regular business hours, and I have to constantly remind myself that she has an independent income. From where, I don't know. I suspect several rich ex-husbands and a good divorce lawyer on retainer, but don't quote me. Ah well, I can at least peer in the window. I cupped my hands around my eyes and put my nose to the glass.

And about fainted. There, in Thalia's foyer display, sat Ilene's train case. No wonder I couldn't find it. Ilene had sold it to Thalia. No, wait a minute. The case had been Ilene's grandmother's or great-grandmother's, and she loved it. I looked again to be sure. Yes, I could see the old gold glimmer of the monogram. Ilene took that case on every trip. When we went to Miami that time, she wouldn't even let the bellman carry it. And some European guy in dark clothes and skinny glasses offered her $200 for it in the lobby. No way Ilene sold that case to Thalia. So how did it end up coyly displayed, with satin camisoles and step-throughs and feather boas snaking out of it, when it should have been in Ilene's apartment, waiting for me to ship it back to Mrs. Brown?

I left a note on Thalia's door for her to call me immediately and went on to my shop. Which was open, as it should be, and full of customers. I tossed my handbag in my office, rolled up my mental sleeves, and got to work.

Work's amazing. There can be all sorts of things on your mind, but get out there with customers and all you're thinking about is the here and now. I highly recommend work to ease stress. If you are one of those unlucky folk who can only visit, rather than work in, a consignment or resale shop, I pity you. Unless, of course, you'd like to come spend the day at Too Good to be Threw. In which case I welcome you.

Well, no, I'm exaggerating about work taking your mind off things. Amidst the fun of matching a necklace to that lady's dress and finding the perfect blouse for the other lady's pant set, I was worried. I still had lots of loose ends and no one to help me tie them up. Sure, I could talk to Polter tomorrow night, but I needed someone now. If only Tom Litwin had proved to be a friend, instead of a Dirty Rotten Dog.

The phone rang. It was for me, Susan said, holding the receiver out to me with one eyebrow raised. I wish I could do that. Raise one eyebrow, I mean.

"Hi, this Wendy Sam."

"Some day you'll have to tell me how you got two names. Most people only have one, like Sam or Dick."

"Hi, Henri. Seems to me, though, I heard some guy call you Harry Grass. Henri Pousse, Harry Grass, that's two names." I couldn't wait to see how he'd explain his shady background.

"Well, now, darling, there's a wonderful, funny, heart-warming story connected with all that. And I'd love to tell you over dinner tonight."

Okay yes I did go have a drink with him last week on only twenty minutes notice, but dinner's another story. I could hear my mother's voice in my ear *You make them call you a week in advance. You don't want them to think you're desperate, do you?*

Truth was, I *was* desperate. For some nice male-female attention, and, if his explanation held any sort of water, for an ear

215

to listen to my clues and help me sort it all out. Henri was charming, and sexy, and eligible, and I wanted to trust him.

"Can we make that coffee, say around five? I have plans this evening, but I'd love to see you." *There, Mom, was that okay? Nice balance between warm and interested but not easy?*

"Let's sit over here," Henri said, and guided me to a love seat in a little nook. The sandwich boutique did have excellent coffee, even if it was a national chain. It was perfectly yet soullessly decorated. I tend to prefer nice homey places like Mocha Mama's, but they close after lunch. "It's quieter."

We settled in, moving the Pelican Press newspaper out of our way and sipping coffee while making small talk. I was trying to get a feel for this guy. Beneath all his attractiveness and suave words, was there a burglar? A thief? A rat? I didn't want to think so, but Tom said the Naples Police did.

"So, Henri, you were going to tell me why you have two names?"

"Let me get us some refills first. A scone perhaps? The apricot are very good."

"No, thanks, Henri, I really do need to be going. But first, Harry Grass?"

He settled in. "Well, to start with, of course I was born Henry, not Henri, thus Harry. I mean, in Iowa? Henri?" He paused. I nodded *Yes yes come on. Tell me you're not a thief and a snitch.*

"And the Grass? It's just a take on my last name from when I was a kid. You know how kids are."

"What, pousse means grass?" I asked. "How would kids in Iowa know that? I don't know that and I had four years of French."

He shifted in his corner of the love seat. It was the first time I'd seen him look less than elegantly relaxed and at ease. "Well, in a roundabout way, yes. But that's another long story, and you said you were pressed for time. Anyway, Harry Grass is just Henri Pousse Americanized.

"To be honest, Wendy Sam, I did have something I wanted to tell you. To apologize for, actually. That reference I made to the things Ilene brought in that last time I'd seen her?"

"The smallish new-ish stuff," I nodded. "That you thought might have been stolen."

He did have the grace to look abashed. "I believe I was somewhat hasty in my assessment."

"Oh?"

"Yes. This morning a lovely lady came in to sell me those precise items, as well as a few more in that vein. With a little subtle prodding, she mentioned that yes indeed, she had known Ilene, and yes, Ilene had taken a few things around to see if she could sell them for her."

"So Ilene was simply acting as a middleman?"

"It appears so. As I said, I was hasty in thinking badly of her. Can you forgive me?"

The crooked smile and the floppy hair did it. "Well okay," I said. "But only if you let me call you Harry."

"If you must," he said, and raised my hand to his lips and kissed it. Right there, in front of God and all those people.

"One more thing, Wendy Sam, and I offer this little tidbit as a way of apologizing. You were asking about Laurence Pease?"

"I was?" I didn't recall mentioning the name to Henri, but I'd been talking to so many people about so many things on Ilene's list, it's totally possible that Pease's name came up at Henri's. Harry's.

"Word has it that Sunshine Improvements is using him as their front man."

"Front man?"

"He persuades the owners of redevelopable land to sell."

"And that's illegal?"

"Not at all. But it seems Pease does a lot of valuations that he never gets the listings for. And for a salesman of the year type, that's very strange. Up until a year, eight months ago, his listings always included every waterfront property he could get

217

signed up. Now, he doesn't seem bothered when those properties are sold out from under him."

"Maybe he's just taking it easy, slowing things down?" I doubted that, from what I'd seen of the man, but it was possible.

"What I hear is he's working harder than ever, trying to find listings. Then they don't get listed. But they do get sold."

"You've lost me. How do they get sold if they're not listed?"

"Private sales. No real estate person, like Pease, involved. No involvement, no commission for him, right? But Pease, so I hear, is living better than ever."

Well, Henri/ Harry wouldn't tell me where he'd heard all this, and we parted. I felt a little better about the man now, and a little less better (can you say that?) about Pease. First, the vegetable name. Then, the cigarette. Now, this information.

Oh yes, and the fact that Ilene's list was written on the back of Laurence Pease's card.

So. Pease goes out and tells people how much their houses are worth, stating a low-ish price, then Barry Cobb's company comes along and buys them for more. Without paying a commission. Why would Pease stand still for that?

Because he was getting paid to. Bribes? Kick-backs? I'm not sure what you'd call them, but I'd bet you anything they were illegal. In addition to being immoral. And that tonic. It was involved in those kinds of sales way too often.

I pulled off the road at the first pay phone I saw. Someday, I'll get a cell phone. Just not today.

"Henri? It's Wendy Sam..."

"How nice it was to see you. We must do it again, only this time I insist on dinner. There's a great..."

"Yeh, yeh, okay, sometime soon. Listen, I'm at a pay phone and there's someone waiting. What was the name of that woman?" There wasn't really anyone waiting, but I didn't want to get side-tracked right now. Later, yes. Probably. But right now, I

218

was on the case.

"Woman?"

"The one that Ilene tried to help sell her stuff for? You know, the smallish stuff?"

Henri chuckled. It was, for all my worry, a warm, comforting sort of chuckle. One I could grow to like. "That's right, you forgot to ask."

"You distracted me."

The chuckle got warmer. "You ain't seen nothin' yet."

Now my face got warmer, and remember, this was August in Sarasota.

"No, really, her name?"

"Penzar. Charlotte Penzar. I noted it particularly, because I knew you'd want to know. Want her address?"

"Morning Has Broken Retirement Estates," I said.

"Well, well, you are quite the little detective, aren't you? Looked that up in the phone book, did you, so quick?"

"No," I said. "I know a friend of hers."

Dom was in his front yard, watering his geraniums, when I pulled in my driveway. He waved and hollered "Alfredo?" to me. One of my all-time weaknesses.

"Great," I said. "If you let me bring the salad."

"Oh no, no, I got great ingredients today, beautiful tomatoes. It's all made already."

Dom knew what the inside of my refrigerator looked like and what my vegetable crisper held. I don't know why I call it a crisper, since everything in it's usually limp or worse. I did tell you we're really close neighbors, right? Fridge privileges.

I showered, changed into something loose and cotton, and went over, bearing a good bottle of wine. The guy in the grocery swore it was a good bottle.

Dom looked at its label a little longer than strictly necessary. Oops, I goofed somehow.

"Nice wine," he said. "We should save it for another

219

night. I've got the perfect wine for Alfredo in a cool ice bath right now."

Such a gentleman. He swung around, trying to hold onto the wine and let me in, and his hip hit the walnut curio shelf. It tottered and fell. A dozen porcelain statues of delicate pastel women with elongated necks and swoopy hands hit the stone floor and shattered.

He stood, paralyzed, above the broken pieces.

"Are you hurt?" I said.

He just looked.

"I'll get a broom and dustpan," I said.

"No. I'll pick them up by hand. Maybe I can glue them."

"Dom, they're shattered. You won't be able to..." Then I looked at his face. Tears were running in his age furrows. He let them, not even trying to wipe them away.

"They were Little Flower's favorites." His voice was very quiet. "That's why I put them here, so people would see them, first thing, when they come in. They wouldn't see her here, but they'd see what she loved." He finally wiped his eyes.

"They kept me company," he said as we put each piece, no matter how small, into a shoe box. "It was almost like having her here. Sometimes," and here he laughed just a little, "I even talked to them. Like I would have talked to her. You know, what the weather's like and what I was going to do that day.

"Otherwise, it's awful quiet here."

Dom was less ebullient than usual as he prepared the fettuccine Alfredo and we sipped the wine he'd had ready. I got the salad out, which was every bit as perfect as mine would have been pitiful, and we sat at the dining room table to eat. Normally, I take my plate and eat out in my back yard, but Dom's too formal for that. Sit at the table, napkin in lap, make suitable dinner conversation.

He needed some cheering up. And how better to cheer a lonely widower up than to ask his opinion? "Dom, I need your

220

take on a situation I found out about today. Do you mind if I kinda ramble, tell you what I'm thinking, see what you think?"

"Oh?" I could hear the interest come back into his voice. Gotta love older Italian men. Tell them you need help, and they perk right up.

"Okay, here's the thing. I think Ilene was onto something big, and she was getting ready to expose some very powerful people in town."

"Wendy Sam, you knew that when the conch shell landed in your living room."

"Well, yes, but I don't know exactly what. And without knowing what, I don't know who. And then I found something else out. Something I didn't expect. I think maybe Ilene didn't expect it either." I fiddled with my wine glass, and Dom noticed and refilled it.

I gathered my thoughts.

"Here's the thing. Ilene had a photograph in her family album that doesn't seem to belong there. One of a old dock and bait store. Before she was born."

"Hell, before she was born don't mean a thing. How old we talking?"

"Late Sixties, early Seventies."

"And what's so special about this photograph?"

"Nothing much. Except it came from an old man who was a snowbird back then. It's a picture of three women in his fishing group. Well, his wife and two other women."

"And?"

"They're standing under a sign for the bait shop that I saw today at Barry Cobb's house."

"So? Cobb is, like, Mr. Sarasota, at least in his own mind. He owns Sunshine Improvements, right, that the guy?"

I nodded. "That's him. His wife is Sarina Jefferson Cobb. Did you know he took her name when they got married?"

"Weird. What'd he do that for?"

"Seems the Cobb name was more desirable than his."

"Names can be desirable?"

"My thoughts exactly, Dom. Anyway, the point is, the sign in this photo is the same sign that has become a coffee table in Barry Cobb's retreat."

"His what?"

I laughed. "That's Nouveau Sarasota for rec room. Why would Barry Cobb, nee Crawford, have an old sign in his room?"

"People like that old stuff. Me and Little Flower, we could never understand that. We liked new stuff. And Little Flower kept it nice. She made plastic covers for everything. I'd have 'em here except the salt air, it plays havoc on plastic."

"Why are you calling your wife Little Flower? Wasn't her name Isabella?"

Dom tucked his chin in and looked up at me through his eyebrows. "That was my pet name for her. I feel kinda like she'd want to hear that tonight, now I've broken her statuettes."

"Aw, that's sweet," I said. "Little Flower. How romantic."

He blushed and took a covering sip of wine. "Not romantic," he said. "Just her name. She was a Fiorello before I married her. That's what that means, Little Flower."

I stared at him, then laughed. "You old coot. You've got the soul of a poet and the excuses of a used-car salesman."

He had the grace to laugh with me. "So sue me. I loved my wife."

"Yes, you did. She was lucky to have you."

"I was lucky to have her. For fifty-six years." He straightened his shoulders. "But she always said, live in the present. So, this sign?"

"Okay. It was in the photo, and it's now in Barry Cobb's den or retreat or whatever. Barry Cobb's name used to be Bartram Crawford." I waited for him to see the significance of this, then realized I hadn't told him everything. Jeez, this organizing-your-thoughts was hard.

"Bartram Crawford, according to Mehitabel Madison Frazier and Ingrid Brown, was the young man who ran the bait shop."

"Well, there you go. He has the sign now, to remind

himself of when he was young. What's the problem with that?"

"The problem is, I think, that Bartram Crawford got Ingrid Brown pregnant."

"Wait, back up. Ingrid Brown was one of the women in the photo?"

"Right."

"Again, so?"

"Ingrid Brown was Inge Johannsen then. Married to someone else. Considerably older than Bartram."

"Wendy Sam," Dom said, getting up to fetch us coffee, "I don't see where you're going with all this. So, some guy who's now rich and famous got somebody else's wife pregnant what, thirty years ago?" He was hollering from the kitchen. "So what? I assume they worked it all out?"

I waited until he came back into the room, carrying two delicate coffee cups, probably part of Little Flower's wedding gifts.

"Thing is," I said, "I think Ilene was Barry Cobb's daughter."

Damn. Dom dropped the coffee cups. Fortunately, neither broke.

"Well, Little Flower's watching over you. She's had enough of your breaking her things tonight."

We mopped coffee off the floor and discussed murder.

"She was trying to expose her own father?"

"I'm not sure Ilene even knew Cobb was her father," I said, sitting back on my heels. "At least not to start with."

"And she died."

"She was murdered, Dom. And I am afraid to find out who killed her. I think the time has come for me to stop poking into it all. But I can't. I can't let a murderer get away with it."

39

I went home, thinking about love, like the love Dom had for his wife, and the love a parent should have for a child, and maybe even, a little, about the love I didn't have in my life.

As I put the Tupperware container of left-over fettuccine in my refrigerator, the phone rang.

"Wendy Sam, you certainly did not leave a very polite message on my machine. And I've been trying to reach you for hours. So what is so important?"

"Thanks for calling back, Thalia."

"I only have a moment. Giorgio will be back in a sec. Speak."

Giorgio? Thalia was out with a Giorgio while I was trying to solve a murder? No wonder she's happy single.

"The train case in your foyer. The one with the monogram. Where'd you get it?"

"Darling, isn't it? $250 and worth every bit of it. Shall I put your name on it?"

"I don't want to buy it. I want to know where you got it."

"Sorry, darling, my sellers count on my discretion. Besides, you think I'd tell a competitor?"

"Gee, Thalia, I thought your customers wouldn't be caught dead in my store. Isn't that what you said the other day? So we're not competitors. Besides, that suitcase was only worth $200 in Miami, and that was to some Eurotrash."

"You called me to complain about my prices?" I could hear someone sitting down next to her and murmuring in her ear and the click of cutlery and glassware.

"Thalia, quit playing games. Where did you get Ilene's grandmother's train case?"

"What?"

"That train case was Ilene's. As far as I know, it was still in her possession when she died. Where did you get it?"

"There must be a thousand..."

"Thalia, the initials on it are E.H.McK., right?"

"Could be."

"It's Ilene's. Did you break into her apartment and steal it?" Maybe she was the one who'd messed around with the bottles on the windowsill.

"What do you take me for? I am highly insulted. I bought that case from some scruffy man. He must have been the thief, not me, I had no way of knowing..."

"Some scruffy guy, huh? Sounds like a thin alibi to me."

She sputtered. I heard masculine mutterings on her end.

"All right, all right. It was that bozo, the one who runs the marina. Where Ilene lives. Lived. I didn't know it was hers. Those aren't *her* initials."

"I want you, first thing tomorrow, to put that case in your back room and leave it there until I pick it up. Ilene's mother specifically asked for it back. First thing tomorrow, you hear me?"

"Wendy Sam, you poor thing. I'm sure it's been a while for you. You probably forget. First thing tomorrow I have better things to do. To Giorgio. And last thing tonight. Actually, within the hour." She disconnected.

I gritted my teeth. She'd earned every syllable, no every letter, of her nickname. Evil Thalia. Yuck. Greed oozed out with her evil. That's what this whole case was about. Greed.

225

40

I hadn't gotten around to visiting the lady who'd sold her house on Ugli Court. I figured that was my next step.

It was a pleasant building, surrounded by oaks that some developer had saved. *Good for you*, I said to the unknown person. *At least you cared about the land.* On the other hand, it was probably just a wise business decision.

A wide verandah had plenty of wicker rockers on it but no sitters. Not strange, considering it was already hot. I pushed the swinging glass doors open and stepped inside to a pleasant lobby, done up like a sitting room. On one side was a wide screen TV. Some toothy blonde was exclaiming over the news. Easy chairs in a semi-circle around the set were full of elderly people. A few looked around at me but most seemed hypnotized by the newscaster's enthusiastic presentation.

At the reception desk with a brass bell sitting on a little platform that read "Ring Me." So I did. A woman stepped out from a door and smiled that automatic commercial smile. It quickly turned into a real smile as she said, "Why, Wendy Sam. What are you doing here?" The woman pirouetted, holding her striped skirt out like a model. "See how perfect it is?"

Ah, mystery of the unknown woman, solved. A customer. I really should get better at names. I snuck a peek at her name badge.

"Karen, it's great. Glad you found something."

"Are you kidding? Too Good to be Threw is the only shop for me. What can I do for you?"

"I'd like to visit Charlotte Penzar. Is that okay?"

"Of course you can. This isn't a hospital, it's a residence.

But I will have to announce you."

Charlotte Penzar was more than happy to see me. No, no, Karen didn't need to leave her post, Charlotte would come down to the lobby. She could use the exercise.

She was perfectly coiffed, clad in a mint-green appliqued pantset and silver slippers, and delighted to see me. She had on one of the flashiest rings I'd ever seen, and as we shook hands, I complimented her on it.

"And it's real," she said. "Always wanted a sapphire, a big showy one. Never could afford it, until now." She flashed her hand back and forth, admiring her ring.

"Actually, that's why I'm here," I said.

She froze. "I'm not buying anything you're selling. False pretenses, huh? Karen said a friend was here. You're a saleswoman."

"No, no, I'm not. I'm sorry, I said that wrong. Biddie Amberson gave me your name. Really, I'm not here to sell you anything. Please."

"Biddie Amberson? How do you know her?"

"I was around to see what they'd done to your house."

"They leveled it, that's what they did. All my roses. Just ripped them out. I can't stand to see it now."

"I know, it's terrible. May we sit? I have a few questions about that."

We found a pair of armchairs. "Why's everyone so interested in my old place?" she asked, as she sat. "It's gone. Like the Ringling Hotel. Gone."

"Yes, that was sad," I acknowledged. The old Ringling Hotel, with its Spanish tiles and circus memories, had been torn down a few years earlier after a bitter and futile battle to save Sarasota's history.

"Biddie said you'd thought the new owner was just going to remodel?"

"That's what he said. But I guess I can't complain. He gave me a good price, enough to live in comfort here and buy my ring." Her good nature reasserted itself and she flashed her sapphire at me again.

"She also said the salesman was well, pushy?"

"No, not really. I mean, it wasn't like he thought I should list it immediately or anything. Said it needed a lot of repairs, and gave me a list. New roof, redo all my bathrooms, screen the porch, all that. I don't have the energy for all that. Not with my health."

"Yes, that would be a bother."

"So that's why, when that other man came around, I took his offer. More than that salesman said, and I wouldn't have to fix anything. Just sell and go. That's what I did. Pretty canny, huh?"

"Mrs. Penzar, who bought your house?"

"Well, I thought it was going to be that man. Nice man. But when I got to the closing, all the papers said Sunshine Improvements. He said it was just his legal name. I didn't know they were going to rip out my roses."

"And the salesman, the one who told you how much all the remodeling was going to cost? Do you remember his name?"

"Oh dear, no I don't. The old brain cells, you know." She patted her hair. "We have a joke around here." she said. "It's not that blondes start out dumb. It's all those years of peroxide."

"Did you maybe save the man's name? On a contract or an estimate or something?"

"Oh, he never gave me anything in writing. But I saved business card. I kept it because it was such a nice picture of him. Would you like me to get it?"

"That would be terrific."

She stood up. "Here I am forgetting my manners. Would you like to see my apartment? It's very nice. I even have my own patio. And room for a rose bush. It's a Princess Di. It's looking exceptionally fine right now. Would you like to see it?"

Who am I to disallow a nice old lady's pride in her rosebush? "I'd love to," I said.

As we walked the corridor to her apartment, she motioned to the steel handrails on both walls. "For us old folks," she said. "Can you believe, when I first got here, I had to use those? No more, though. This place agrees with me. Love it. Don't even have to cook. But I might, tonight. They always serve fried fish on Fridays. Think I'll have me a Lean Cuisine instead."

Her apartment was just what I'd expected. Furniture brought down years ago from Up North, dark and too big in the tiny rooms. She proudly showed my the living room, her bedroom, the little extra room, the patio. The rosebush in its pot and a café table with two chairs filled it.

"Coffee?" she said. I nodded. "Please." Little did I know how caffeinated detectives must be. Which made me think of Traitor Tom. I pushed the thought out of my mind.

Mrs. Penzar chatted on as she made the coffee. "You know, you're the second person who asked about my selling my house."

I barely heard her. There, centered on the plastic waffle place mat on the kitchen table, was a blue glass bottle with one perfect rose in it.

"Gorgeous, isn't it?" she said. "I always think the Princess Di rose is the prettiest."

"The bottle," I said. "It, umm, it really shows off your rose perfectly."

"Doesn't it? Milk? Afraid I only have skim."

"No, thanks. Where'd you get such a pretty bottle?"

"Oh, that old thing. It's an old medicine bottle. But it's perfect for Princess Di. That's why I'm keeping it."

"Keeping it? Does someone want to take it away?"

Mrs. Penzar sat our coffee mugs down on the table.

"Oh, just Chloe," she said. "She left message after message on my machine. I finally got so tired of it, I left a message on hers. Said I'd thrown it out, that I didn't have it, and there was no sense in calling me every day about it. I didn't like lying, but that bottle's just too pretty to recycle, don't you think?"

"Chloe gave the bottle to you?"

"Well, it had tonic in it, you see. One day, I was out in my rose garden, this was before I sold the house of course, and I, well, I almost fainted. Shouldn't have been gardening in the heat

229

of the day, but black spot, you know, it needs watching for." She examined the leaves of the cut rose in the bottle carefully. "Anyway, Chloe saw me and helped me. Got me back in the air conditioning, then went out to her car and got me this medicine."

"You took it?"

"Why yes. It was all natural. Herbs, you know. Took the whole bottle. Then when I moved here, I brought it, because I knew I'd have a Princess Di. It's just perfect for a Princess Di. Oh, but you wanted that man's card." She got up and rummaged through her junk drawer. "Here it is, right where I left it when that other young lady asked for it."

It was Laurence Pease's card. "Handsome man, don't you think. But so perky. I wasn't feeling good then, some sort of dizzy spells, and he was too perky."

I finally heard what she'd said twice. "Someone else asked about this man?"

"Why yes. Just a few weeks ago. That nice lady. She gave a talk on antiques, and very interesting it was, too. She even had on old-fashioned clothes. A pretty little rose-bud print dress. Well," she said, indicating the blossom in the bottle, "You know I love roses."

"This lady?" I said. "Was her name Ilene Brown?"

"Why, yes it was. Do you know her?"

"Yes, yes I did."

So. Ilene visited all the people on her list. I still wasn't sure what Blowfish Bayou had to do with anything, and Loquat remained a mystery, and of course that *Epazote/ St J. AM!* line was puzzling. I'd even looked up epazote in the dictionary, thinking maybe it was an exotic fruit or something, like loquat, but no dice.

I muttered under my breath as I drove to work. *Blowfish Bayou, Epazote, St J, AM, Loquat.* I even tried fiddling with the letters of epazote. Zapotee. A play on Manatee County, up around Bradenton? Didn't make sense. Peatoze. Some reference

230

to Laurence Pease? That, unfortunately, made more sense. He was going around giving low estimates and scaring seniors about the money they'd have to invest in fixing up their houses, then Barry Cobb came along and bought them. While Chloe was dosing them with who knows what kind of tonic. This was not turning out at all well. And Ilene was killed for knowing this. I was getting in over my head. I was a shopkeeper, for heaven's sake. That's not a dangerous occupation.

Blowfish Bayou, Epazote, St J, AM, Loquat. I have to solve this, I thought, *before whoever killed Ilene comes after me.* This was getting serious. And I couldn't go running back to That Tom Litwin. I mean, I might be in danger, but a girl has her pride.

The store was perking along, and lo and behold, both Chloe and Thalia were shopping. They greeted me, and I looked hard at both of them. Had they come in together, or was it a coincidence? Chloe, who passed the potion around like a poisoned apple, and Thalia, who said she'd gotten Ilene's train case from Beeton. Which I hadn't completely swallowed. How would some beer-swilling idiot like Beeton even know who would buy an antique valise?

Just in case Chloe was spying on my progress, I decided not to ask Thalia if she'd put the case away for me. I hoped she wouldn't mention it in front of Chloe. But then, what if they were in this together? *Help,* I shouted in my mind. *Oh Tom, why'd you have to be such a bastard. I need your help!* As if in answer, the phone rang. And damned if it wasn't Tom. Then I had a brainstorm. I could flush out whatever was going on with a little improv.

"Tom, how nice to hear from you." I turned to face both women.

"It is? I was just..."

"You did? Found a full bottle?" Chloe's head swiveled around towards me. Thalia took a step towards me, still holding an Armani jacket in her hand.

"What are you talking about, Wendy Sam? It's just I

231

wanted to..."

"You're going to have it analyzed?" Thalia's eyes got big. Chloe's face went pale and she put a hand out to steady herself on a clothes rail.

"Analyzed? What's going on?"

"Tomorrow? Why, yes, I can go to the lab with you. First thing?"

"No, today," Tom sounded like he was getting frustrated. "Joshua. I called to remind you about picking up Joshua."

"Certainly. I won't forget. That's wonderful news." I hung up while Tom was still talking.

I smiled as serenely as a madonna at Chloe and Thalia. "Looks like I'm close to figuring this all out," I said to them both.

"Good, that's good," Chloe said and practically ran out the door. Thalia put the Armani jacket back on a rack, the wrong rack of course, and looked at her wrist. "My, the time. Must go," and fled.

She wasn't wearing a watch. Maybe I was stirring things up, getting things moving. Looked to me like Thalia was involved, too. The reaction when I mentioned a full bottle, getting its contents analyzed. Were they working together, Chloe and Thalia? Is that how Thalia ended up with Ilene's grandmother's luggage?

The phone rang again. Probably Tom calling back to find out what that had been all about. I picked the receiver up and said, "I haven't forgotten Joshua."

"Who's Joshua? Is this Too Good to be Threw? Is Susan there?"

"Oh, sorry. Yes." I gave the call to Susan.

I was parking my car at the elementary school, doing my best to stay out of the way of the slo-mo parade of Mommies in mini-vans when it occurred to me. I'd never met Joshua. *How would I know which kid to take home?* I giggled to myself. What if I picked up the wrong kid? It wasn't funny. I was just nervous.

232

Turned out to be no problem. The principal's office had three kids sitting in chairs, book bags at their feet. Two were girls, one was a boy. Ergo, Joshua. "Joshua?" I asked. The boy stood up and I could see his resemblance to his father.

"You have to sign me out," he said. "Picture ID." He motioned to the woman behind the counter. She frowned at him. "Please. Ms. Miller, I'm Joshua Litwin," and he held out his hand.

Obviously, the school secretary had gone over his manners with him. Good for her.

"How's school so far?" The new year had just started a few weeks earlier. I've never understood why Florida schools go back in August, the hottest month of all.

The kid looked over at me with distaste, then he must have remembered the secretary's lessons. "Fine, thank you, ma'am." Well, so much for that conversation. Five minutes later I tried again.

"So, Joshua, what'll we do this afternoon?" I asked.

He was watching cars go by. His father's child, all right. I swear I could even see the adult jaw line in this boy's profile. "Dad says you live on the beach?"

"Well, near it. Just down the street. We can go there if you want."

"He kicked his book bag. "I brought a swimsuit. I couldn't fit a towel in, but Mom said you'd let me use one of yours."

So his mother knew about me. Well, of course. She'd want to know her child was in good hands. Besides which, what did I care? I was only doing a favor I'd promised to do before things changed. I'm sure this was the only time I'd see this boy, and I'd never have to deal with his mother. Or his father, except for when he came to pick Joshua up.

We stopped on the Circle for ice cream. He wanted the whole works, he got it. Then we changed and spent a while on the beach. At first he was shy, but he relaxed like kids do. Even brought me a few shells and whined when I said it was time to go. He perked up when I told him it was pizza for dinner.

233

By the time we were showered, Polter was there with all the ingredients. Joshua was fascinated when Polter tossed the dough in the air and made the round crust. "This is how real pizzerias do it," Polter said. Joshua tried his hand at it but dough ended up everywhere. Good thing Polter's smart enough to have made a double recipe.

We got Joshua de-doughed and seated at the breakfast bar with a knife and some tomatoes and were talking over his head. Polter knife flashed as he separated the broccoli into separate stalks. "Trees," Joshua said, wrinkling his nose. "You're not going to put trees on the pizza, are you?"

"Yes, young man, I am. Good for you and good on pizza." Polter seemed unfazed by the kid's disapproval. I, on the other hand, was worried he wouldn't eat it and I'd have to find the jar of peanut butter for PB&Js, which is what my mother fed me when I wouldn't eat whatever was for supper. I held up a bunch of asparagus and asked if they were okay.

The kid rolled his eyes. "Spears? I'm not eating any pizza with trees and spears on it. Where's the pineapple?"

Polter looked aghast. "You put pineapple on your pizza?"

I started snapping the asparagus spears anyway. I'd put them on the adult side of the pie. Polter casually said, "You know, that's really what Pousse means. Your friend? He said it meant grass? It's stalks, or spouts, like grass stalks. He was kind of right."

"So Henri Pousse, Harry Grass, is also Harry Spears. Patty was gonna Google him."

"Teoma," the kid said. I looked up, startled, expecting to see him choking or something. He was calmly sawing his tomatoes into mush. "What?" he said when he noticed my stare.

"What did you say?"

"Teoma. Better search engine than Google."

These kids nowadays.

"Wait a minute," I said. "Gary Somethingvegetably. We have Jerry Karrote, we have Laurence, Larry Pease, and now maybe Harry Spears, spears as in asparagus? What is the deal here? Who was Ilene afraid of?"

234

"Who's Ilene?" Joshua asked.

"Never you mind. Hey, did you know Ilene's got satellite TV? Why don't you go watch while we finish up this pizza and make a salad?" Polter asked.

"I don't eat salad," the kid said.

"Fine, no salad. Go watch TV."

I shook my head as Joshua headed for my TV room in the back of the house. "You'd make a lousy parent," I said. "Did you hear yourself? "No salad, yes TV? Isn't it supposed to be the other way around?"

"One night won't hurt him. You can't talk about things around kids without them hearing it all. I had a thought."

"You have a million thoughts, Polter. Is this one that's shareable? Oh, I forgot. All your thoughts are shareable. This one doesn't have anything to do with animal sex, does it?"

"What's wrong with animal sex?" he asked in an aggrieved tone. "You got something against little furry puppies and little fuzzy ducklings?"

I had to laugh. "Okay, okay. So. Your thought was?"

"There's another vegetable."

"For the pizza?"

"In this case, Wendy Sam. Keep your mind on it."

Precisely what I was trying hard not to do. I had the tape recorder all hidden in a slightly-opened drawer near where I planned to sit Pease down, and I even had a few leading questions in mind. I was getting a little nervous, but I figured if I forced things to a head, they'd be over soon, and I could let Ilene rest in peace.

"Gary Beeton."

"The marina guy? Oh, Beeton. Beet. A vegetable."

Polter nodded. "So, Beeton, Karrote, Spears. But did Ilene know Henri Pousse's real name was Spears?"

"Probably not," I said. "I think he avoids it pretty good."

"But you found out because..."

"Because Thalia told me so. Said she ran into his brother in some restaurant."

"Kind of far-fetched, don't you think? Think Thalia was lying to you?"

I thought. She could have been. She was trying to persuade me that Ilene was involved in stolen goods. To throw suspicion off of Chloe? Off of Pease? I was getting more confused than ever.

"Okay," I said. "Say Ilene didn't knew Pousse was Asparagus, I mean Spears. So it has to be Beeton, Karrote, or Pease."

"Can't be Pease." Polter was sliding the loaded pizza into the oven.

"Why not? He gives low prices and high repair estimates to people whose houses Barry Cobb then buys, he smokes, it's his card the list's on, Ilene went to see him the day before she died."

"He smokes?" Polter smiled. "That makes you a murderer nowadays?"

"Long story," I said. "Why can't it be Pease?"

"You said it yourself. Ilene went to see him the day before she died. But she talked to her mother the day before that."

"And mentioned Gary Vegetable to her mother then. Before she'd encountered Pease."

"Bingo. We have twenty minutes 'til pizza. Get out that list again."

We pored over the card with Ilene's turquoise words on it. "Okay, Polter, do your thing."

"St J? Saint something? Saint Jerome? He was the one with all the arrows, right?"

"No, Jerome was the one who took the thorn out of the lion's paw," I said.

"I'm wrong?" Polter said. "Okay, what's Saint Jerome got to do with this list?"

"I can't imagine. Maybe it's Saint Joan? Joseph?"

"That's it!" Polter exclaimed. "Port St. Joe. Development town, up near Apalachicola."

"No, doesn't sound right. All the other things on this list are real local to Sarasota. Saint John?"

"Saint John's River's closer. Did you know it flows backwards? South to north, I mean?"

"Interesting, Polter, interesting. But not local."

"Then there's Saint John's Wort."

"That's it, that's it." I was ecstatic. "An herb, right?"

"For memory," Polter said. "Yes."

"So the tonic could be Saint John's Wort."

"I don't think that would hurt anyone though. You said they were dizzy. Not forgetful."

"Oh." The oven timer dinged. We'd forgotten the salad. Joshua didn't mind, and he very quietly ate all around the broccoli on his slices, piling the greenery as small as possible on the corner of his plate without mentioning it. Polite kid. Raised right.

The door bell rang, and it was Patty. "Results," she said. Henri, Harry, whoever he is."

Joshua was sent to the TV room again, which he didn't seem to mind, and the three of us sat down. I told her about our theory that St J meant Saint John's Wort then offered her some pizza. Patty insisted she wasn't hungry, but the last two slices disappeared as she spread out her notes on the Googling of Henri Pousse. "Hey, the asparagus was a brilliant idea," she said.

"Okay, here's what I got. Nothing on Henri Pousse at all. Including," and here she looked over her half-glasses at me, "no criminal record."

Good. I hadn't wanted to believe that of him.

"Now, Harry Grass. He's either a bull mastiff who won Best of Breed in 2002 (and who's a girl dog, by the way. Such an impolite word they use.) Or he runs a garage out of his home in Vancouver BC, that's Canada. Sounds like a good mechanic, too."

"You found that all on the Internet?"

"Yup. Now Harry Spears. Harry Spears ran for political office in 1924 in Tennessee, is known as a great catcher of grey snapper in Marathon, was one of the Little Rascals in the nineteen-twenties or a director at Majestic Studios in 1914, depending on which web site you believe. Oh yeh, and he married

Mayme Van Horn in Kansas in 1914, too. Busy little devil."

"So no Harry Spears, our Harry Spears." I didn't know whether to be relieved or disappointed.

Polter brightened. "Harry Spears? Punt leader, 1966, Gators. Jersey number 34."

We women looked at him in amazement. "Are you sure?" I said.

Polter looked hurt. "Hey just because I got a saint wrong, doesn't mean I don't know my U of Florida stats."

"1966? So he'd be, say 55-ish now? Could be the same guy." That was possible, but where it got us to know that Henri Pousse, the antiques dealer that Ilene had on her list, was a punt leader, whatever that was, I didn't know. I said so.

"Could be that the AM on Ilene's list was the other shop," Patty said.

"Amelia's Memories?" I didn't think so. Unless Ilene was just listing where she'd heard about tonic in blue bottles, Amy's story.

"AM also means ante meridiem, don't forget," Polter said. "Latin for before midday, before noon. Most people don't know that. Drives me crazy, how people say twelve a.m. What they're really saying is twelve before twelve. Makes no sense. Even like 9 a.m. in the morning. AM means morning. They're repeating themselves. Nine in the morning in the morning. Cripes."

"Morning?" Patty said. "*Epazote/ StJ/ AM!* means in the morning? Were these people supposed to take their tonic in the morning? Is that it?"

"Morning. Morning has Broken."

They stared at me. "The retirement home," I said. "Where Charlotte Penzar lives. The Ugli Court woman."

"But Ugli was already on the list. Why would Ilene note it down twice?" Patty said.

"No, you see," Polter pointed at the list. "It's on the same line with *Epazote/ StJ*. And it has an exclamation point after it. Maybe the connection's at the retirement place."

"I don't see how," I said. "I was there today. Seemed like a perfectly normal place to me."

The doorbell rang again. It was Tom. Tom Litwin. The Cad.

"Hi Wendy Sam. Got off early, so I figured I'd take Joshua off your hands."

It was barely seven. "Okay," I said and let him in. I noticed Patty palming Ilene's list that we'd all been sitting around. Isn't it great to have girl friends who understand?

Polter stood. "Guess I'll be going." Men friends. They're the ones who just look for the closest exit. He kissed me, patted me on the cheek, thanked me for the pizza even though he brought it and he made it, and beat it out of there fast as his Birkenstocks would go.

"Joshua's watching TV," I said, going into the kitchen. I turned the water on as hard as it would go and started banging around plates and glasses.

Tom didn't take the hint. "Thanks for watching Joshua for me." I nodded, my back to him.

"I didn't get a chance to tell you about Henri Pousse. Seems he's not the same guy the Naples police mentioned. Far as I could find out, this Pousse is clean. Funny thing, though, he was Harry Spears. Football hero."

"Gators," I said. "1966 punt leader."

"Well, yes. You a sports fan?"

I turned around, rolled my eyes at him, and turned back to the sink.

"I forgot. You're a detective now. How's it going?"

"Fine," I said. "You better go get your kid. He's probably watching porn."

"Wendy Sam, I don't know what I did, but..."

"You didn't do a thing. We're just not compatible." I dried my hands on my butt and went to get Joshua.

Tom took his son and left. I don't look at him. Couldn't stand to see the hurt look in his eyes.

Patty was still on the couch. "So?" she said.

"So what?" I said.

"Gotcha. See ya." She got up to leave but as she got to the door, she turned around and said, "You're making a mistake. Elsie told me about asking him to watch over you, but that's not what's going on. Just because she thinks it is. He was helping you because he wanted to spend time with you. Don't blow it, Wendy Sam. That's all I have to say."

Friends. I need 'em like a hole in the head.

I grabbed the car keys. I needed a sunset again, but a different one, not my home sunset. I needed to get out of my regular routine. I went to my second favorite beach on the south end of Siesta.

I pulled up to the dunes of Turtle Beach and got out of the car. Behind me, the picnic area and playground on the north side of the lagoon were empty of families now, and not a single boat was being retrieved from the canal.

I climbed the steps of the wooden crossover and paused at the top, looking over the narrow beach. To my left, the bayside condos were mostly closed up, sitting empty until their owners came back in November or December. To my right, the trailer park was similarly deserted, lying in its summer slumber. I'd have the beach to myself, it seemed. I climbed down to the sand and wiggled my toes in its soft coolness.

I walked north, searching the tide line for tiny intact shells. Nervous shore birds kept just ahead of me probing the water's edge for their dinner.

The Gulf waves were, as usual, gentle and caressing, overlapping in a white-noise rhythm. The sun was close to the horizon. My attention was on the way the light came through the water and the turquoise, sky-blue, and Gulf green it made, so I didn't hear anything until it was too late.

41

I awoke because I was cold. It was totally dark and I was lying in sand, one leg in the water. My head hurt and for some reason I couldn't see out of my right eye. I tried to sit up. I was nauseous and sweaty. I wiped my hand across my face. It came away sticky. In the faint starlight I could see the darkness in my hand. Blood. I couldn't see out of my right eye because there was blood.

I felt delicately around my hair. More stickiness, mixed with sand. Someone had hit me. Come up behind me on the deserted beach, silently, and hit me.

I had to get up, had to go find help. I scrambled like a crab, trying to right myself while ignoring the stabbing pain. There was a piece of waterlogged wood next to me in the sand. I picked it up to take with me. It was probably evidence. At the very least, I could use it as a weapon if my assailant was still around.

Turtles nest at Turtle Beach, and when they hatch, they head for the nearest light, which should be moonlight on the waves. There are no artificial lights near beaches in August. Usually that's good. But now, I could barely see the steps to the dune walkover. I crawled up on my hands and knees, praying there was someone to help in the parking lot.

There wasn't. My car was the only one in the lot. Past the playground and the beach restrooms, across the road, through a parking lot, there was a restaurant with cars and people. I could see twinkling lights in the trees and they were swaying as in a breeze. But this is Sarasota in August. There are no breezes. I got halfway there before I collapsed.

241

42

I awoke. I was still in the park drive. The lights at the restaurant were still on but they weren't swaying anymore. There was only one car in the restaurant lot now. It was much later. I'd been laying there, on the pavement, for a good while and no one had seen me. August in Sarasota. The town's as empty as it ever gets.

I crawled over to a fencepost and pulled myself up. The pain was less now, but I was more sick to my stomach. If I could only get across to the restaurant, someone could help me. It seemed to take hours, but finally, I reached the car and leaned on its hood. And promptly threw up all over it.

"Christ, fuckin' drunk," I heard a young male voice. "God damn, why me?"

I looked up, trying to apologize. It must have been the dishwasher. He was in shorts and a faded tee shirt, sneakers with their tongues hanging out like some obscene tropical flower, and a ball cap. He stepped back when he saw my face.

"Jesus, lady, what happened?" He had a white apron balled up in his hand and tried to pat the blood off my face. The apron smelled of Clorox.

"Can I sit down?" I asked as my legs gave way and I nestled next to his front tire. "Would you hold this?" I handed the piece of wood to him.

If you are ever bashed in the head late one night, don't ask the paramedics to call a certain detective for you. He will not be at all sympathetic. Even after the ambulance has left and he's driving you home.

"I told you and told you to let me finish this investigation,

242

but no, you had to traipse around town stirring up nests of cotton mouths," he was saying.

"There's money involved here, Wendy Sam. Lots of money. More money than you and I would ever have all our lives. You don't go playing Nancy Drew when there's millions involved."

"Where's the wood?"

"What?"

"The wood, the piece she bashed me with?"

"Who bashed you? Did you see?"

"I didn't see anything. I was looking for shells and watching the sun set, and then it was now. I think I blacked out a couple of times. Where's the wood?"

"Jesus, woman, what does it matter where the wood is?"

I looked at him incredulously. "It's evidence. Or a clue. I can't think which right now."

43

Then I was in my bed. Tom was sitting across the room, in the white rocker. There was a pink bra hanging over the arm rest. I have always intended to develop neater personal habits, but believe me, if you hang up clothes all day long in a consignment shop, you soon lose the taste for doing it at home.

Tom stood up and blew out a candle on the mantle. He opened the shade and there it was, glorious Florida sunrise. I winced.

"You're awake," he said.

"Yes, Detective, I am. Brilliant deduction." Then I felt like a shit. Here I got the man out late, made him drag me home and tuck me in bed, and he'd obviously spent the night in my charming but not overly-comfy rocking chair. "Sorry," I muttered.

"Coffee?" he said. I nodded and winced. For some reason, I'd assumed I was all recovered. Obviously, I wasn't.

I struggled out of bed when Tom left the room. I was still in my clothes from yesterday and that made me feel better. At least Tom hadn't undressed me. I got to the bathroom, washed my face and rinsed out my mouth, and felt around on my head. It was still way too sore for me to even try brushing the sand out of my curls so I didn't. I pulled off my salt-and-grit laden clothes and wrapped my Chinese robe around myself and went out into the living room.

Tom had placed two cups of coffee on the dining table. There was a plate of pastries there as well, on a plate I recognized as one of Signora Dom's legacy. So Dom had been over. I wondered how much he'd told Tom of my activities. Not the conch shell I hoped. Or the sign at Cobb's house. Or Ilene's train case that Thalia somehow had. I didn't believe her story about

Beeton selling it to her.

"Where's Joshua? Didn't you have him last night?"

"Thank you, Tom, for rescuing me from those overzealous EMTs who wanted to take me to Sarasota Memorial for observation. Thank you, Tom, for coming to get me, and bringing me home, and watching over me as I slept."

I was instantly contrite. "Yes, Tom, I'm sorry, of course a thousand thank-yous. I am deeply, deeply mortified that I neglected to properly thank you for saving my, my, my rear end."

He grinned. The sun shone. The coffee was a thousand times better than when I made it. It was almost worth being slugged in the head with a piece of driftwood.

"At the risk of sounding less than grateful, could you answer me two questions, Detective Litwin?"

"Have a pastry. Dom brought them over. Remind me to call him in a minute. He was terribly worried."

"Okay, okay. Dom's a dear. Okay. First, who's with Joshua? You said his mother was away."

"Neighbor. Nice family, Joshua goes to school with their daughter."

"So, like, you could have had him stay with them yesterday, rather than with me?"

"Well. Maybe."

"What do you mean, well maybe?"

"Well, if he'd stayed with them, you wouldn't have gotten to know him."

I stared at him. "You mean the whole thing was just so we'd, like, bond?"

"Didn't you?"

"I sat in the midday sun on the beach, to bond with the kid of a man I'm mad at? And ate a banana split for a man who's a cad and a bounder?"

"I didn't tell you to eat a banana split."

"Excuse me, Tom Litwin, but one doesn't order just one banana split. They come in pairs. Like the ark. All those calories, for nothing," I mourned.

245

"What, you don't like banana splits?"

"I love them. See these hips? These are not fat-free sorbet hips. And no, I'm not mad at you. Anymore."

"Thank God." I do wish he'd stop smiling that smile.

"And another thing."

"Name it." He opened his arms wide. I fought the impulse to fling myself into them. Actually, with the headache I had, flinging was not on the agenda. But it's the thought that counts.

"Where's my wood?"

He lifted his coffee mug to his mouth and grinned behind it.

"Your wood?"

"Yes, I distinctly remember asking you to take charge of my wood."

He raised his eyebrows.

"Tom Litwin, where is the piece of wood that she bashed me with?"

He got serious. "Wendy Sam, tell me why you say *she bashed me.* Do you know who hit you?"

"No. It just happened."

"So why *she?*"

"Oh." I saw what he meant. I had all these male suspects. Mark Four, Pease, Beeton, even (although I couldn't imagine it) Henri. Oh, and Barry too. Can't forget Barry. So what made me say "she"?

"Footsteps," I said.

"You heard the person coming up behind you?"

"No. I mean footprints. When I awoke, in the water."

"You were *in the water?*" His voice got amazingly high-pitched there.

"Just one leg. It's okay," I said, putting my hand on his arm. "I got out."

"But you might not have. You might have drowned."

"Nonsense. Anyway, footprints. Next to me when I got up. Definitely female."

"Long gone by the time I got there." Tom sounded disappointed.

"How long was it, exactly?" I was curious. Not every sunset you end up smashed in the head, throwing up on a stranger's car hood, being rescued by the man you love to hate.

"Dunno. I got there around 11. Medics called me because you kept saying my name."

"What, they look things up in the phone book?"

"Wendy Sam, I am a homicide detective. It stands to reason that any EMT in town would recognize my name."

"So's where the wood?"

"Wendy Sam, we can't get fingerprints off sodden wood."

"That's not the point."

"And the point is?"

"Ilene was murdered. Why else attack me? I want that piece of wood. I'm going to have it mounted. With a brass plaque."

"A brass plaque?"

"That says *I was so right so there.*"

He burst out laughing. I fell in love. Patty was right. He'd been there because he wanted to be, not because Elsie told him to be.

Don't you hate it when friends are right?

The phone rang. Tom was still laughing and shaking his head, so I answered it.

"Wendy Sam, I'm so sorry. I tossed it."

"Thalia? You tossed the train case? It was Ilene's family heirloom."

"No, no, I have the case. I tossed the bottle. The one that was inside. It smelled awful."

"Thalia, start over. What bottle?"

"Inside. There was a bottle, inside, with some foul liquid. I threw it in the Dumpster."

Ilene's train case had a bottle inside. That smelled bad.

247

Ilene had put the bottle in her train case. Why?

The phone call at Ilene's, the day she'd died. Some man, mad that Ilene wasn't on her way to him. Someone who'd needed a couple of hours to run tests.

"Thalia, thanks,'bye." I scurried, if that's what you can call a gingerly-careful scuttle, to my bedroom. I snatched up the bra handing on the rocker and threw it in my laundry basket, then pawed through looking for the shorts I'd worn that day, the day I found Ilene dead.

I have a very large laundry basket. The shorts were there at the bottom. The name and phone number were in the pocket. I brought it out to the kitchen, to Tom.

"Look," I said.

He read it. "Sam Bennett." And a phone number.

"Where's that area code?"

"Gainesville," he said.

"Gainesville? As in the university?"

"Probably. Why?"

I was dialing as I explained to him about the phone call. "Sam Bennett, please."

"Analysis Lab, Sam Bennett speaking."

We talked. He told me Ilene had requested an appointment then not shown. An appointment to analyze an unknown fluid.

"Why you?"

"I am, after all, the premier source for organics in the state," the man said. "It's my field."

"I'm wondering where Ilene would have gotten your name."

"Any number of places. I am written up in many journals." The man was sounding more and more like a pompous ass, but I was trying to be polite.

"Would you have a record of her call to you?"

"Of course. This is a state lab. Just a minute."

While I was waiting for him to look it up, I glanced over at Tom. He was drinking coffee, eating pastries. Coffee, I finally realized, he had made. While I lolled in bed. Just like my dream man. Well, not quite. My dream man got out of our bed, not off the hard wooden rocker in the corner of my bedroom. I did something I'd never done before in my life. I winked at a man.

He silently toasted me with his coffee mug.

"Yes, it says here, Nancy Lindauer. A nurse at, let me see, Morning has Broken Retirement Estates. Does that help?"

Nancy, my customer. Nancy, who solved the item on the list. *Epazote/ St J/ AM!* Ilene's note meant *ask Nancy.*

"Yes, thanks, it does. Can you tell me just one more thing? Does the word epazote mean anything to you?"

"Of course. An herb. Chenopodium ambrosiodes. Also called West Indian goosefoot or Mexican tea. Actually, Mexicans usually call it herba de Santa Maria. Used as an anthelmintic."

"Huh?"

"It kills worms."

"It kills worms?"

Tom was signaling frantically to me. "Could you hold on just one moment?" I asked in my most ladylike tone. I could hear the squawking on the other end as I hissed to Tom *What?*

"Ask him what else it's good for."

"I was going to. Jeez."

"Mr. Bennett?"

"Doctor."

"Oh, sorry, Doctor Bennett. Is epazote used for anything else?"

"Well, many things actually. Interesting thing is..." I could feel a Polter-type moment coming on. Useless Fact City.

"...it's used in a lot of Mexican cooking. Things with beans, most often."

Tom was waving again. I turned my back.

"One more thing, Doctor. Can it be harmful?"

"Oh goodness me, yes indeedy. A heavy dose can make people dizzy. And people with kidney problems, why, it's very dangerous."

I said thanks, goodbye. Tom was clenching his fists above

his head like some sports fan.   "What?" I said rather crossly. I could feel the headache creeping back.

"Good girl! Right questions! Bravo!"

"Brava, actually."

"What?"

"Oh, that's right. You haven't come under Polter's spell yet. It's brava for women. Bravo's for men."

Tom shook his head. "You win. Brava it is. So what did the man say?"

"Epazote's an herb. From Mexico and Central America. Also called goosefoot. Which Chloe grows, I saw it in her garden. It makes people dizzy. And wormless. Oh, and you don't give it to people with kidney problems."

"What?"

"Kidney problems," I repeated. "You don't give it to people with kidney problems. Like Otto Bruniger. I think Barry wanted Chloe to give the tonic to Otto, but Chloe found out he has kidney problems, and wouldn't do it. That's what the business card with Otto's name on it was all about. Barry wanted Otto's house and Chloe wasn't cooperating.

"And that's not all. Bonita made dinner for Ilene one night, which included a sauce she called fruit and beans herba de Santa Maria. Epazote. Ilene must have recognized the smell. And looked up the contraindications on the Internet. She knew Chloe was conspiring with Barry Cobb and Laurence Pease to buy waterfront land and build the kind of houses Ilene despised."

"So that's what that phone call was about yesterday? Getting the tonic analyzed? I wondered what you were doing."

"I was trying to figure out what was going on. Chloe and Thalia were listening on my end. They both got spooked. Chloe knew there was something wrong with her concoction."

"Jesus, woman, maybe that's what led to the attack on you." Tom looked really mad.

"But it wasn't Thalia. She was worried only because she'd thrown the bottle away."

"So you think it was Chloe who hit you?"

250

I didn't want to think so. But I was pretty sure those footprints were a woman's. But I could be wrong. After all, I'd just been hit in the head.

"There's a couple of other things I need to tell you, Tom."

"I'm not gonna like this, am I?"

"Probably not. Here, have another pastry."

He shook his head. "Talk to me."

Well, by the time I got done showing him the letter that Ilene wrote the day before she died, the one that said *it's gone beyond greed,* and telling him about my last conversation with her when Ilene said *Chloe thinks she knows what she's doing but she doesn't,* he was pacing the floor. I decided that, after all, the conch shell incident didn't need to be told. I was afraid that pulsing vein in his right temple would go into double time. As Elsie said, men like a bit of mystery. As Jeanne Lockerbie told her granddaughter, you don't need to tell all your business.

"So Chloe is the one who attacked you," he said. "I'm going to go out there and arrest her."

"Don't be, umm, hasty." I was going to say "silly" but decided that wasn't the best word to use with a steaming homicide detective. "Ilene didn't think Chloe knew what she was doing, and I think that's true. "Besides, don't you need like evidence or something? You said you couldn't get fingerprints off my wood. Heck, I'm not even sure that piece of wood's the weapon. And I'm not sure about those footprints, either, the female ones."

Tom was sitting again now. He put his elbows on the table and his head in his hands. "Even if everything you say is true, still, the only crime I have is your attack. The official stance is that Ilene's death was an accident. And nothing else you've looked as is a crime. Laurence Pease may be setting oldsters up for an easy sell to Barry Cobb, Chloe may be passing out potions that are too strong or something, but all that's not illegal."

"Oh my God." I stared at him.

"What?"

"Barry Cobb. Cob as in corn cob. Corn as in vegetable.

Gary Somethingvegetably is Barry Cobb. Ilene was afraid of Barry Cobb. *He doesn't care about anyone, just his wallet.* That's what Ilene told her mother."

"Don't you mean anything? He doesn't care about any*thing* but his wallet? Any*one* doesn't make sense."

"That's just it," I said. "Ilene had the photo, she knew the Blowfish Bayou story, she saw the photo at Cobb's office the day before she died. After she talked to her mother, after she wrote the note to me.

"I think she figured it out. That she was the daughter of the man she hated, the man whose sleazy operations she was uncovering. She figured it out right before she died. He killed her. Oh my God. It's horrid that he killed his own daughter. But that she realized he was her father, just before he murdered her. My God." Tears filled my eyes.

Tom put his hand over mine, which were clenched tightly together and patted.

After a little bit, Tom said quietly, "What's this about photographs?"

That's right. I hadn't told him about the three pictures. Once I did, he was up on his feet, rinsing the breakfast dishes. "Get dressed," he said. "We're going to see Barry Cobb. You are going to ask him some questions."

"Me? I thought you didn't like the way I asked questions?"

"Somehow," he said, drying his hands on the dish towel, "I think you've learned a lot recently."

44

He ate breakfast on Saturdays at his club, Sarina's maid told me. He was probably there now.

He was. He was eating an omelette, manipulating the heavy cutlery as though he was a surgeon. He looked up in surprise as I approached the table. The only reason I was admitted to the private dining room was Tom's badge. Tom stayed in the foyer and sent me in alone.

Now this I know is true: any well-bred man will instinctively at least start to stand when a lady comes up to his table. Cobb didn't move a muscle.

"Yes?" he said. He knew who I was, I'm sure, but he kept his face as blank as he must have when doing his deals.

"Mr. Cobb," I said, "May I have a moment?"

He gestured at his breakfast. "Perhaps another time."

"Just one question."

"Which would be?"

"How well did you know Ilene Brown?"

His eyes went even emptier. "Brown? Name doesn't ring a bell."

"Well then, how about Ingrid Johannsen?"

"That's two questions. If you'll excuse me." He picked up his knife and fork.

"Here's a third. Blowfish Bayou?"

He laid his silverware down carefully. "That's what I named my company after. BB. Blowfish Bayou. Anyone who's anyone in the county knows that."

"Does anyone who's anyone know why you named your company that? Because Blowfish Bayou was the summer of your life? The summer you loved Ingrid Johannsen?"

253

"You really must excuse me." He raised his hand and a tuxedoed waiter hurried over. "This young lady needs you to show her the way out."

"He doesn't know."

"What?"

"That Ilene was his daughter."

"He must have," Tom said as we sat in his car outside the club, "otherwise there was no reason to kill her. Just because she found out things that were underhanded but not illegal? Nah. It only makes sense if he was afraid of being exposed."

"In this day and age?" I asked. "What would be the big deal to admitting you had a daughter thirty years ago with some woman who was someone else's wife?"

"Sarina."

"What, she'd be upset? I don't think Sarina gets upset. It would cause wrinkles."

"She'd divorce him. And there goes all his money. Not to mention his standing in the community."

"But Sunshine Improvements. BB Construction. They're all over town. Barry Cobb must have enough of his own money now, outside of his wife's fortune."

Tom looked grim. "Those kind of people," he said. "Losing half of his money to his wife, and losing the use of all her money? He'd be a failure. Even if he still had what we'd consider a fortune. Barry Cobb couldn't let his wife find out that Ilene was his daughter."

"But he didn't know. I could see it in his eyes. He has no idea."

"Wendy Sam, you're learning fast. But I am not going to exonerate a man because you thought he looked innocent at breakfast."

"Can you do that?" I said. "Arrest a man for a murder the police say isn't a murder?"

"That's not what I'm going to do. I'm going to charge him

with the attack on you."

I frowned. "I still think it was a woman. I'd hear a man sneak up on me, don't you think?"

Tom Litwin shrugged, then reached in under his jacket and readjusted his holster. "I didn't say I thought he attacked you. That's just what I'm going to charge him with."

Tom dropped me off at home, telling me to rest, that a bash in the head was nothing to sneeze at. I assured him I would, then waited ten minutes so he was sure to be off Lido Key before I grabbed my keys and my aspirin, told Dom I felt fine and that I had to go see Chloe and headed out Route 72 once more. I had it all figured out.

45

Chloe was packing when I got there. The kitchen was untouched and so was the living room, but her bedroom was torn apart and there were boxes spilling clothes and shoes over most of the floor space.

The curtains had been taken down and folded neatly on a chair. The bed was stripped to the mattress, so I guessed Chloe was leaving today.

"You're only taking your clothes?" There was a smudge on her cheek and the hem of her tee shirt had been used to wipe her forehead.

"The rest, he can have."

"Your herbs? You're leaving them all behind?"

Chloe made a scary sound, one she meant probably as a sarcastic laugh. But it came out as a cry from the heart, a jagged ripping sound I hope I never hear again.

"My herbs? You think I want them? I should burn them. I don't deserve to be an herbalist. I just took his recipe and made it. Never checked, never examined the side effects or contraindications. He said it was all right, it was harmless."

"You couldn't have known."

"He said it would just make them realize they needed to be in a home and I believed him. Because I wanted to. Because he said he'd give me my land if I helped him."

"Chloe, you weren't to know. How could you?"

"I could have looked it up. Double-checked." She motioned to the living room with its bookcases full of reference books. Two or three were out and open, face down on the footstool in front of her reading chair. "Hell, I could have looked it up on the Internet." That terrible sound again. "That's what

Ilene did, right? Before he killed her."

"But he gave you the recipe. You trusted him. You shouldn't have, but you didn't know."

Chloe slumped down onto the bare mattress. "The first rule of herbalism," she said in a monotone, "is *first do no harm*."

"I thought that was doctors."

She looked up at me with dull eyes.

After a while, she said "Do you know what the second rule is?"

I sat down beside her on the bed and put my arm around her. "You didn't break it on purpose. You thought you were helping. And thank goodness no one died."

"No one but Ilene. Our friend."

I was silent. There was nothing to say.

"She died because I didn't follow the second rule."

"She died because she was thrown down the stairs."

"She died," and Chloe broke down. "She died because, because I should have known. The recipe was wrong. Because of the second rule."

"What's the second rule, Chloe?" I pushed her hair out of her face and kept my hand on her cheek, the way you do with a fretful child.

"Never use the seeds when the roots will do. Never use the roots when the leaves will do. Never use the leaves when the flowers will do." She sighed.

"Chloe?"

She struggled to her feet and stood facing the bare window, looking out on the land she had longed for all her life. Her herbs and plants sat still out there in the glare of a tropical summer. Most of them were so pretty.

"There's an order of toxicity, Wendy Sam. The flowers, then the leaves, then the roots. And last, the seeds. The seeds are always the strongest, the most dangerous. Never use the seeds when..."

Chloe turned back away from her land and towards me. "Oh hell. It was greed. I did it so he'd sign the land over to me.

257

Justifying that old people need to be watched over, that was just my excuse. Ilene was right. People should have a choice, not be forced into it."

She continued, "By the time I figured out it was too strong, the harm was done. And I had to keep quiet about it. And no one was really harmed. You saw, Wendy Sam, you saw. I wouldn't give the tonic to Otto Bruniger because of his kidneys. And I was trying to get all of the bottles back."

Her cell phone rang. Chloe made no move to answer it. So I did.

"Wendy Sam, is that you? You're with Chloe, right? That's where Dom said you were going. Are you okay?"

"Of course," I said. "Did you want to talk to her? How did the arrest go?"

"Hon, sit down."

"What?"

"Barry Cobb didn't kill Ilene."

"What? What happened?"

"I"m sure he didn't kill her."

"So why did you arrest him?"

"I thought he had. But he hadn't. He didn't even know, Wendy Sam."

"Tom, you're not making any sense. And you're scaring me. You sound terrible. What's wrong?"

"Barry Cobb is dead. He killed himself with the officer's gun. On the street, in front of a crowd. He killed himself, Wendy Sam."

Oh my God. "He killed himself to avoid arrest? But you just said you were sure he didn't kill Ilene. Tom, tell me what's going on."

I could hear him take a big breath, as though what he had to say next had to all come out at once before he broke down.

"He didn't kill her, but he let her die. He found her and she was still breathing. But he left, he left her because he was afraid of his reputation, of losing his money."

"What?"

"He was there early that morning, Wednesday. He was driving his wife's car, he had an appointment and he needed it that morning. He figured he'd stop by and see who this woman was, the one who was nosing around his business."

"And?"

"She was there, on the ground. Still breathing, he swore. He could have called for help but he didn't. He thought only of his reputation, and how the whole story would come out, and he turned around and left her there. Figured it was meant to be, that she'd tripped and fallen, that she was dying. He left her to die. Alone."

"So, that's murder, isn't it? Letting someone die, not getting help?"

"Doesn't matter now. He didn't know, Wendy Sam."

"Tom, what are you talking about?"

"Barry Cobb never knew Ilene Brown was his daughter. When I told him, he grabbed the officer, grabbed the gun, and put it to his temple. He killed himself, Wendy Sam, because his greed killed his daughter. The daughter he never even knew he had."

I looked up. Chloe had turned around towards me, and she was silhouetted against the strong August sunlight. I couldn't see her expression. She reached down and started unpacking the box closest to her. I told Tom I'd see him later and pressed the button to end the call.

I drove home as fast as I could. Tom was sitting in my backyard having a staring contest with Birdie.

I put coffee on and hugged him.

"I'm sorry," I began.

"For what? For finding out your friend was, indeed, left to die on her own? Maybe she could have been saved. If that bastard had been less self-serving."

"Chloe seems to be staying."

Tom looked up at me. "She didn't mean any harm," I said. "She stopped once she figured out the tonic was wrong, that

259

Barry was using it just to get people's houses."

Tom's phone rang.

"Yes, all right, give me the address." He motioned to me for paper and pencil. "Twenty minutes."

Corinthia had called the police station when she heard on the news about Barry's suicide and asked to speak to the officer in charge. He was to meet her at her house immediately. I went along. Tom wanted me to.

She was sitting in an old kitchen chair under the shade of a dusty citrus tree in her front yard. She was surprised to see me. We hugged, I insisted she stay seated, and Tom went into her kitchen to bring out two more chairs. A mongrel slunk out from the shade under the porch and growled at him, but Corinthia yelled, "John Galt, you hush!" and he did.

At her request, Tom told her what happened.

"Well, of course Barry had a child. Everyone knew that."

"Everyone except Barry it seems. Why didn't he know?"

The old woman sniffed. "Prob'y didn't care to know. Lotta young men like that. Always been that way."

"How did you know?" Tom asked.

Corinthia looked over at him with scorn. "Hey, Mr. Police, you never been black. You black, you listen an' you watch. White folks. That Bayou place?"

"Blowfish Bayou?"

"That a bait shop. Where you think white boys get bait? They ain't goin' out, catchin' it. That's black boy work. Black boys sell the bait, they know all about that Barry. Our boys know, we all know." She waved her hand around indicating the whole neighborhood.

"So you knew Barry, Bartram, got this woman pregnant. Did you know what happened to the child?" I asked.

"In good time, in good time. All comes back on you, you live long enough." Corinthia rearranged her legs. "Ah, it's an achy day. I gotta get movin' or I'll freeze like this."

260

"Corinthia, I'm sorry, we're keeping you too long. But when did you figure out that Ilene was that child?"

"Got eyes, han't I? Written in her face. That girl was a Crawford, no doubt."

"You knew other Crawfords, besides Barry?"

"Lordy yes. The father George and the grandfather Samuel. That Samuel, he was always a cheat and a liar. Lie just for the sake of lyin'. Passed it down to his son and grandson. I'm ashamed of him, I am."

"Ashamed?" That was a strange reaction. "Why would you be ashamed of Samuel Crawford?"

"Well, it's his house I'm sittin' in, in't it?"

Tom and I stared at each other.

My voice came back first. "This house belonged to the Crawfords?"

"Why yes honey. Why else you think Barry wanted to get it out from under me? It's his family home!" She laughed and slapped her thigh.

"Can you imagine, honey?" She was as tickled as I've ever seen her. "Him wantin' this old shack, when he lives out there on that hifalutin Key? Knowin' him, he just wants it to spite me. Prob'ly tear down this tree, this one right here." She patted its trunk. "Samuel told me years ago, when we were young, Mrs. Potter Palmer planted this self-same loquat. 1917, 1918, thereabouts. Right before she died. A historic tree right here in my front yard."

Loquat. The final item on Ilene's list. Barry Cobb wanted Loquat, Corinthia's house.

46

The night passed more swiftly than either Tom or I wanted. But all the events leading up to that night weighed heavily on us, and we just held each other. I had a dream.

Coins of bronze and gold glittered overhead as Ilene walked towards me. Her pale hair was tinged with green by the sunlight passing through the old live oak trees and she brushed aside long grey tendrils of Spanish moss on her approach. Her dress was gauzy, grey like the moss, spangled with bugle beads and sequins like the sun-struck leaves over our heads.

She came right up to me and stood there.

"You're dead," I said.

"I am? I don't feel dead."

"You fell down the stairs. You don't remember?"

"I found my father. I wasn't looking for him but I found him. It was horrible." The bronze and gold were now on Ilene's cheeks, twinkling off her tears.

I reached out to touch her, and the Spanish moss and her grey skirts wafted around her as she receded.

"I don't want him as a father." The coins moved across her body. "Don't let him be my father," the wind whispered.

"He's dead now too," I called after her.

"Good." The word was a longing for sleep.

I awoke in a puddle of hard Florida sunshine with Tom at my side. I felt guilty for being glad of another human being's death. His, not hers. Hers I would mourn for the rest of my life.

But later. First there was coffee to be made and one less task to do. I hurried Tom off to his house, his job, whatever. I was preoccupied. About an hour later, when I was sure he'd be in the middle of something, I left a message on his cell that I was going to make a sympathy call on Sarina.

To give me an hour or two. I would get a confession.

Then I left, happy that I didn't have a cell phone, because he couldn't call me back and tell me not to.

Amazingly, when I pulled into the Cobb estate, Sarina's silver Mercedes sat alone on the circular drive. No friends or family the morning after your husband kills himself with a policeman's gun in the middle of downtown? *What kind of people are these, that don't come to comfort a new widow?*

She answered the door herself. "I gave Ilse the day off. She was getting on my nerves. All that crying and moaning for *Barry*. Not a tear for *me*. Come through, I'm on the patio."

This is a new widow? She had on a floral short set, high-heeled sandals with gay pink flowers, and a layer of expensive-smelling sun block. She snatched up a tiny chrome cell phone as we walked through the house, and we settled on two lounge chairs, side-by-side, facing the early-morning sun. There was a bottle of wine in an ice bucket. Sarina laid the phone down and poured two glasses of wine. It was just barely blush. I took a sip. It tasted like warm peaches and dewy raspberries had tiptoed hand-in-hand through a god's nectar.

"It's so unfair," Sarina said in reply to my simple words of sympathy. "For him to leave me in this awkward position. So terribly unthoughtful. I mean, you see how it is. No one knows what to say to me so they don't say anything. Not even one phone call." She gestured to the silent phone.

I felt a momentary pang of sympathy but then she went on, "It's very worrying to know that the man you devoted your life to propping up, that he'd cared so little. That he'd do this, well this embarrassing thing and leave me to deal with it."

She took a sip of her wine. "Mmm, good, isn't it? Something new Julius at the Cellar recommended to me."

The woman was crazy. Maybe this hadn't been such a good idea after all, to come here alone to get her confession.

263

"Tell me about Ilene," I said.

"Oh, such a silly young woman. Laurence Pease called me, told me she was noising around his and Barry's deals. He seemed to think I could do something about it."

"And you couldn't?"

"Well, what was I to do? I don't even get over there," she said, indicating the mainland across the bay, "very often. Well, once in a while, of course, but mostly, my friends are here."

Except, of course, they weren't. Which is why we were sitting here alone.

It was time for me to do what I had to do. "Sarina, tell me about Ilene's fall."

She got a crafty look on her face.

"It was after the Midnight Pass do. I had had a glass or two of champagne, and I decided to stop at her place on the way home. It's next to some boatyard."

"Yes, I know."

"I was going to talk to her, tell her to leave it alone."

"Where was Barry?"

She shrugged. "He always stays late at these things. The men, they sit out on the patio, smoking cigars, making deals, you know. Besides, we'd driven separately because of my hair."

"Your hair?"

"I'd had it done in an elaborate style, the only thing that looked right with my dress, and Barry never puts the top up on his XLR. Refuses to. Refused to. I can't get used to saying that."

She didn't seem perturbed by having to use the past tense, just annoyed. "So I had the Mercedes, anyway. She was there, loading her car. Pretty thing, she was. Funny, I'd never bothered to find out what she looked like before."

"You mean, since you'd found out from Laurence that Ilene was asking around about Barry?"

She turned towards me, puzzled. "No, I mean since she'd arrived in town. Couple of years, wasn't it? Never interested enough, I guess."

"Why would you have been?"

264

"Well, she was Barry's daughter, wasn't she? Most women would be curious."

I couldn't believe this. Sarina knew Ilene was Barry's daughter. That made her all the more a monster.

"How did you know that?" I asked her.

"Know what? That she was his daughter?"

I nodded. She looked at me as though as I was crazy.

"Daddy. Daddy had a whole report done on Barry, before we got married. It was in there, that Barry'd had a child with some woman, even her name. Daddy's lawyers, well they're mine now of course, they kept track of her. That's how I knew she'd moved to Sarasota. The lawyers said to just ignore her. So I did. It was easy. I mean," and here she laughed, "we don't exactly move in the same circles do we?"

"I told her," Sarina said, "I told her to mind her own business. That Barry was a good husband, and if he wanted to fool around with that Chloe, he was welcome to. Wasn't any of her business. I was the wife, and it didn't matter to me, so why should it matter to her?"

"But your husband wasn't seeing Chloe," I said. "He was using her to poison people. So he could buy their houses."

Sarina made a scoffing noise. "Nonsense. I don't see any dead bodies, do you?" She went very still. "Except for his."

"And Ilene's," I reminded her. This was surreal. Here I was, sipping wine by a luxurious pool on a luxurious island having to remind a murderer that she killed someone.

"Well, but that was an accident. I was just trying to persuade her to leave it all alone."

"How did it happen?"

Sarina was in her own little self-justified world. "It was completely an accident. She was traipsing up and down those stairs, carrying things, and she wouldn't listen to me. I was standing below her and she just stood there, waiting for me to get out of her way.

"I said to her, I said listen, I've been a good wife, what he does is his own business, besides, I said to her, you can't go

265

around telling people, telling them your own father's doing that."

So that's when Ilene learned she was Barry's daughter.

"Then she lost her footing and fell." Sarina shrugged and fiddled with her Bulgari bracelet. "I tried to catch her, but that flowerpot came down. All over my dress," she added. "I tried to brush it off."

So that's how the flowers were scattered all over Ilene.

"She just laid there. Not moving. She must have broken her neck or something, right?"

I didn't answer. Tom said the medical examiner said she hadn't, that it had been a blow to the head, said she must have landed on her head.

"I had to make it look like a murder. Otherwise they'd think Barry did it. So I picked up the flower pot and smashed her like a murderer would. Then I took that nasty old suitcase of hers. So it would look like a robbery, right?"

She seemed to want me to tell her she was clever.

"But then I got worried about that suitcase and threw it in the trash bin. And then I went home.

"That pretty dress of mine, though, I don't think you'll take it on consignment," she mourned. "It got all dirty." She was more concerned with her couturier gown than her murdering her husband's daughter.

"You don't take a hint very well, do you, Wendy Sam Miller? I write you that note and throw it through your window. You ignore it. Then I follow you all the way to that stupid beach and give you my famous underhand stroke with that nasty wet wood, and even that doesn't bother you. I mean, it's miles to that beach. We have perfectly lovely beaches right here, or even over by you. But no, you have to ruin my entire evening, driving down there to that beach. Very thoughtless of you," she said.

"So anyway, Ilene. The famous daughter. Such a clumsy little thing. Just like a Crawford. Very awkward people.

"Well," she said, making a brisk *brush-my-hands-of-this* motion. "You see, it was all an accident. And it was Barry's fault. If he had just kept his daughter in line, none of this would have

266

happened."

I stood up and asked if I could use her cell phone. As I dialed, I said to Sarina, "Ilene didn't know she was Barry's daughter. And Barry never knew he even had a daughter. Until they told him yesterday. That's why he killed himself. Because you didn't tell him Ilene was his daughter." My connection went through. "Tom?" I said. "I'm done here. I'll wait with Sarina until you get here."

About the Author

Kate Holmes has been involved in the consignment business all her life. Her mother opened two shops, Pin Money, on Long Island New York in the mid-1950's and Kate grew up learning the business.

She opened her own shop, One More Time, in Columbus Ohio in 1975. She began writing an industry newsletter in 1983 and published the first edition of Too Good to be Threw: The Complete Operations Manual for Consignment Shops in 1988, which is still in print and available at www.tgtbt.com, along with her other Products for the Professional Resaler.

Kate helped the National Association of Resale and Thrift Shops start their very first conference, served on their Board of Directors, and is still tickled that she received both the Renee Rivers Award for Outstanding Service and the very first Educational Service Award.

Recently, she was honored with a lifetime membership in NARTS.

Kate sold her shop in 1995 and retired to Sarasota in 1998, where she continues to advise the industry through her Web site at www.tgtbt.com.

Has all this intrigued you?
Interested in starting your own
consignment, resale, or thrift shop?

Well, I can't promise that you'll start solving murders, but I can foretell that you'll have a wonderful career ahead of you!

Everything you need to know, and things you didn't even know you needed to know, are in the
Products for the Professional Resaler published by
Katydid Press and Too Good to be Threw.

Take a look at our Web site at www.tgtbt.com,
which has a lot of free info, tips, links, and a
Products Page with our publications on it.
And lots more besides!

If you would prefer a paper copy of our Products for the
Professional Resaler catalog,
please send a long SASE to
Too Good to be Threw,
4736 Meadowview Blvd., Sarasota FL 34233.

Give the gift of
The Picker Who Perished
to your favorite secondhander today!

❑ Yes, I want _____ copies of *The Picker Who Perished* for $12.95 each.

❑ **Include me in your mailing list** so I can find out when the further adventures of Wendy Sam Miller, owner of the fictional Too Good to be Threw, are available.

❑ **I want to learn how to run my own shop!** Send *Too Good to be Threw: The Complete Operations Manual for Consignment and Resale Shops* for $69.95.

Include $3.95 shipping for one book, and $1.95 for each additional book. Canadian orders use US funds, please.

My check or money order for $ _____ is enclosed.
Please charge my ❑VISA ❑Mastercard ❑Discover
Card # _____
Exp. Date _____ Signature _____

Name _____
Address _____
City, State, ZIP _____
Phone _____ Email _____

Or FAX (941) 922-5902
Make your check payable and mail to
Too Good to be Threw
4736 Meadowview Blvd., Sarasota FL 34233
www.tgtbt.com
(941) 924-4142